Crash Landing

Li Charmaine Anne

annick
press
toronto • berkeley

Cover art by JB Gallego, designed by Sam Tse
Edited by Kaela Cadieux and Jieun Lee
Interior design by Sam Tse
Expert read by Diamond Yao, Anna Zeitner, and Elijah Forbes
Copy edited by Dana Hopkins
Proofread by Mary Ann Blair
Cantonese review by Ambrose Li

Annick Press Ltd.

We acknowledge the support of the Canada Council for the Arts and the Ontario Arts Council, and the participation of the Government of Canada/la participation du gouvernement du Canada for our publishing activities.

ONTARIO ARTS COUNCIL
CONSEIL DES ARTS DE L'ONTARIO
an Ontario government agency
un organisme du gouvernement de l'Ontario

Library and Archives Canada Cataloguing in Publication

Title: Crash landing / Li Charmaine Anne.
Names: Li, Charmaine Anne, author.
Identifiers: Canadiana (print) 20230525008 | Canadiana (ebook) 20230525016 | ISBN 9781773218427 (softcover) | ISBN 9781773218410 (hardcover) | ISBN 9781773218434 (EPUB) | ISBN 9781773218441 (PDF)
Subjects: LCGFT: Novels.
Classification: LCC PS8623.I33 C73 2024 | DDC jC813/.6—dc23

Published in the U.S.A. by Annick Press (U.S.) Ltd.
Distributed in Canada by University of Toronto Press.
Distributed in the U.S.A. by Publishers Group West.

Printed in Canada

annickpress.com
licharmaineanne.ca

Also available as an e-book. Please visit annickpress.com/ebooks for more details.

To Ma Mi, who was my favorite person.

All my achievements are yours as well.

Contents

Don't I deserve stories?

September 2010

CHAPTER 1

The edge of my skateboard's deck smacks against my shin. I swear and flip the hair out of my eyes, and sweat splashes all over my face. At this rate, I'll never land a kickflip. Which is embarrassing because eight-year-olds on YouTube land kickflips all the time.

I sit down on my board in front of our garage in the laneway behind the house. It's Labor Day Monday, the last day before school starts, and it's scorching hot. It's almost over—the summer I landed my first ollie. Not like I had anyone to celebrate with, what with David in Korea and Wendy having no interests outside of music and yelling at me to recycle.

I lift my ponytail and fan the back of my neck. I want to lop off all my hair, but every time I mention it, Ma Mi makes a big fuss. Last week, she told me that having short hair will "confuse" people into thinking I'm a boy and that when I grow up it will be unprofessional to go into a job interview like that.

"But I want to be an artist, Ma Mi, not a stockbroker," I'd told her, rolling my eyes. "Artists are *supposed* to look out of the ordinary. I would look *less* professional as an artist wearing a pantsuit."

Wendy, of course, had to chime in. "But Ga Jie, being an artist isn't a real job. I'm a concertmaster and I don't get paid for it."

"No one asked you, Wendy."

Ma Mi told us to be quiet and eat our choy.

I look at the laneway and imagine myself skating it. Actually skating it. Like the videos I watch on YouTube every night: fish-eye lenses of talented people dancing across the urban landscape, nailing harrowing stunts against a backdrop of epic music. Sometimes I don't know what I like more, skateboarding or watching skateboarding.

Kunnng! A familiar sound cuts through my humid frustration. I'd recognize that sound anywhere: it's a skateboard's wheels rushing on concrete. I block the sun out with my hand and peer down the laneway.

A girl skates toward me. A girl. She looks my age, and Asian, too. I rarely see other Asian girls skate. I rarely see other *girls* skate. And the way she zigzag carves her way down the laneway slope, absorbing bumps and cracks like it's as easy as scratching an itch, I can tell she's the real deal. I watch her crouch and the way the muscles in her ankles tense. She rides up the ramp to the neighbors' garage and—*bam!*—busts out a pop shove-it with *ridiculous* air: the board spins a quick 180 under her feet, and she catches it and rides back down the ramp fakie. Her body is still and confident, the board controlled and precise despite the massive pop she got off the tiny ramp.

Nope, this girl isn't a poser.

She rides goofy, like me: right foot forward, left foot back. I get a better look at her as she rides closer. She's lean and athletic. Long black hair with bright red streaks held back with a bandanna. No helmet, of course (I swear, I'm the only teen skater who wears one). Plaid board shorts and a black band tee with a neon shoelace belt. Skate shoes with a healthy scuff. She's also . . . good-looking. Good-looking enough for me to notice that she's good-looking. I'm thinking about what that even means when her bright eyes fall on me, and before things get too weird, I cough out a "hi."

She slows down. Now she's close enough for me to hear the scratchy sounds of loud music playing through her earphones. She stops and stomps the tail of her board so that the nose lands neatly in her hand. When I do that, my board just hits me in the crotch.

"Hey." Her board graphic is all scuffed up—more evidence that she's a legit skater.

Hi," I say again, my mind blank. I've stuck to skating in the laneway all summer for a reason: to avoid embarrassing myself in front of *real* skaters like her.

She juts her chin out at my board. "Sick designs."

"Thanks." She means the doodles I've drawn all over my grip tape with paint pen. I feel my face redden. I hope this doesn't make me look like someone who cares more about having a cool-looking board than skating on it. But I've always had the urge to doodle on blank things, and the big black blankness of the skateboard's grip tape was too tempting. Hence the crosshatched tree leaves and fish and lizards and other random crap on my board.

As if she senses my thoughts, she asks, "You skate?"

I mumble, "Um. Kinda?"

She makes a hybrid laugh-scoff noise. "You can't 'kinda' skate. You're either a skater or you're not." She gestures at my board. "C'mon, show me your moves."

My ears hammer with blood. "I don't have any, uh, moves. I just started this summer, so I only know how to ride and ollie and tic-tac."

But her eyes flash knowingly. "You were trying to kickflip earlier."

My eyebrows jump up into my overgrown bangs. "You were watching me?!"

She laughs. I'm a little offended but not in a bullied way. And the way she laughs, it's like a thin layer of gentle teasing over a thicker layer of genuineness. Like, *it's okay, you're cool.* She says, "Come on then. Show me your kickflip."

I stand up and walk over to the patch of grass I'd been practicing on. I feel like a potato because she looks so cool and I'm over here wearing sweat shorts and my P.E. T-shirt. I prop my feet onto my board, dig my back foot into the tail, and place my front foot loosely on the nose bolts. I count to three in my head then slam down the tail. The board pops up and I kick my front foot diagonally against the nose. My foot rolls the board over slowly, like a lazy old cat, and I land on the graphic on the back of the deck. My wheels spin, laughing at me.

But the skater girl isn't. "I think it's the flick," she says, thoughtful, analytical. "Show me your ollie. And do it on the road. Rolling," she adds.

I swallow. I'm not good at rolling ollies. Too much speed still sketches me out. But there is something about this girl, something about her eyes. It's like they're physically prodding me: *Do it. Do a rolling ollie. I dare you.*

So I do it. I give myself a gentle push to gain some moderate speed then pop off my tail and drag my front foot toward the nose to pull it up. My wheels barely hop off the ground. I catch my board, but my balance is sketchy and I step off immediately after landing.

My cheeks burn, but the skater girl just nods. "Yeah, it's your front foot. Your ollie's a little rocketed. Don't think of it as dragging your foot up, think of it as kicking *forward.*" She jumps on her board and does the most graceful ollie I've ever seen. Barely any force on her pop, just a flick of her back foot. The board floats up like a magic carpet and her front foot hooks against the nose pocket, leveling it out. "You've got the basic idea down, though!" And she sounds like she means it. "Can you do a shove-it?"

I shake my head.

"Backside and frontside 180s?"

I shake my head again, my face even hotter than before. I wait for her to say something mean, but she doesn't.

"Master your ollies first. They're the foundation to everything," she says. "Then try shove-its. *Then* kickflips."

I nod the way I nod at music teachers and driving instructors.

She shrugs. "Then it's just practice, really." She holds her board by the nose, makes a running start, throws down, jumps on, and bombs down the laneway, busting out a powerslide as she turns the corner.

So that's it then. A mysterious skater girl randomly drops into my neighborhood and then leaves, and now I'll never see her again. I can't help but feel bummed. Is it possible to miss a stranger you just met?

I push the thought away and get back on my board. Right: ollies. I do a small one while rolling. Then another, a little faster. I crisscross the laneway, over and over, so completely engrossed in ollieing that I almost don't hear the wheels approach.

The skater girl has done a full lap around the block. She kicks up her board, brushes a red strand of hair away from her face, and smirks. "Hey, you're getting better already."

I smile back. "Thanks."

"I'm Ash, by the way. I live on this block now."

"I'm Jay," I say. "I live here too."

She cocks an eyebrow at me. "Jay? Is that a nickname?"

I frown. "How can you tell?"

"Is it?"

I have to give it to her. "You're right. It's a nickname. I hate the name my parents gave me so last year I started using my initials: J.W. But it was too much of a mouthful, so my friends started calling me Jay. Guess what my real name is."

Ash stares at me for a full two seconds before stating, without a beat of hesitation, "Jessica."

My jaw falls open. "How did you know?!"

She laughs. "Well, you're obviously Chinese, and Chinese parents tend to use the same names over and over. Like Jessica or Amy. Or Vivian. Or Joyce."

"How do you know I'm Chinese? I could be Korean. Or, like, Thai."

"Right. *Are* you Korean?"

I glance sheepishly to the side. "No, I'm Chinese. Cantonese, to be exact."

"Same," she says. "I'm Ashley, Ashley Chan." Here she makes a face. "I hate it too. It's so . . . *blonde*. So I tell people to call me Ash, like from *Pokémon*."

I stick out my hand. "Well, it's nice to meet you, Ash."

She stares at my stuck-out hand. "What are you, in a business meeting?" She closes my hand into a fist and bumps it.

I say, "So you just moved here? Where's your house?"

She gestures vaguely behind her at no house in particular. "I'm supposed to go to a new school tomorrow. George Vancouver."

"I go to George Van!" I say. "Hey, I can show you around."

"Yeah?" A smile tugs at the corner of her mouth.

"For sure."

"Cool. Tell me which teachers are hardasses and which kids I should avoid."

"The teachers aren't so bad," I say. "And the kids . . . well, we're nerds, mostly."

She nods. "Cool, cool." Her voice drifts and her eyes fall downward as she fidgets with her feet. "Cool," she says again. "My old school was a bit of a mess. So. Yeah. Nerds are good." She grins. I'm not sure what she means by "mess," but I decide it's too early to ask so I just nod.

She seems to appreciate that. "You seem cool, J.W."

"It's Jay."

She winks. "Right. See you tomorrow, Jay." She tosses me a smile and jumps back on her board. I watch her until she turns the corner of the laneway. Suddenly, I'm excited for tomorrow. I don't even remember the last time I felt excited for school.

. . .

"You were up late last night," Wendy says in her trademark accusatory way, complete with narrowed eyes and judgmental eyebrows. We're walking to school together, my sister in a flowy new-school-year dress, me in shorts and my dad's old polo.

"I was reading my AP English textbook," I mutter. It's a lie; I was bingeing how-to-kickflip videos on YouTube, as always.

Wendy rolls her eyes and huffs. "So. You think I should do Model UN or Environmental Club this year?" She scrunches up her nose as if to squeeze the answer out of her face.

"I hear Model UN has really good food at their conferences."

"What do you know? You're not in it. You're not in anything."

"You asked for my opinion. And for your information, I'm in band and I write for the newspaper."

"You wrote *two* articles last year, and one of them was a cartoon."

"Hey. People love my cartoons." I tsk. "Maybe you shouldn't do Model UN *or* Environmental Club. You did Student Council and Environmental Club last year and got so burned-out. Maybe just chill this year."

Wendy stops dead in her tracks, which is what she does when she wants to be all dramatic about making a point. "Ga Jie. I'm in *Grade 11*. And I want to get into an Ivy League. I can't just 'chill.'" She does air quotes in my face. I sigh and pull her along. That's Wendy for you. Nineteen months younger than me, an overachiever, and the darling of the family.

Wendy grumbles about clubs until we get to school. Ultimately, she decides to ditch Environmental Club because "all they do is pick up garbage, it's not like they actually change things." I mumble a see-you-after-school and dash down the hallway before she can change her mind.

As I make my way to the grad lounge, I look for Ash, but I don't see her yet. I imagine us walking down the hall with our skateboards, how we'd stand out.

Here's the thing: George Van is not your typical public high school. For one, our teachers like to boast that they work at a diverse school, but is it really "diverse" when most of us are Asian? Second, while in most movies, nerds are the minority, here, caring about your test scores and volunteering hours is mainstream. Wendy says it's because we're on the West Side and that's just the vibe here.

The grad lounge is a decrepit couch, a wobbly coffee table, and a crusty microwave stuffed into what used to be a janitor's closet with the door knocked down. It's exclusive to Grade 12s, and everyone in my year has been looking forward to it since Grade 8. By the time I get there, a crowd is already crammed onto the couch, smushing the poor pile of polyester into oblivion. Almost spilling over the edge is David.

I met David Yoon Kim in Grade 5, when I beat him at a spelling bee and he cried. Because before I had the audacity to come along, David won everything—chess meets, math competitions, everything. He was in the other class, so I didn't know him well, and he flat-out ignored me for several weeks after the spelling bee. But I kept saying hi to him in the hallway because I felt bad, like I'd stolen his lunch money or something. Then one thing led to another and now he's my best friend. I never did spelling bee again, but David continued his winning streak until he retired in Grade 7. David's one of the top students at our school, which is one of the top schools in the district. So, naturally, my parents love him. He bows to them every time he sees them, the suck-up.

I smack David's timetable away from his face. "Sup, Dave, you asshole. How was Toronto and Korea?"

"Hey yourself." David moves aside so I can sit on the last free corner of the couch. David had gone straight from school to a college prep program in Toronto. Then went straight from Toronto to Seoul to spend the rest of the summer with relatives. He only got home yesterday, after a summer of messaging me when I was asleep and me messaging him while he was asleep.

"Toronto was hot, Korea was even hotter," David says. "I missed the rain. How was your summer?"

I shrug. "Did a lot of skateboarding."

"I'm glad you're alive," he says. David has the same opinion about skateboarding as my mother, as in, he thinks it's suicidal.

"So, what do you have planned for the paper this year? I had this idea about pairing caricatures of teachers with movie villains and—"

David holds up a hand in his "bitch, please" way. "Gonna stop you right there, Jay. First, that's an awful idea. Second, I'm not running Journalism anymore."

I scowl because Journalism Club is the one thing that David and I have consistently done together all through high school. "Then who's doing it?"

David shrugs. "Are *you* interested?"

I shake my head. Vigorously.

"Well, I guess it's dead then. But whatever. I need to focus on being Student Council President." He points to the wall. Posters of his bespectacled, dimpled face are plastered everywhere. He's wearing a red cape and there's a cartoon crown copy-and-pasted over his head. *King David for*

Prez. "No one else is running," he says, grinning, "so it's an automatic win."

I cringe. "What did you use to make that, Word Art? Jeez, you should've asked me for help." He smiles awkwardly and I shake my head. "Anyway. Dave, I was hoping we could, like, *have fun* this year, you know? It's Grade 12. It's our last year in this dump. We should make it count."

He scowls at me. "'Make it count'? Way ahead of you, dude. I'm in AP Physics and—"

I groan. Loudly. Several people look at us, but I ignore them. "Not like that, Dave. I mean, it's time we have some *experiences*. Remember that bucket-list thing we did in Grade 8 for our time capsule project?"

He scowls at me even harder. "Oh my god, you remember that thing?"

"You don't?"

He shrugs. "It was silly. We were thirteen. It was full of kiddie stuff like 'go to a house party' and 'get our first kiss' and 'go on a road trip.' Dude, you don't even drive."

"I have my learner's permit!"

He sighs and goes back to reading his timetable. "Jay, don't tell me you think *High School Musical* was real. Besides, I don't care about any of that stuff. I just said those things to sound cool. Well . . . maybe a first kiss *would* be cool but—"

"Hey, David!"

I turn around and it's Min Chen and Sophie Lang. Min is small and slouchy with tight ponytails and a wardrobe that mainly consists of shades of brown. Sophie is her opposite, eye-catching in a long rainbow sundress and fire-red hair. She's one of the few white kids at our school and she towers over us. I've never talked to either of them much because I find Sophie obnoxiously over social and Min sometimes forgets to add the *s* to her plurals, which is a pet peeve of mine.

"Oh hey!" David brightens up and beckons them to join us. He says to me, "We were all in the program together in Toronto. Isn't that wild?"

"David made those lectures bearable," Sophie says, rolling her eyes. She looks at me. "Hey, we're in band together, right? You play percussion?"

I nod, even though saying I'm in band is a bit of a stretch. I spend most of band class catching up on homework because percussion never gets any interesting parts.

"So which calc class are you guy in?" Min asks, and the three of them start comparing timetables. That's when I spot her—Ash, skateboard tucked under one arm, backpack slung over the other. She stands in the middle of the hallway holding her locker assignment with white-knuckled fingers. Weight on one leg, eyebrows furrowed. I didn't know you could look cool and stressed at the same time. I jump up and wave her over.

Ash perks up when she sees me. She comes over and we fist-bump again. "Fuck," she breathes. I wince because to be honest, I'm not used to such casual f-bombs. "So this is where the goddamn Grade 12 lockers are. I like how segregated this place is. Did you notice A-wing is all white people?"

I feel everyone else's eyes on the back of my head, so I gesture vaguely behind me. "Guys, this is Ash. I met her yesterday. She just moved onto my block."

There's a mumble-cloud of heys from the group. Ash's eyes dart curiously around the lounge space. She points at David's poster and laughs. "Wow, what a cheesy poster."

Min and Sophie stare at David, and his whole body stiffens.

"Uh, this is David," I say quickly, waving at him. "He's running for Student Council."

". . . and I could use your vote?" David chuckles nervously.

It's Ash's turn to go stiff. "Shit, sorry," she mumbles. "Um, yeah, for sure. Good luck." She slaps on a squirrely, nervous smile.

"Well! I need to get to English," Sophie says, breaking the silence that follows.

"Me too." Min follows her out.

David awkwardly moves past Ash. "I'll see you at lunch, Jay." He gives my shoulder a halfhearted pat.

I'm left with Ash. She jostles her knee. "Well shit, I fucked up, didn't I?"

"David'll get over it. He's cool." I hope so, at least.

Ash and I compare schedules, and it turns out we have AP English together. I'm surprised, but she snorts and says, "Just because I skate doesn't mean I don't read." She has a point there.

I go to my first block alone: Open Studio. It took me a summer's worth of begging for Ma Mi to let me take this course. In return, I promised her I'd take at least one AP class.

Open Studio is pretty awesome because it's essentially a do-whatever-you-want class where you put together a portfolio. There are a few mandatory assignments, but you get a lot of freedom interpreting them. It's run by Mr. Templeton, a small, gray-haired man with a wardrobe that makes him look like a gnome. He spends fifteen minutes outlining class expectations then dumps piles of university viewbooks on the tables and tells us we have free rein for the rest of the class.

Everyone digs into the viewbooks, and soon the room is buzzing with discussions about grade point averages, portfolio specifications, and which city is more prestigious, London or New York. "Art school is just a backup anyway," someone says. "Ideal is architecture, but my parents really want me to go into engineering."

I open my sketchbook and tap my 5B pencil against it. *You have to think about your future, Jessica. How will you feed your children?* I don't want any children, Mom. *That's what you think now. What if you change your mind?* I sigh and, unable to push away the loop of Ma Mi's voice in my head, grab a viewbook. The cover—a beautiful canal with colorful houseboats—takes me by surprise. I grab a few more viewbooks from that pile, which no one has touched because everyone took the North American ones. I look at photos of London, Barcelona, and Amsterdam. I flip through some programs, and one catches my eye: Bachelor of Fine Arts in Digital Media. Sure, people don't need someone to paint portraits of them anymore, but the world needs designers. I think about how, over the summer, I'd visited skate shops just to look at the deck displays. Someone had to design those. And I think about the skateboarding videos I watch every night before I go to sleep. Someone had to shoot those and set them to music.

I walk up to Mr. Templeton, who's mindlessly sharpening pencil crayons at his desk. "Hey, Mr. Templeton, would you mind if I do a *digital* portfolio?"

He doesn't take his eyes off his pencil-sharpening. "What would that look like?"

"Like graphic design. Or film."

He pauses his sharpening for a bit then resumes. "Just make sure you meet all the course requirements. Everyone needs to do a public space project in term two. A mural, installation, or something that interacts with public space."

When lunchtime rolls around, I find Ash and we sit with David, Min, and Sophie in the cafeteria. The three of them talk about their eccentric calculus teacher and I focus on my burger. Ash just watches and listens, so I guess she already ate. Then David says something along the lines of "cheesecake seconds" and everyone but Ash and I get up.

"You don't want cheesecake?" I say to her.

"School-board cheesecake?" She wrinkles her nose. "No, I wanna show you something." She pulls out a piece of paper. It's a printout of an e-mail, and the printer needs more toner. I squint to make out the words:

Hello Ash,

We are stoked to inform you that your video submission for the BC Next Gen Skaters Contest has been accepted. Congratulations, you are now in the preliminary round! Please send us your next submission video by November 30, and we will vote on final contestants by early next year.

We want to tell you that your submission was very impressive, especially for an athlete your age. Our only suggestion is to use a higher quality camera for your edits. We look forward to your next video.

Cheers,
The BC Skaters Guild

"Wow. What's the BC Skaters Guild?" I ask.

Ash's eyes go wide the way people's eyes do when you admit to never having watched a famous film franchise. "Only the hottest, raddest skate collective in the province. I'm their hugest fan, and whoever wins this video contest will get to compete in an invitational next spring. I've been following this contest since I was, like, fifteen. The first time, I couldn't make the first video deadline because I sprained my ankle real bad. Then last year, shit happened and I didn't make the second video deadline." She looks away. "This is, like, third time's the charm, y'know? Third time *better* be the charm."

I say, "You need a better camera, I see."

She grimaces. "Yeah. I don't have the money for a real camera. I have a cheap fish-eye lens, but all I got is a friend's point-and-shoot."

We sit there staring at our food trays for a moment, and then it strikes me. "Hey. I can help you film."

She turns to me. "What?"

"I think my dad has an HD camcorder. He bought it for when we went to Hong Kong and never used it. It's not a VX1000 or anything, but it's way nicer than a point-and-shoot and I can ask him to borrow it."

Ash's gaze shifts to the side. "I dunno. I don't want to waste your time."

"I want to practice using digital tools," I say. "And I *love* watching skateboarding videos. Like, I'm *obsessed* with them. I've always wanted to shoot some myself, but I don't skate well enough to."

"It won't be as glamorous as the videos you see on YouTube," Ash says. "There's a lot of bailing. And swearing."

I shrug.

"We'll have to ride around town, go to different places. You got money for bus tickets?"

My parents keep a stack of them in the sideboard by the living room, and as far as I know, they don't keep count. "No problem."

"It might take hours just to capture a few seconds of footage. It's a grind."

"Wow, you *really* don't want my help," I say, laughing.

But she doesn't laugh. "I just don't want to waste your time," she says again.

"Well, if you let me use your videos as part of my digital art portfolio, then it's not a waste of time."

"Well..." Ash blinks. "See, I *really* need to win. First place in the invitational gets a grand, for one. But more than that, this might be my big break, you know? Like, if I do good at this contest, there might be sponsorships. And contracts. And bigger contracts, with more money. I need that. I need to move out as soon as possible. *Fuck*, I gotta move out..." She looks away.

"If you're not confident in my video skills, we can do a test run," I say. Because I'll be honest, I've never shot a video in my life; I just have cinematographically incredible videos playing in my head all the time.

In the car. When I'm listening to music. When I'm trying to fall asleep.

Ash is quiet for a few seconds, thinking, then says, "Okay. Sure. Let's try it. Can you start right away?"

We won't have exams or projects for a while. "Yeah."

A grin slowly spreads across Ash's face. "Sick."

. . .

Ash e-mails me a link to her video submission after school and I watch it after my parents and Wendy have gone to bed.

The video fades in from black with the snarling opening riff of a Runaways song. The camera tracks Ash pushing her skateboard, red tendrils of hair ribboning out behind her. She approaches a six-stair and clears it with a massive, boned-out ollie. Now *that's* an opener. I lean forward hard on my elbows, trying to identify as many tricks as possible. Frontside boardslide. Ollie into manual, kickflip out. Slappy back lipslide. No comply fakie bigspin over a parking block. And whoa—a tre flip! There are several clips of her carving the hell out of a massive bowl, shots of powerslides and reverts down a laneway. More flips, grinds, and slides. And then her ender is a gutsy 50-50 down a handrail. The camera zooms cartoonishly to her grinning face and it's pure happiness. If only the camera and the editing were a little more polished, this could belong in an action movie.

I sit back, my body rippling with stoke the way it does after an epic video. *This* is what skateboarding is all about. Style and creativity. Freedom and expression. Seeing the urban environment as an empty mural and your board as painting pictures that will never stay still.

I replay the video several times over until "Cherry Bomb" gets stuck in my head. I go to bed shortly after one in the morning, ghostly frames of skateboarding tricks leaping through my dreams.

CHAPTER 2

I wait for Ash to take me on a skateboarding adventure, but she says she needs to practice more first because being in front of the camera sketches her out. I'm stoked, if a little impatient. So I spend my free time watching filmmaking tutorials on YouTube, and I actually read the owner's manual for my dad's camcorder. No learning by pressing random buttons—I'm taking this seriously.

I only have AP English with Ash, so for several weeks I don't see her often. She seems to float through a few groups at school as if checking them out, but she doesn't stay with any for long, even the one small group of goth kids we have. She sits with David, Sophie, Min, and me a few times. But she rarely eats and doesn't stick around. I notice she goes off-campus most lunch hours, maybe to skate.

One day, I catch her practicing flip tricks in the tennis courts. So I start bringing my board too, hoping to see Ash with hers at lunch. Well, I carry it most of the way because I'm afraid of falling on my face in front of the whole school. The first time I ask Ash whether I can skate with her, she's stoked. "Fuck yeah," she says. "It's nice to have a buddy." And it is. Having an extra set of eyes makes a big difference. I don't have to take videos of myself to see whether my ollie has lifted all four wheels off the ground. Instead, Ash spots everything.

"You're not bending your knees. You gotta jump higher. Like, suck your knees up into your chest. Exaggerate it, it'll make a difference. There you go!" By that Friday, my ollies have grown exponentially in height. I think Ash is stoked too because she starts asking me to skate with her at lunch. We stick around school because I don't want to be late for class, and when I land my first ollie up a curb, I feel like I can fly. Ash smacks her board against the ground in applause, and it's so loud the bangs reverberate off the courtyard walls.

Then, one day in mid-October I find Ash waiting by my locker after school. She lifts her chin at me. "Hey. Got time?"

I look at her, confused.

"There's this cool spot in East Van I wanna hit and the weather's good today. You think we can drop by your place and get the camera?"

"Uh." Usually, when I go out, I tell my parents at least two days in advance. Ash looks at me expectantly. I don't want to seem uncool. "Sure."

I knock on my dad's office after school. I always ask him for permission to go out because unlike my mom, De Di doesn't ask me a gazillion questions. Which works out because if Ma Mi grills me, I can tell her I did ask an adult, and shouldn't parents have equal say in their children's affairs?

"When will you be home?" De Di asks when I tell him I'm going to a friend's to finish a project.

"I don't know."

"Wendy has a rehearsal tonight. I was planning an early dinner."

"I'll eat dinner with my classmates. They mentioned they might get McDonald's. Can I borrow your camcorder? I need it for the project."

"Okay. Keep your phone on, okay?"

"Yes, De Di."

"Don't be out too late."

"Yes, De Di."

When we get on the bus, Ash beelines for the back row and sits by the window with her shoes and board against the seat in front of her. I sit beside her, suddenly anxious that I'll have nothing to say for the next half hour. I've never hung out with her like this, one-on-one, without skateboarding or AP English as a conversation starter. So I take out the camcorder and fidget with it.

Ash glances over. "Your dad's got such cool stuff. What does he do again?"

"He's an engineer," I say. "Well, he was. His firm downsized him out during the recession a couple years ago and he's been consulting from home ever since. What does your dad do?"

Ash looks out the window again. "Oh, same thing. Construction or something."

"My dad came here to study engineering, but I sometimes wonder if he really *likes it*, you know? Like, did he choose it because he's passionate about buildings, or did his parents want him to be an engineer? Or, maybe he saw a particularly well-done pamphlet at a job fair once."

Ash just looks at me and shrugs.

"Does your dad have a random dad-hobby like photography?" I ask.

"No, he's boring."

"I think my dad's bored," I say. "He likes to give off the impression that he's busy, but I think he just reads the news all day."

Ash laughs. "See, my dad just drinks beers after work."

My dad, on the other hand, is more of a coffee drinker. Like me. He doesn't say much, just sits in his home office most of the day, drinking endless cups of coffee and fiddling around on his computer. He only leaves the room when the sun's about to set, when he goes to the back porch to yell at me to come inside before Ma Mi gets home. Ma Mi often works late because she thinks working is one's sole purpose in life and preparing for it is the only way children should spend their time. If she saw me filming stuff for a friend instead of studying or researching universities, she'd throw a fit.

We get off at a moderately busy commercial area in East Van. Ash jumps on her board right away and zooms into an alley. There's rush-hour foot traffic all around, so I run after her, carrying my board under my arm like a poser. Well, at least I'm not mall-grabbing it by the trucks.

The alley is splashed on all sides with colorful graffiti. It attacks my senses and I stand and stare for a moment, digesting everything, before Ash yells, "Yo! Over here!"

"Dude. This is sick." The street art will make this an awesome shot.

Ash does shove-its and no complys on a bank leading up to a garage door. Then she points to a five-stair coming out of the back entrance of a restaurant. "I'm gonna kickflip that."

Ash straight airs the stairs first with a solid ollie. But when she tries to kickflip, she misses catching the board and takes a hard slam. We keep sessioning the stairs, but the landing is sketchy and it's hard for her to get enough speed.

"Hey, why don't you try more stuff on the bank?" I say. "It'll look super cool with the art in the background." I crouch down—hell, I get on my elbows, alley dirt be damned because I'm sure I can squeeze in a shower before my mom sees me tonight. Tilt the camera up. Hell yeah it looks cool.

Ash scowls at the bank, hands on her hips. "Bank's kinda mellow though. I really wanna wow the judges with bigger stuff."

"Aren't you practicing the ten stair at the skate park? Just wow them with that," I say. "This is a great spot to show off style."

She nods and we launch into a more chill session. Well, Ash makes it look chill. Her heelflips and kickflips are textbook. Then she tries a boneless, but instead of stepping on the ground, she stomps the garage door. The *fwum* sound it makes is so satisfying. Ash does a few takes and on the cleanest one, I resist the urge to yell with excitement so I can pan up to the art after the shot.

I don't notice how long she's been skating until I see the battery icon on the camera blinking. At the same time, a woman leans out of one of the back doors and yells, "Hey, what's going on here?"

I stand up so quickly, all the blood rushes out of my head and I get dizzy.

"Nothing!" Ash says equally loudly.

"Stop banging on the door!" the lady barks. "You kids should go home and do your homework."

Ash scowls.

"My battery's dead anyway," I say to her quickly before she can yell back at the lady. "Maybe we should go."

She shrugs and yawns. "Fine. I'm wiped anyway."

We walk down the street, carrying our boards because we're both pretty wiped. I notice that there are a lot of barbers and hairdressers in this area. They're all kind of grungy-looking, with handwritten signs propped out on the sidewalk advertising their prices.

"Whoa, ten dollars for a haircut. Seriously?" I point to one sign.

"You need a haircut?" Ash says.

"I've always wanted short hair," I mutter.

Ash looks at me thoughtfully. "I think short hair would suit you."

I push my bangs off my forehead. Ma Mi *has* been nagging me about my bangs lately. And even if she hates it, it's just hair. I can always grow it back. In time for graduation, even.

I walk in and get seated immediately. The clientele is mostly Asian seniors, and the man getting his head shaved next to me is snoring in his chair. A woman drapes a cape over me and says in a no-nonsense voice, "What you want?"

"Short," I say.

"How short?"

I place my hand right below my ear.

"Short like man?" says the hairdresser.

"Yeah," I say. "Short like man!"

When my hair is done, I nudge Ash, who is curled up asleep on one of the chairs. As we walk down the street, I catch her sneaking glimpses at my head.

"Hey, thanks for waiting for me," I tell her. I've never felt so . . . *light*. Who knew hair could weigh so much?

"No problem," she says, looking at her phone. "Any time spent away from my dad is time well spent."

"What's so bad about your dad?" I ask.

She shrugs. "Your hair looks good. I was right. Short suits you."

. . .

I wake up to Wendy throwing a pillow in my face. "Ma Mi's in the shower. Get up before she realizes you're not dressed."

Something feels weird and not quite right. Just when I get up and rub my eyes to unstick them, Wendy squeals. "Holy crap, your hair!"

"Oh. Right." I ruffle the top of my head. My hair's so short it sticks straight up.

"Ma Mi's gonna be hysterical." Standing in my doorway, Wendy's eyes glitter with excitement. She will never admit it, but she loves watching me vs. Ma Mi drama.

I take a deep breath before I walk downstairs to the kitchen. "Jo sun,"

I announce as the warm scent of freshly brewed jok slaps me in the face. "Good morning."

Ma Mi drops a pot lid on the counter and the clang makes Wendy jump. "Aiya, Jessica! What did you do?!" She looks like a cartoon, staring at me with eyes the size of spatulas. But her seriousness is compromised by the frilly Hello Kitty apron she's wearing over her work blouse.

I casually take my seat across from De Di, who hasn't looked up from today's edition of the Chinese newspaper. "You kept telling me my hair was getting too long. So I cut it last night when you guys were at Wendy's rehearsal."

"I said I would bring you to Mrs. Ly's this weekend!"

"This was just ten dollars. Not bad, huh?" Mrs. Ly has been doing our family's hair for eons, but a few years ago when I'd asked for short hair, she'd given me the ugliest bob ever and I haven't dared to return since.

"Where did you go? I thought you had a group project!"

"We walked to McDonald's and I saw this place."

De Di takes a noisy sip of coffee and turns a page. "Haircut looks neat and tidy," he says. "Maybe it'll help her focus in school."

"But what if people think you're a boy?" Ma Mi's forehead folds into an accordion of creases.

"She doesn't care," Wendy says. "She thinks it's edgy and we're boring for not liking it."

Ma Mi makes exasperated noises as she shovels jok into a bowl. She hands the bowl to Wendy, who frowns. "But I want toast."

"I heard on the radio that rice is healthier than wheat," says Ma Mi. Wendy dejectedly takes the jok, but I walk past Ma Mi and get bread before she can give me a bowl. I've never been a fan of the stuff and honestly, who cares if I get fat. Fat is more cushion to land on in a skate bail. I make my toast, Wendy makes cups of tea for herself and Ma Mi, and I pour coffee for myself and De Di.

"So. Jessica." Ma Mi sits down with a sigh, obviously trying to push past the subject of hair. "How is AP English?"

My parents talk to Wendy and me in Cantonese, and for the most part, we answer back in English. I spread marmalade on my toast and De Di passes me the English newspaper. "We still haven't met the regular teacher yet," I tell Ma Mi. "He's apparently new to the school but he's been on medical leave since September. The sub's been making us read random short stories and write reports."

"Medical leave for a month?" De Di chuckles. "Only in Canada."

"And how are you doing?" Ma Mi asks.

"I got an A on my last report."

"See? I told you it would be good to take an AP course. In fact, I think you should have taken more than one!" The look she gives me is somehow hopeful and condescending at the same time.

I open the newspaper to the crossword. "I'm not interested."

Ma Mi sighs. "Ah Nui, I don't want to be one of those moms who pressure their kids so much that they jump out of buildings. But sometimes I worry about you. You're so ... unwilling to consider other things. Ah Mui, can you get me some milk from the fridge?" Wendy gets up. "Ga Jie," Mom adds, looking back to me, "why don't you try something outside of art?"

"How many times have we gone over this, Mom? I want to major in art."

"Art is good, but it wouldn't hurt to have a backup plan. Something stable and well-paying."

"I'd rather be poor and do something I like than be rich and do something I don't like."

She shakes her head. "Aiiii. You've never been poor. Do you know how many kids would love to be where you are? What about business school? You don't need advanced science classes for it and it's stable and well-paying."

"I don't want money," I tell her. "I want excitement. Travel. To meet new people and do new things."

"Then you'll need to find money to do that la."

"Hey, everyone." Wendy holds the fridge door open. "You think we can switch to almond milk? Way smaller carbon footprint than dairy."

De Di chuckles and says to Ma Mi, "Don't worry. Wendy will take care of us in our old age."

"I want to go to school in Europe," I say, and my parents momentarily pause their chewing. After that first day of school, I had brought home all those European viewbooks to show my parents. De Di had seemed intrigued, and Ma Mi, for the first time I can recall, was surprised I had something academic I wanted to do. But they told me to think carefully because I'd have to get a scholarship to even afford it, and even then, there are so many cheaper options nearby. Maybe not the kind of program I *want*, but programs with *better earning potential*. So think *really, really* hard about it, they'd said.

"I want to go to Europe," I say again. "You asked me to think about it, and I did, and I want to go to Europe."

Wendy scoffs into her jok. Ma Mi and De Di resume their chewing. Then Ma Mi says, "Look at the local universities. They're very good, top-ranked in the country, with art programs, too. You could live at home, save money."

"I don't want to live at home."

Ma Mi purses her lips and sips her jok. I don't think my mother has considered the prospect of having an empty nest. The way she was raised, kids live with their parents until they either get married or something extremely important requires them to move out. My parents have made their peace with Wendy leaving—after all, her plan is to go to America, get into an Ivy League, and accomplish Great Things. But they must have assumed I would stay home, earn a respectable degree at a local university, get a respectable job in the city, and take care of them when they're old.

Ma Mi sips her tea and says, "You'll have to do your own laundry, cook your own food, clean the bathroom, clean everything."

"That's fine." Chores are a fair price to pay for freedom. I just haven't figured out how to convince my mother that I'm not some naive princess who doesn't understand that.

De Di peers over his newspaper. "I'm sure Ga Jie can take care of herself." I can't help but smile back at him.

After breakfast, I get a text from David asking if I need a ride to school. *no,* I tell him, *ash and i are skating to school.* Then I write out a longer message: *ugh, my mom now wants me to do BUSINESS SCHOOL.* David replies: *join the club.*

When I get to the back gate, Ash is already there practicing her flip tricks. "Hey," I say, "your board's stopped squeaking."

"Yeah, I fixed my bearing situation." Her breathing's tight, eyes focused on her feet. "Switched them out for brand-new ones someone was just giving away on Craigslist. Will have to replace my deck in a few weeks though. It's losing major pop."

I look down at my own board. It's a complete put together done by a guy at the store. Cost more than a hundred bucks. While I don't know anything about parts and tools and DIYing, Ash constantly buys and trades stuff on Craigslist. "Don't you worry about getting ripped off?" I asked her once. "Not if you know what you're doing," Ash had said. "I'd rather do the research and assemble my own board. The Internet is free."

We ride out of the laneway and onto the main road. I feel more confident riding with someone, even if she's way faster than me.

"Did you see the video I sent you last night?" Ash yells over her shoulder. It was of an up-and-coming female skater named Gabby from Seattle. She only started uploading videos last year, doing intermediate tricks.

Now she's progressed a ton and has amassed thousands of subscribers, even a sponsor.

"Yeah! It was sick," I yell back. "You can totally do the same. Your tricks are even higher level. Just gotta upload more footy."

"That comment section though," Ash says, shaking her head. "Wow."

"I've got all the classics memorized by now." I dip my voice down to its most douchey. *"If I get a sex change, I'd be sponsored too. Female skateboarding is a joke. That's a funny looking kitchen."* Ash laughs.

We kick up our boards and walk the rest of the way when we get to within a block of the school. "You need to teach me how to assemble a board sometime," I say.

Ash scoffs. "Dude, you get straight As. You can figure it out."

We stop at the top of the steps in front of the main doors. Ash sticks around like she senses I have something more to say. It takes me a while, and then finally I remember: "I brought my laptop to school. I wanna show you the edit I was talking about." Ash had given me a hard drive of clips from her video submission to play with, and I'd sort of remixed it into what I thought was a stronger video.

Ash gives me a wide grin. "Cool."

The bell rings. People push past us.

"So, I'll see you in English, I guess," I say.

"Yeah." Ash nods and slips into the crowd. I wave, but she's already dashing off in the direction of the Woodworking lab.

David, Sophie, and Min are clustered around the Grade 12 lockers when I get there. David has bags under his eyes. He'd lost the Student Council presidency to Samantha Zhao, who had run on a whim. This had surprised everyone because Samantha is one of the FOBs, and most FOBs stick to themselves and don't like getting involved, probably because getting involved means speaking English. Samantha had told everyone she was going to get her parents to buy a bunch of fancy new stuff for the school, which sounds too good to be true. But she drives a Ferrari and wears brand name everything, so people must have believed her.

David still got into Student Council . . . through his backup position as Events Coordinator. Which is the perfect position for someone who hates parties. "You guys are all coming to the Halloween dance, right?" he asks us when I get to my locker. I shake my head, trying not to laugh because George Van school dances are a joke. David scowls at me. "You're not going?"

"Have you ever seen me stoked about a school dance? Besides, I don't have a costume."

David groans. "But you *have* to come! Imagine being Events Coordinator and no one shows up at your event coordinations. What kind of event-coordinating is that?!"

"I told you, you should've just done Journalism Club," I say unhelpfully as Sophie and Min mutter goodbyes and head off to their next class.

David says, "Dude, *I need you.* Besides"—he crosses his arms and cocks his head all sassy at me—"you're the one who said Grade 12 is supposed to be about experiences. You've never been to a school dance before, so *experience it.*"

I sigh. "Telling me no one else is going is not a great selling point."

"Then bring someone. Bring . . . whatsername."

"Ash?"

"Yeah. Ash. She has cool vibes. Maybe she'll class up the place."

I laugh, but David's right. Ash *does* have cool vibes. "I still don't have a costume though."

He rolls his eyes dramatically. "Wear a garbage bag. Seriously, I need all hands on deck."

When I text Ash about the dance, her response is *will there be booze,* no question mark. When I reply that I highly doubt it, she texts *ehhhh* and agrees on the condition I find us both costumes.

I sketch out costume ideas in my notebook while we wait for the real AP English teacher, who is supposed to show up today. Ash sits next to me and watches my edits on De Di's laptop. I flick my eyes to her from time to time: she's deeply focused, hunched over with her chin in one hand, fingers obscuring her mouth.

Finally, she says, "Dude, this is sick."

"Really?" I let go of a breath I didn't know I was holding.

"Yeah." Something about the way she says "yeah" tells me she really means it. "You made my edit look like crap." When she sees my face, she laughs and adds, "I mean that in a good way! That's some sick color correction. It's a totally different feel. Makes winter feel like summer. Who knew chill music makes skateboarding look even gnarlier? And that boneless?" I had snuck some alley clips in there. "Damn, you were right, J.W. That's one sick shot."

I smile. I try to think of something to say, but a deep, growling voice behind us interrupts everything.

"Put your fancy electronics away before I confiscate and pawn 'em because the union can't negotiate half a dime."

The class shuts up and spins to face the door. Ash slowly closes the laptop and slides it over into my lap. A short, wiry man stands at the classroom entrance with his hands in his pockets. He's bald with an impeccably groomed beard, small dark eyes, and a look that says he lives in a world of perpetual disappointment.

"I'm Mr. Hussein and I will be your Advanced Placement English teacher." His voice is bigger than he is, booming across the class. "Let me make one thing clear." I feel Ash trying to stifle her giggles next to me. "I will have no bullshit in this class. You're all smart—allegedly—if you got into this class. And I've heard some wildly impressive things about this school, so my expectations are up here." He points to the ceiling. "Which means I expect nothing short of excellence from each and every one of you. I intend to run this class like a college course, so I won't chase you down for every missed assignment. I won't call your mommy and daddy to discipline you. When the final comes around and you've done zero work, that's on you."

Ash stops giggling. Mr. Hussein picks up a stack of papers from his desk and begins handing them out. "Let's get down to business. Everyone, pick a partner. I don't care whom. Pick your best friend, and if they screw you over, too bad. Then pick an author from this list. You'll read a major work by that author, write a two thousand-word paper, and do a presentation in front of the class. These presentations will happen throughout the year. Once you have your partner and choice of author, I'll assign you a random date."

People start muttering to each other. The kids with reputations for being the smartest suddenly get attention. I look at the author list. Some of the names I recognize: William Shakespeare, T. S. Eliot, Charles Dickens. Others, I don't: Angela Carter, Toni Morrison, Susan Sontag. I groan.

"Tell me about it," Ash mutters beside me. "Most of these are dead white guys with nothing interesting to say. Except maybe Oscar Wilde. I say we pick one of the ladies, like Mary Shelley." Her finger traces down the list and halts near the end. "Oh hey, let's do Virginia Woolf!"

"Let's?" I say. "Are we partnering up?"

She gives me an are-you-serious look. "Did you have other plans?"

I shrug. "Virginia Woolf, it is."

We go to the library to pick out our books. I go to the W section and pull out the skinniest book there. "How about this one?"

Ash makes a face. "*The Waves*? Didn't care much for that one. I want *Orlando*."

"There's no *Orlando* here."

We're the only ones in the stacks. Everyone else is at the computers discussing page counts and SparkNotes. Mr. Hussein walks by, and Ash tells him we can't find the book we want.

He nods thoughtfully. "Interesting choice. I would have thought *Mrs. Dalloway* would be your entryway into Woolf."

"*Mrs. Dalloway* is an excellent commentary on early modern feminism, but a presentation on it will put everyone to sleep," Ash says. I hear a lift in her voice, something that has never appeared with any of the substitute teachers. "We want something fun. A romance."

A faint suggestion of warmth twinkles in Mr. Hussein's eyes. "I see."

"Wait, we're reading a romance?" I've seen girls swoon over Mr. Darcy and Edward Cullen and I can't imagine being one of them.

"Relax," Ash says. "It's not cheesy."

"My partner works at a bookstore," Mr. Hussein says. "I can probably find you two copies." He then gives Ash and me a presentation date near the end of the year.

"So what kind of uncheesy romance is this story?" I ask Ash when we're alone again.

"Oh, it's super interesting. It's about a man who becomes a woman but stays the same person."

"How is that romantic?"

"It was inspired by Virginia Woolf's lover, Vita Sackville-West."

"Vita." I frown. "Is that a woman's name?"

Ash waggles her eyebrows. "Exactly."

CHAPTER 3

When I get home, I upload my edit to YouTube now that Ash has given it her blessing. It's only forty-five seconds, but the views start trickling in. Nothing wild, but throughout the night, the numbers slowly climb. For the fun of it, I send the video link to Gabby, the skater girl from Seattle, in a private message. I don't expect her to respond, but almost immediately I see a comment from her username. All she's written is *SIIICKKK*. Then, I get a private message: *yo ash you're killin it im gonna send this to all my friends*. I text Ash to tell her and she responds: *fuckkk yeahhh!!!* Sure enough—maybe because Gabby shared the video—the numbers climb even faster. I can't contain my excitement, so I text David the news, but he doesn't respond.

I don't have much homework, so I rewatch one of my favorite movies, *Spirited Away*. I know it's supposed to be a kids' movie. The first time I watched it I was seven and it terrified me. But since then, I've rewatched it at least once a year and every time I do, I notice something new, or something takes on a new meaning. I wish anime was taken more seriously instead of being labeled a nerd genre.

The next day as Ash and I skate to school, I tell her I have an awesome idea for a costume if only I had the right clothes and some fabric.

"Then go buy clothes," Ash says.

"I don't want to buy new clothes just for one night."

"Duh, don't. Go to the thrift store."

I've never even been to a thrift store, and there aren't any in our neighborhood. "Where's a good thrift store?" I ask. "Maybe one with bedsheets, so I can get some cheap fabric."

She thinks for a bit then says, "We can go to my favorite one downtown. Wanna go after school?"

I have an invitation from David to study for tomorrow's geography test at his place. Geography is one of the few classes we have together, and studying with David almost always guarantees a good grade. But so far Ms. Gill has been an easy teacher and I'm not worried. I tell Ash, "You don't have to come with me, you know. Like, if your parents want you home or something."

She laughs. "My parents don't care. Besides, we can get some cool shots in Gastown while we're there." It boggles my mind how easily Ash can change her plans. Her parents must be super chill or something.

As for me, I text David that I won't be coming and then phone De Di. I tell him I need to get materials for a school project at a big art store downtown. He grunts and tells me to be home for dinner.

It's been a while since I've been downtown. We used to visit Chinatown every weekend or so when I was younger, when the only major Chinese grocery store was there. Then Richmond got super developed and now there are tons of places to buy Chinese groceries south of the Fraser River. De Di avoids downtown now because the streets are narrow, parking is expensive, and Ma Mi says the people lumbering about on drugs make her nervous.

A man in a tie-dyed T-shirt with a guitar slung over his shoulder climbs aboard our bus without paying his fare. If I had been riding with my parents, they would have muttered something about the transit authority not using their brains by not installing turnstiles. My parents have lived here for decades, but there are some things they're still not used to. Such as the honor system, people who sit in cafés for hours without buying a drink, and why everyone's obsessed with making marijuana legal. The guitar man croons an atonal ditty at the back of the bus and everyone pretends he doesn't exist.

We get off just before Waterfront, where tourists and people who live on the street move around like water and oil refusing to mix. Ash throws down and skates east toward Gastown. I follow her. I'm not nearly as fast or confident, but I'm getting better at absorbing all the bumps and cracks. Going faster helps, plus slightly unweighting my feet now and then.

The thrift store smells like wet towels. While everything is categorized by size and gender, you have to flip through each individual hanger because there's only one of everything. I'm embarrassed to admit I've never bought clothes at a thrift store before. When we want cheap clothes, De Di drives us over the border to the outlet malls in Washington.

"So what are you planning for costumes?" Ash asks as I claw through a tub of bedsheets.

"You'll see."

"Better not be anything embarrassing."

"Oh no. It's gonna be epic." I'm about to walk off with a bedsheet when I notice something in the corner that's even better: an old chef's uniform. Hell yeah this'll be epic.

My chef's uniform and some clothes I want to alter come out to less than twenty-five dollars. Ash picks out a toque and some arm warmers for under seven bucks.

We leave the thrift store and pass one of those "medical" pot stores where a bunch of guys are smoking outside. They whistle when we pass them. I'm pretty sure they're just whistling at Ash because I look like a preteen boy. I try to ignore them, but Ash yells at them to fuck off. They tell her to fuck off too because they were "just giving compliments, why you gotta be bitchy?" Then one of them screams at her to do a kickflip in an obnoxious, assholey voice. Without missing a beat or saying a word, Ash jumps on her board, lands a perfect kickflip, and flips them off with both hands. She rides away, and I toss a middle finger at them too before I ride after her.

It's the golden hour, and the vintage streetlamps and cobblestone of Gastown are bathed in straw-colored light. Ash dares me to hippie jump over a chain hanging between two iron poles. Gastown is full of those, but the pavement is sketchy and I violently shake my head no. Ash lands it with no problem though, jumping over the chain and landing back on her board on the other side. Then she does it again with a 180 body varial, then she ollies it, and then she even half cabs over it. So fuck it, I try as well. My board flies backward and almost gets run over by a car. The driver yells at me and I apologize profusely, feeling myself going red. Ash sees how shaken up I am and squeezes my shoulder. "Hey, it happens. But you sent it! That's awesome."

Afterward, we walk east to the bus stop and pass the Downtown Eastside. I watch where I step in case there are needles and clutch my camera bag to my chest. We get to a block where people are selling random stuff on the street—jeans with the price tags still on, unidentifiable knickknacks, bongs, and what I recognize from Personal Development class as a crack pipe. Ash picks up her board and carries it through a part of the crowd where a good portion of people are just lying on the sidewalk—sleeping or dead, I don't know.

As we wait at a bus stop, I feel exposed and antsy. Of course, the bus is late. I'm torn between looking around to stay aware of my surroundings and avoiding making eye contact with anyone. Every minute, someone runs across the street without looking first and there's a barrage of honks and profanity. When the bus finally arrives, I'm relieved that there's a barrier between the outside world and the fare-paid zone. A second later, I'm disgusted at my own thoughts.

I had ripped a few YouTube videos onto my iPod so I watch them with Ash on the bus ride home. I can tell that she's tired, and without asking, she lays her head on my shoulder. I tense, but she's not that heavy. We watch our favorite female skaters: Leticia Bufoni. Vanessa Torres. Alexis Sablone. Marisa Dal Santo. I like listening to Ash explain why her favorite skaters are so good. "It's all about the style. The ease. The steez. The ease of steez." She admits that she dyes her hair red because she wants a signature, a brand. "Like how Leticia Bufoni wears headbands in her videos."

The bus passes people clumped together under awnings and tents and tarps. I gesture at a group huddled in front of an abandoned storefront. Some of them stand at weird angles, swaying and drooping. "Why do you think they're all like that?" I ask. "Like they're falling asleep on their feet."

I say it like it's a funny observation, but Ash doesn't smile. "They're high," she says.

It's getting dark. I text my dad to eat dinner without me. There will probably be questions when I get home, but I'll just say I was wandering downtown for inspiration. Which isn't untrue. We cross back over to Kitsilano on the Burrard Bridge. The sky is dark and gray, and soon, tiny flecks of water glance across the windows. We just missed the rain.

. . .

A few nights before the Halloween dance, Ma Mi finds me in my room sewing, my music on full blast. I don't notice her until she walks into the room, arms akimbo. I jump. "Jesus! You scared me."

"Do not take the Lord's name in vain." She scowls at the mess of fabric on the floor. "What is all this?"

"School," I say, avoiding her eyes. "It's for Open Studio." Her eyebrows arch in suspicion. I cave. "It's for a thing I'm doing for David."

"Oh. David." She relaxes a little. "I haven't seen him at all this year."

"Well. You know David. He's busy. Got his hands full with Student Council and stuff."

"You've made a new friend, haven't you?" Ma Mi says. "The one that lives on our block? De Di says the two of you skateboard to school together."

I look away. "Yeah, that's Ash—Ashley."

"Is she Chinese? Korean?"

I roll my eyes. One of the first things Ma Mi asks when I meet someone new is what race they are. If they're Asian, she wants to know what type of Asian. Which always weirds me out. "Yeah, she's Cantonese."

"Cantonese. Hong Kong? Mainland—Guangdong?"

"I don't know."

Ma Mi flips over some of the fabric on the ground with her toe. "De Di says he sees her skateboarding in the middle of the day. I hope she's not skipping school. I hear a lot of Grade 12s do that, skip school."

I look down at my sewing. Ash has actually invited me to skip school more than once. Last week, she had walked up to me after my Math class, dark circles under her eyes, and said, "Wanna get out early?" Nervously, I'd said no. She'd shrugged and left without saying anything. I don't get how she's so blasé about skipping because the school calls your parents if you don't show up for class. My mom got a call once because there was a mistake, and I came home to a freakout.

"Be careful who you spend time with," Ma Mi says. "It's your last year la. Very important."

"Weren't you listening? I'm doing this for David."

"Which means you have to focus on your grades," Ma Mi says. "I'm sure David is doing something very interesting, but if it's not for school—"

"Don't worry, Ma Mi."

Ma Mi lingers at my door for a few more seconds then sighs and leaves.

. . .

The night of the Halloween dance, I find Ash waiting by my garage, shivering in her costume. But the moment she sees me, it's like she suddenly stops feeling cold. She whistles. "Whoa, you really outdid yourself, J.W."

I grin back. I'm proud of our costumes. Ash's isn't too eye-catching—her hair's tied back and she's wearing an oversized white T-shirt with a light green stripe sewn across it, paired with pink shorts—but that was her one request: "I'll dress up as whatever if it's not super uncomfortable or embarrassing." Meanwhile, I turned my chef's jacket into a white kimono, tied it with a wide purple scarf, and paired the set with knee-length blue baggy shorts I found in the boys' section of the thrift store. It's super DIY compared to the pro-level *Spirited Away* cosplayers I see on DeviantArt, but we're instantly recognizable as Haku and Chihiro if you know the movie.

"Dang, now I wish I was Haku," Ash says.

"Too bad. I look more like a guy," I say.

Ash chuckles. "I thought Haku was a girl at first. He's so androgynous, I love it."

"No one's gonna recognize who you guys are going as." We turn around to see Wendy, who is shutting the back door behind her. She wears eyeliner whiskers and cardboard cat ears. Which is a low-effort attempt, in my opinion. I'm surprised Wendy is going to the dance at all. Maybe David convinced her, too.

"I'm sure they will," Ash says when she catches my worried look. "There are so many Asian kids in this school—someone must watch Studio Ghibli movies."

When we get to the school gym, they're blasting that Black Eyed Peas song about tonight being a good night. It echoes with desperation into the empty auditorium. Strobe lights flash across orange streamers and unoccupied space. The only people here are Student Council folks and their friends. Ms. Osborne, the vice principal and dance chaperone, stands yawning next to a table piled high with cans of pop, bowls of chips, and jumbo boxes of Hallowe'en candies.

A ghost—a literal bedsheet with two holes cut out of it—darts toward me and I recognize its gait as David's. "Oh my god, thank you for coming!" His voice rushes out of his eyeholes like it's a dying spirit clamoring for escape.

"That's what she said," Ash mutters next to me.

The ghost looks at Ash then back at me. "So . . . what are you two supposed to be?"

"Seriously?!" I exclaim. "Chihiro and Haku from *Spirited Away*!" When David's eyeholes stare blankly back at me, I say, "I showed you the movie in Grade 8, remember? I was bawling on the couch?"

"Oh. The movie you showed me after my piano competition? I fell asleep during that, remember? I was so tired." David chuckles awkwardly while I roll my eyes. Then he says to us, "Enjoy the party, I guess. Please don't make a mess because I'm the one who has to clean it up. Now if you'll excuse me, I have to make sure those Grade 8 reps don't eff up the foam tombstones. Man, I just *love* my job!"

David floats away. Ash and I stake out a position near the chips and candy. We stuff our faces and wash it all down with off-brand pop. Non-Student-Council people slowly trickle in now that it's half an hour after the official start time and they're therefore fashionably late. The DJ is in his own world, giant headphones clamped around his ears as he blends one top 40 teen track into the next. The teens in question stand in a rigid clump by the stage, as if any small movement would constitute dancing and should be avoided. I try to look over their heads for David, but it's like he's become his costume and disappeared. Meanwhile, the pop I drank makes a beeline to my bladder.

The girls' washroom is rowdier than the actual dance—a cacophony of people doing their eyeliner and taking photos with their phones. Sophie and Min are in a corner with some other girls. I go into a stall, do my business, and when I'm done they're still there, deep in conversation.

I go up to them. "Hey, you guys seen David?"

"Probably in a room blowing up balloon," says Min. "That's, like, most of his job."

"Hey, Jay," Sophie says, "help us settle a debate. Who do you think is cuter, Austin Tang, Trevor Brooks, or Kevin Kim?" The other girls peer at me like I'm about to break a tie on a game show.

"Uh." I hesitate. "I dunno. None of the above?" I don't really think any of the guys at our school are "cute."

Sophie scowls. "Seriously? Not even Kevin? Guy could be in a K-pop group."

"I say Trevor," says one of the other girls. "Love an emo guy."

"I'm gonna look for David," I mutter.

I hear one of the girls say, "Hey, David's gay. That's a theory, right?" as the washroom door swings behind me. I stop and consider going back to ask what makes her think that, but then I shake it off. Some people just really have nothing better to talk about.

David is still MIA when I get back to the dance floor, which is marginally more energetic now. I find Ash in the same place, chewing on gummy worms. "Sup?" she says to me.

"Just had a *fascinating* conversation in the girls' washroom about who's cutest," I say, "Austin, Trevor, or Kevin."

"Kevin Santos?" I shoot Ash a look and she shrugs. "Well, he's certainly better-looking than Kevin Kim in my Shop class."

"I just don't get why boys are so fascinating," I say.

Ash laughs. "That's 'cause you're like me. You'd rather do stuff than stand around and talk."

"Ew, I don't want to *do* any of those guys," I say.

Ash's laugh is full-blown. "I mean stuff like skate and hang out."

We stand there watching bodies bob off beat for a few more moments. Then Ash elbows me lightly in the arm. "Y'know, if you want to leave, I know somewhere we can go."

"Where?" More people are here now. Still far from a full house, but enough to be respectable for David.

"There's a small thing at a skate park in East Van."

"That's far," I say. "We won't get home until late. My mom . . ." I trail off and wait for Ash to groan at me. But all she does is plunge her hand into the chip bowl.

"You can tell her you're staying over at David's."

"David's a guy. She doesn't let me stay over at guys' houses."

"Then tell her you're at Sophie's or Min's." She shrugs again. "Or we can just stay here. Up to you."

"Right. But . . ." Then I remember my time capsule project and it hits me: I've never skipped school, gone to a party, tried drugs, had sex, or done any of those *Dazed and Confused* things. Maybe, for once, I should do something daring. Something "bad." It's my last year of high school, after all. Shouldn't I have some stories? Don't I deserve stories?

"Fuck it, let's do it."

Ash's eyebrows go up. Is she surprised? Impressed? I can't tell.

I still can't find David, but he's probably busy anyway. We slip past costumed bodies, down the hall, past the washrooms, and into the chilly night. I'm rehearsing lies in my head to tell my mom when something out of the corner of my eye makes me stop. "Holy shit."

Two people are making out behind the big tree just outside the staff room window. It takes me a second to place the guy, a skinny dude with floppy curls. He doesn't go to George Van, but I recognize him from Wendy's orchestra. And he's kissing Wendy. Ash starts giggling, which Wendy hears. She sees us and shoves the guy into the bushes like he's a hot potato.

Wendy runs toward me and snarls, "You can't tell Mom and Dad! Swear to me you won't tell them about Justin!"

I smirk. "You do know this one's going into the blackmail deck."

But Wendy's eyes are even more on fire than the jack-o'-lanterns decorating the gym. "Don't you dare! If they knew—" She lowers her voice. "If they knew I was seeing a guy, and a Black guy at that—"

"What?" I laugh. "Our parents aren't racist."

"They're absolutely racist!" Wendy says through her teeth. "Jeez, have you never heard De Di talk? 'Black people are lazy.' 'Black people are only good at sports.'"

"Huh." Behind Wendy, Justin is still standing awkwardly next to the tree, hands stuffed in his pockets. I'm glad he can't overhear us.

Wendy sighs loudly. "So. What do you want?"

"Tell Mom I'll be home late because I'm helping David clean up," I say.

Wendy frowns at me then at Ash. "Where are you guys going?"

"To a party," Ash says. "Wanna come?"

"What party?" Wendy whirls on me, eyes wide. "Jay, what the hell are you trying to pull? Won't David be pissed?"

"David's too busy to be pissed. Just cover for me, yeah? And have fun with Justin. Use protection or . . . whatever." Maybe I've had too much sugar, but I find myself caring little about consequences. Ash shouts at me that the bus is coming. We sprint for it, and I feel so light I think I could float up into the sky.

"Wendy seems like she's living her best life," Ash muses once we sit down on the bus.

"I'm surprised she even came to the dance. But now I know why," I say, still a little shaken that my sister has kissed a boy on the lips. In fact, I'm surprised Wendy is dating at all. It's almost like she's cheating on her textbooks.

"She's really good at music, right?"

"Yeah. She plays violin in a youth orchestra. She's the concertmaster," I say.

"Do you play anything?"

I shrug. "I play percussion in band. Mom tried to put me in piano lessons alongside Wendy, but I hated practicing. You?"

"Nah. My dad made me do piano lessons. But instead of making sure I practiced while he was at work"—she snickers—"my por por took me to the park to skateboard."

I laugh. "Your por por sounds cool. Jeez, what is it with Asian parents wanting so desperately for their kids to learn classical music?"

Ash shrugs. "I think it's an assimilation thing. Like, you want your kids to be sophisticated and Western."

"So, I'm guessing you don't play anymore?" I ask.

Ash laughs, but it's a different laugh. A heavier laugh. "Nah. My dad broke the piano."

"Wait, what?"

"He asked me to play 'Für Elise' one day, and when I couldn't, he threw a hammer at my hands. But I was too quick. He missed and broke the keyboard instead." She chuckles.

I stare at her. "Dude, what the fuck."

She points at something out the window. "I've heard good things about that skate shop. We should go sometime."

The skate park Ash brings me to is a nest of noise inside an otherwise quiet residential neighborhood. I've never been here and I have to convince my legs to keep moving forward instead of running away. Excited voices echo through the night. Aluminum cans crinkle as they're thrown against the ground. And there's a heavy, skunky smell that I recognize as weed from our excursion downtown. Tinny music plays from someone's phone, which they've stuck in a mug to amplify the sound.

Most people aren't in costume, and no one is dressed as an anime character. I brace myself for weird stares and hidden laughter. But people either ignore us or give us polite nods of acknowledgment before going back to skating, drinking, smoking, or hanging around. There's a big tree strung with glowsticks in the middle of the park, and a bunch of non-skaters sit under it, talking and drinking. The tree looks like a bioluminescent coral reef—magical.

Ash casually walks up to a tall blond guy wearing a fox onesie and glasses. He throws up his hands with glee when he sees her. They fist-bump each other and even hug. I hang back, fumbling with my pockets, until the guy notices me, too. He stares at us, and then a grin slowly spreads across his face. "You're from that anime with the really good music that won all those awards!" He hikes his thumb at us and shouts, "Aren't these kids killing it?" We get a few whoops. I don't think anyone recognizes us, but a group of girls who are sitting under the glowstick tree shoot "aww, such cute kids" faces at us.

"This is Simon," Ash says, and the tall fox guy gives me a dorky wave. "I was in the same class as his brother Dezzy. We all used to skate together. Speaking of—"

"He's grounded," Simon groans. "Again."

"Hey, thanks for getting me that shift at Burger Truck last weekend," Ash says, bumping his arm with a fist.

Simon seems friendly, if a little smelly. I'm guessing he smokes. He thrusts two cans of beer into our hands. "Cheers," Ash says.

Simon clinks cans with her. "How's your new school?"

Ash glugs down five big gulps of beer and shrugs. "It's kinda nerdy, but Jay's cool." She looks over at me and her smile is lit up by the glow-sticks. "Jay made these costumes all by herself."

"Way to go, Jay!" Simon gives me a fist bump.

I knock back a large gulp of beer and almost choke. Bitter liquid leaks out of the corner of my mouth. I turn around quickly to make sure no one sees me.

Ash takes me around the park, saying hi, introducing me to people whose names I instantly forget. She tells me her main group of friends aren't here. A few people tell Ash that her latest edit was sick, and Ash immediately points to me. People give me fist bumps, and it's like me being in a nerdy anime costume doesn't matter. I watch skaters dip in and out of the bowls, mesmerized by their graceful movements and occasional bails. Then I hear a cloud of noise and it's Ash arguing with Simon and a few guys. Someone thrusts a board at her. She shakes her head a few times then grabs it. She makes a running start toward the bowls and leaps on.

I panic for a moment—I don't want to be alone with strangers while Ash skates, but no one's even looking at me because they're all staring at her. She carves the bowl like it's butter then throws the cleanest 5-0 grind on the coping. A few people stomp their boards. She flies out, pumps toward a pile of beer cans, and ollies over them. Clean. The banging boards crescendo, and Ash is bombarded by fist bumps. I wish I had my camera.

Simon walks up next to me and takes a big drag off whatever he's smoking. "She's a beaut, eh?"

"Yeah," I say. "She's super talented."

Ash throws a sketchy tre flip. Tre flips are when you combine a 360 pop shove-it and a kickflip. That is, you flip the board and spin it around at the same time. I expect her to trip up, but she lands it, just barely. She returns her borrowed board and I follow her to sit down under the glowstick tree with the other people who are hanging out around the mug-phone. Ash nudges me with her knee and nods at the park. "Wanna have a go?"

I shake my head. Hard. "Are you kidding me? I've never dropped in ever in my life."

Her eyebrows shoot up. "Never? Shit, we gotta come back here with Dez and Matt and teach you."

I'm about to laugh off the offer, but Ash's attention is already stolen. There's a game of SKATE happening: a challenger does a trick, and if the next person can't do it, they get a letter. Spell out SKATE and you lose. Two guys do rock paper scissors and the winner shouts for trick suggestions. "Laser flip!" Ash yells. One guy laughs and says, "Fuck you, Ash!"

A guy leaves his pod of friends by the stair set and approaches us, holding a beer. He doesn't look like the other guys. He wears a cardigan and has wiry glasses perched on his nose. The way he looks at us, all serious and focused, makes me feel like a textbook.

He stands over us. I watch him. Ash, eyes glued to the SKATE game, doesn't notice him, and he doesn't notice me. "Hey," he says.

Ash doesn't take her eyes off the game. "Hey."

"You're friends with Dezzy, right? Simon's little brother?"

"Yeah."

"May I?" He gestures at the empty space on Ash's other side, and she shrugs. He sits down. The SKATE players both land their nollie back 180s and Ash whoops.

"I'm Blake. I go to culinary school with Simon," says the guy.

"Cool." Ash watches the next skater throw an unexpectedly elegant old-school boneless.

"I went to Mackenzie, too." Ash's eyes flicker with neon blue as they follow the skaters in the park. Blake presses on. "I dropped out in Grade 12 though. Moved out at seventeen and finished the year in distance ed. That's probably why we've never met."

Finally, Ash's eyes shift to him. "Huh, probably. You got your own place at seventeen?"

He shakes his head. "Crashed with friends. But boy was it glorious." He smiles. "I saw you skate. You've got balls. Heh. I don't think I've ever said that to a girl."

There's an awkward pause, and then Blake slurps in a breath and says, "You guys want a joint?"

Ash perks up. "Aw yeah. I never say no to weed."

Blake pulls out a baggie with a cone-shaped joint in it. He sticks the joint in Ash's mouth and cups his hands around the tip. There's the click of a lighter and a flare of fire. Ash tilts her head into his hands, and the way he stares at her sketches me out a little. Wisps of smoke float from his hands, turning violet under the glowsticks. Soon, the air is thick with a pungent sweetness.

Ash throws back her head and exhales a thick cloud of smoke into the sky. Blake's still watching her, but so am I. Then I clear my throat and say, "Hey, can I take a puff?"

Ash raises her eyebrows at me. "You smoke?"

"No, but I've always wanted to try." I've been curious about shrooms and weed ever since learning about them in our antidrug classes, which were probably less effective than our teachers expected them to be. I'd gone home to read forums where people described their feelings of intoxication, and I've been waiting for someone to hand me a joint at a party ever since.

Ash hands me the joint. "Dude, pass to the left," Blake says from her other side, but Ash ignores him.

"Take a breath," she says. "Then do a short sip from the filter and then gulp back another lungful of pure air." She mimes the movements as she describes them, but my head's all cloudy from the beer, and her words don't land. I take the joint though, holding it awkwardly, scared that I'll either burn my fingers or drop it and set the park on fire. Forgetting what Ash told me to do, all I get is a mouthful of harsh, hot air and soon I'm coughing and choking up a storm.

Blake laughs.

"Shut up, we're seventeen," Ash says as I pass the joint to him.

Blake leans on an elbow and faces the sky. He holds the joint with long, slender fingers, his hand relaxed. It actually looks cool, the way he knocks back his head and takes short puffs followed by a long draw. "I liked your tailslide," he says to Ash. Ash didn't do a tailslide, she did a 5-0.

"Thanks," Ash says, and I'm surprised she doesn't bother correcting him. Instead, she burps loudly, but Blake doesn't seem to notice. She asks, "You skate?"

"Yeah, but just to get to school and work and stuff. How's the weed?"

"It's chill. Good shit."

Blake leans over her. "It's a really nice strain. An indica-dominant cultivar bred by some OG hippies on the Island." I wish the joint would circle back to me, but he uses it like a baton as he talks.

"What does that mean?" Ash asks.

"Indicas are the mellower strains and sativas are the more cerebral ones, but this one's a hybrid that combines the best of both worlds. You feel relaxed but not sleepy, and you get all the mental stimulation of a sativa without the anxiety that's usually associated with them." Blake sucks on the joint. "So. What do you do? Other than skate, that is."

"Listen to music and read books, mostly." Ash says. "Jay's gotten me into a few movies."

Blake says, "I like books more than movies, personally. I prefer using my own imagination."

"Some movies let you do that," I say. Blake's eyes flick to me for a moment before going back to Ash.

Ash says, "What do you read?"

"What do *you* read?"

"Well, last week I borrowed *On the Road*."

Blake's eyebrows jump up. "Holy shit, you read the Beats? Wow. I'm a huge Kerouac fan, myself. Did you know he wrote that manuscript—"

"On one continuous sheet of paper." Ash nods and grins. "Yes. I've read the Wikipedia page. Pretty sick."

"Man, wouldn't it be cool to go on a trip like in *On the Road*? Just drive to who knows where, conked out on acid."

"You'd need to have really good music," Ash says.

"Right. Well, what kinda music do you like?"

"What kinda music do *you* like?"

"Y'know. Punk. Hardcore. Metal. The works."

Ash nods slowly. "That's a good sound."

I make a mental note to look up the Beats when I get home, but I doubt my brain—marinating in a stew of drugs and alcohol—will remember.

Blake and Ash keep talking about the subgenres of punk music like I'm not there, so I watch the guys skate instead. I don't get how they can throw themselves into reckless tricks with no regard for safety. Maybe it's a dude thing, to be reckless. I've seen YouTube comments saying that's why men's skateboarding is ahead of women's. I just hope it's not something inborn, something you're stuck with. Sometimes, I wish I was a guy. Maybe if I was a guy, Ma Mi and De Di would let me stay out late instead of having a heart attack every time I get home after sunset. My life could be full of risks and adventure instead of my current rotation of homework, movies, and occasional cosplaying.

Ash lobs words at me, but she sounds like she's speaking underwater so all I do is grunt in response. The joint's back in my hand. I try to perfect my inhale, but whenever I hold the smoke in for more than a second, I collapse into a coughing mess. *Oracular Spectacular* plays in the mug-phone. People get louder. If I close my eyes, I can hear every single instrument from the mug-phone. They swirl together on the backs of my eyelids. I get dizzy so I open my eyes. Skateboarders spin tricks in slo-mo, grind boxes and rails in slo-mo, fall over themselves and gurgle expletives in slo-mo. I don't remember "Time to Pretend" being this long. When I'd first heard it on the radio a few years back, I had thought it sounded strange, but now, it's beautiful. The whole night is beautiful. The glowsticks, the music, the skateboarders lapping the park, the company—well, at least the company I came with.

I want to tell Ash how beautiful everything is. I turn around to hear Blake say, "It's rad you like Violent Femmes."

Ash says, "It's cool you know them."

Blake snorts. "Of course I do! It's *Violent Femmes*. Y'know, it's so hard to find people who appreciate punk these days. *Real* punk, not Avril Lavigne."

They stare at each other for a bit. I can't see Ash's face from where I'm sitting, only Blake's, and maybe it's the weed clouding my perception, but he has a face like a pug's and I've always found squishy dog faces off-putting.

He says, "I'm in a band, you know. Wanna go somewhere quieter and listen to some music?"

Ash turns around, a silhouette backlit by the glowsticks. She says to me, "I'm gonna be over there by the trees, yeah?"

I squint and nod. My mouth feels like a desert, so I grab a lukewarm beer from a near-empty six-pack under the glowstick tree. It's getting chilly so I roll myself into a ball. There are fewer people skating now. Most are sitting with friends, drinking and talking.

I stand up and the blood drains from my head. I almost black out. I blink, sway, and take a moment to stand still. I want to go home.

I spot Ash and Blake standing inside a grove of trees, each wearing one earbud. They can't see me from their angle, but I can hear them. "The asshole thing about this province is you're not legal until you're nineteen," Blake says. "But that doesn't mean you can't get the ball rolling. You got money?"

"I pick up a shift here and there at Simon's restaurant."

"You thinking of college?"

"Not until I have more money."

"Good. That's smart. Everyone says you should go to school first, but not everyone has parents who have ten grand just sitting around."

Ash laughs.

"If you want my advice, pick a trade," says Blake. "You don't have to sit in a classroom for four years and trades pay better than whatever an English major makes anyway. You can learn hair or nails or something."

"Or fix cars."

"Or fix cars. You know a lot about cars?"

Ash shrugs. "Cars are just skateboards on steroids."

Blake laughs.

I frown. Ash has never told me what she wants to do after high school, just that she can't wait to be done with it. I hug the shadows because I feel like a creep watching them, but I also need to tell Ash that I want to leave.

Then Blake takes a step forward, and his hand wraps around Ash's neck and jaw.

He pulls her face toward him. His hand is huge. Ash's finger hooks onto one of his belt loops and pulls him toward her. His knee finds the gap between her legs.

I force myself to turn around and walk back to the party. I sit under the glowstick tree until Ash and Blake come back after what seems like forever, bumping elbows and laughing.

CHAPTER 4

The next morning, I wake up all loopy. Turns out David sent me a bunch of texts last night:

yo where are u?

hey I can't find you where u at?

JAY. Where the heck are u???? dude srsly.

I text back, *i'll explain on monday.* David doesn't respond at all, which makes me uneasy, but after sitting at my desk nervously for a few minutes, I realize there's nothing I can do.

So I spend the rest of the weekend with headphones clapped on my ears, rushing through homework and then sifting through the clips we collected in Gastown. One line—Ash's hippie jump body varial over the chain followed by a switch no comply 180 and then a pop shove—was particularly steezy. But the pop shove is atrociously tiny on my screen because I was stationary when I was filming. I chew my lip. I'll have to learn how to follow.

On Monday, I don't see David in the lounge so I go straight to geography. He comes in just after the bell, nods at me, and sits down on the other side of the room. We learn about glaciers and, suddenly, the period is over. I watch David out of the corner of my eye, but instead of approaching me, he just shoves his books into his backpack and leaves. I catch up with him in the hall. He keeps walking. "Hey, David."

He stares at his moving feet. "Hey."

"How was the dance?"

As if on cue, a group of guys pass us with a holler and one of them claps David on the shoulder. "Dude, you are *legendary*!" David gives a timid smile in return.

"What was *that*?" I say.

His mouth is a thin, straight line and his eyes point ahead. "Eh, you missed it. I did a thing at the dance."

"What kinda thing?"

"A dance kinda thing."

I try to imagine David dancing, but my mind draws a blank.

He clears his throat. "I was trying to find you. You totally disappeared."

"So did you," I say.

"I had stuff to do." A pause then he asks, "Did you leave early?"

I clear my throat and focus on putting one foot in front of the other. "Yeah. I'm sorry. I wanted to say bye to you, but I couldn't find you. And honestly, I was getting bored, so—"

"So you went home," he says flatly.

"Well . . . no." I can't lie to David. I'll lie to my parents because I didn't choose them as my adult overlords. But I chose David as my friend.

"Then where the heck did you go?" His forehead folds into a dozen little crinkles.

"We went to a party."

"We?"

"Ash and I."

"Oh." He frowns. "Whose party?"

"A friend from Ash's old school," I say. I add, as jokingly as I can, "What is this, an interrogation?"

David grunts. "No. Whatever. It's fine. You showed up and that's all I asked for, right? I gotta . . ." He tips his head to the boys' washroom and ducks in.

At lunch, I find Ash in the cafeteria. By now, we've established that the corner table near B-wing is our spot. Sophie and Min sit there too, mostly out of habit because David isn't available for lunch half the time due to his extracurriculars. Ash is the first one there today, eating beans straight out of a can. I grimace. "Isn't that cold?"

She shrugs. "Fills you up." She licks her fork. "So. How was losing your weed virginity?"

"Pretty cool, I guess." I have to admit that listening to music high is pretty awesome. But it's not something I want to do every day.

Ash smirks. "And now that I have a dealer boyfriend, we can get as much weed as we like. Well," she amends, "he's not exactly a dealer. He works at a quasilegal dispensary."

"Wait—he's your boyfriend?"

Sophie and Min sit down at our table just as Ash nods. Min stares at Ash's beans.

"Hey, where were you at the dance?" Sophie says to me. "David was looking for you but you just, like, disappeared."

"I just left early," I tell her. "We talked. He's okay."

But Sophie and Min exchange uneasy glances. "You missed his thing, you know," Min says into her dinner roll.

"Was this dance really that epic?" I say.

Sophie and Min exchange another glance. Sophie shrugs. "You kinda had to be there."

We eat our lunch in awkward silence. Then Ash mumbles something to me and all I catch is "outside." She slips away from the table and chucks her empty can into the recycling bin before power walking out the door.

"Did she seriously eat a can of bean for lunch?" Min says.

I ignore her. "Hey, is David okay?" I ask Sophie.

"I don't know." Sophie avoids my eyes and pushes her food around her plate.

"I was looking for him, you know. It's not my fault I couldn't find him."

Sophie shrugs. "I think—I think he was just really stressed about the dance. But it all worked out, I guess."

We eat in silence. Then Min says to Sophie, "Hey, so did you watch *Brotherhood* or no?"

I'm relieved because I've only seen the original *Fullmetal Alchemist* so have nothing to contribute to the conversation. I eat as fast as I can and mutter, "See you later."

David is nowhere to be found, so I go old-school. I write on a piece of notebook paper, *Hey David. I'm sorry I left the dance. Your dance must've been pretty cool. Tell me about it sometime? <3 Jay.* I slip the note into his locker.

At the end of the day, I catch a glimpse of David shutting his locker on his way out. He must have seen the note, but he doesn't bring it up.

. . .

I ask my parents for risers and larger, softer wheels for my board. It's so I can follow better, but I tell them it's for safety because the bigger your wheels, the easier it is to roll over obstacles and not trip and die. The risers, on the other hand, prevent wheelbite.

"Do you seriously have time to skateboard so much?" Ma Mi asks. "Shouldn't you be studying?"

"Finals aren't until June. And filming skateboarding stuff is part of Open Studio," I say. Well, I can only really use it for 10 percent of my grade, but Ma Mi doesn't need to know that.

She looks at my dad, who shrugs. "Safety is important."

Ma Mi sighs and gives me her approval.

I don't have a safety reason for camera accessories, though, and if there's one inexcusable thing, it's a shaky shot. When I tell Ash this, she crosses her arms, furrows her eyebrows, and says, "My dad's got a bunch of random scrap in the garage, I'll see what I can do."

And sure enough, she comes to school the next day with a DIY camera handle. "Holy shit," I breathe. "You're a genius."

Ash shrugs. "Three years of Shop. You learn a few things." When she sees me peer at the handle, she smirks and says, "That's from my dad's golf club. I've never seen him golf in his life. Still"—she winks—"don't tell him."

Remembering the piano–hammer incident, I nod gravely.

With the November 30 deadline coming up, it's time to shoot as much as we can. The precious few hours between school ending at three and my mom coming home at six are a hustle. Ash takes me to a few skate parks. I've never dared step into a skate park by myself because I'm scared of being called a noob. Maybe it's because I'm with Ash, who is so obviously legit, but people are way nicer than I'd imagined. Not that I do much anyway; I just cruise around, following Ash with my camera.

One time, a guy with too many piercings and tattoos to count shouts and starts walking toward me. I feel a moment of panic, but all he does is say, "You gotta shoot lower. It'll look better. Can I?" I give him my camera and he films Ash's boardslide, showing me how to zoom in on the end of the flat bar when Ash lands the trick. He's right, it does look better. More pro.

"Thanks," I say.

He grins. "Good luck!"

Because I'm not willing to skip classes or stay out way past dark, Ash sometimes borrows my camera and gets one of her friends from her old school to film street shots across the city. I'm a little disappointed that her friend—a guy who likes doing derpy faces into the camera—doesn't have the exact same shooting style as I do, but it is what it is.

When it rains, we practice flat-ground tricks in my garage. It's during one of these sessions that I land my first shove-it. It takes me hours just to get the back foot motion down and another several hours of getting confident enough to land with both feet on the board. But one day, my body feels especially flexible, I'm hyped for some reason, and I land it, and it's the most incredible feeling in the world. Ash bashes her board on the ground so hard that for a moment I think it'll break.

On sunny days, we take our breaks at the local playground at the top of the slide, looking at the North Shore mountains. I eat leftover snacks and Ash smokes cigarettes. She tells me she's been smoking on and off since Grade 9, whenever she has access. Now she gets her goods from Blake. I try a cigarette, but it just makes my head spin and my throat itchy.

"So, what's your plan after graduation?" I ask her, handing back her cig, my eyes brimming with cough-tears.

She shrugs. "I dunno. Move out. Work. Buy a car. Drive to skate comps."

I cough some more, remembering her conversation with Blake. "No school?"

"Nah. Too expensive."

"You could get a scholarship." If Ash doesn't go to school, she'll be my only friend—heck, maybe the only person in our grade—who won't be going to university next year. Which, for some reason, feels weird.

Ash has nothing to say about scholarships. Just takes a long drag off her cigarette.

I had expected her to talk incessantly about Blake, but to my pleasant surprise, she doesn't. In the past, whenever I met a girl with a boyfriend, their boyfriend was all they could talk about. As if having a boyfriend was their entire personality. But Ash's lack of gossip ironically piques my interest. I ask her, "So, what's it like dating Blake?"

Ash laughs and a plume of smoke explodes in my face. I brush it away. "What's it *like*? What do you want to know, you pervert?"

"I'm just curious. I don't have other friends who date."

She shrugs. "It's fun. We talk, listen to music, get high. We went skating a few times, but I don't think he likes it because I'm so much better than him." She laughs. "Now that it gets darker earlier, we mainly stay home and watch movies, but I like that I have a second place I can crash at."

"I thought he hates movies and only likes books," I say. "I thought you guys had a thing about the Beats."

Ash snorts. "The Beats are overrated, to be honest. They're just white dudes ripping off jazz. Their stuff *sounds* profound, but it's honestly garble disguised as high-brow shit." She flicks ash off her cigarette.

"But you like Blake," I say.

Ash nods. "Yeah. People our age tend to be shallow. Focused on mundane things like school and work and money. Blake's all about living a life that's worth it, a life based on experiences."

"Like getting high and watching movies?"

Ash either doesn't hear my sarcasm or chooses to ignore it. "He thinks we shouldn't waste our lives working. He's got this sick plan: spend your summers tree planting then live off-grid in a van away from people because people suck." I nod out of politeness. "He's also okay with polyamory, which is awesome."

"What's that?"

"It's when you date more than one person and they all know about it and consent to it."

I frown. "So like cheating?"

Her eyes widen. "It's nothing like cheating!" she says loudly, in her I'm-stoked-to-tell-you-about-this-thing-I-just-learned way. "*Everyone* consents to it. That's the difference."

I'm still frowning. "But why would you want to do that? Don't you want just one special person for yourself?"

Ash shakes her head vigorously. "That's just selfish and possessive, in my opinion. Did you know humans aren't naturally monogamous? Like, that's a real scientific theory, that monogamy is a recent invention. And it makes sense because, like, something like half of all marriages end in divorce."

"Huh."

"Yeah."

That's something I like about Ash. She talks about things from a perspective that I've never heard of before, and even if I don't agree with what she's saying, it's always interesting to think about.

Ash chucks her cigarette and continues. "I can't imagine being with *one* person for the rest of my life. I can't imagine *one* person checking all my boxes." She rolls back and forth on her board. "What if you like Bob's nose but hate his eyebrows? Or love Sally's hair but hate how loud she chews?"

I laugh. "You shouldn't date people because of their eyebrows."

"You know what I mean!"

"And are you saying you'd date a Sally?" I say.

Ash shrugs. "Those were hypothetical names."

"I know. But would you? Date a Sally, I mean. A girl."

Ash stares off into the distance for a moment. "Maybe."

"Huh."

She flashes me a cheeky grin. "Maybe if she was hot. Like, really, really hot."

I laugh.

. . .

At school, most of my attention is focused on learning all the Adobe programs. But I'm the only person in Open Studio interested in this sort of thing, and Mr. Templeton's PC is too old to handle the software without lagging. When he sees me struggling to draw a square on a skate deck template one day, he taps me on the shoulder and says, "You know, I hear they just installed some iMacs in Mr. Hussein's classroom because he runs the yearbook class now."

"Really?"

"Uh-huh."

There are only three iMacs, and the Yearbook kids use them all during my Art block, so I spend every lunch hour in Mr. Hussein's room. He doesn't mind as long as I'm quiet. It's easier to focus here, and sometimes Ash will sit with me and read a book while I do my stuff. When Mr. Hussein leaves the room, we watch skate videos on YouTube.

One day, Sophie and Min stumble in, arms linked, when Ash and I are alone. "David said you'd be here," says Min.

Sophie peers at my computer. "Whatcha doin'?"

I exit out of YouTube and pull up Adobe. "Working. Where's David?"

"Putting out another Student Council fire." Things have more or less gone back to normal between me and David. I think he just decided to pretend nothing happened, and to be honest, I'm not even sure what, if anything, *did* happen.

Ash stands up. "I'm going out for a smoke. Wanna come, Jay?"

I feel Min and Sophie watching me. "Maybe later?"

Ash nods, sticks a cigarette behind her ear, and slips out of the room.

"Who smokes?" Min mutters when Ash is out of earshot. "It's so gross."

"You're gross," I say jokingly. Min ignores me.

Sophie says, "So this year's band trip—did you hear? We might not get to go if not enough people sign up."

"That sucks." The annual band trip is the biggest reason why I'm in band. Actually, it might be the only reason. It does suck, sometimes, to see Wendy go on all those Model UN and youth orchestra trips. She's away the weekend of the band trip, too, at a conference in Victoria.

"Well, now you all know how I feel," Min says grumpily. "My mother has never allowed me to go on ski trip. Until this year. And now it's canceled."

"My family's going to the French Alps this Christmas," Sophie says. "I was thinking if the band trip does get canceled, you guys can come with us." I look at Sophie, surprised, because we've only really started talking this year. But she looks genuine. So maybe she just likes skiing that much.

Min snorts. "My mother would never let me. And that sounds super expensive."

Sophie sighs, and they switch to talking about *Fullmetal Alchemist*. My eyes hurt from staring at the computer screen, so I go out to find Ash. She's practicing tre flips underneath the awning by the gym. Ash can do them but not as consistently as she'd like. Even in the throes of tripping over failed tre flips, Ash's limbs have a graceful bounciness about them that I can never imitate. She's one of the few people I've seen who looks good in skinny jeans that taper at the ankle. They make her dredged-up skate shoes optically enormous in contrast. It shouldn't be a good aesthetic, yet somehow I dig it.

"Hey," I say.

She stops and tic-tacs toward me. "Hey."

"Your channel's really blowing up," I say.

"No shit. It's all thanks to you." I've been uploading clips regularly, even the sketchy, grainy ones with the horrible angles. And it's been working. Ash has hundreds of subscribers now. She says it's because I'm consistent at uploading, but I think it's because Ash is a good skater, period. Not a good skater "for a girl." Just a good skater.

Ash lights a cigarette.

"Hey. Why do you like smoking?" I ask. "Not judging you or anything," I add quickly.

She taps off the ash and shrugs. "Wards off hunger. Excuse to go outside." She takes another long drag.

I guess that's all the answer I'll get. "This weekend's supposed to be sunny," I say. "Wanna hang out?"

"Actually"—Ash flicks her cigarette into a puddle and stuffs her hands into her pockets—"There's this stairwell I used to session on in my old neighborhood. I've always dreamed of landing a kickflip over it. Could be a really good ender for my video. Come with me to shoot and I can introduce you to the guys."

"The guys?" I imagine a crew of smoking, swearing white boys in flannel shirts who call each other "pussy" when one of them can't land a trick.

Ash says, "They're a little quirky but they won't bite. I can even get Blake to introduce you to one of his friends, you know. Like, if you're into that."

I blink. "What?"

"You know." She shifts from foot to foot. "If you're into that." When I stare back blankly, she waves it off. "Never mind. I'll come by after lunch on Saturday?"

I say yes before I can change my mind.

. . .

I tell my mother I'm going over to David's on Saturday to finish a science project. It's getting easier to lie to her. I don't feel great about it, but I don't feel awful either. Telling Ma Mi the truth will only send her into a frenzy of worry, and I know work has been stressing her out lately. So long as I don't take too many bus tickets from the living room sideboard, she won't notice anything fishy.

After that time in Gastown when the lady yelled at us in the alley, I'm a little nervous. I've seen enough Internet videos of skaters getting in trouble for skating in public spaces. People think we're doing property damage or that if we get hurt, we'll sue them. But to my relief, the staircase Ash wants to use is at the back of a warehouse, and it's the weekend so no one's working. And it overlooks a parking lot so there are no cars. Still, I'm glad that Ash designates Dezzy as her spotter.

Like Simon, Dezzy is tall and lanky, with long blond hair. A rabid fan of metal, he wears all black. No graphic on his shirt or anything, just black. He wears a helmet (also black), which makes me feel less dorky about always wearing mine. He looks intimidating from a distance, but once I meet him, he's a mini-version of Simon, all fist-bumping you like he's known you all his life.

Logan has a cigarette constantly burning in his mouth and looks like he just stepped out of the nineties, with his hair shaved short and an oversized T-shirt and baggy jeans. He's quiet, stocky, and serious-looking, but when I eke out an ollie he nods approvingly. "Nice."

I recognize Matt as the derpy-faces guy. Like Dezzy, he looks intimidating at first: long dark hair, black nail polish, lip piercings, and a chain hanging off his pants. But up close, I see he's wearing a family-friendly Vancouver Aboriginal Youth Arts Camp '09 T-shirt. He breaks out into a toothy, goofy grin when Ash introduces us.

It's a steep seven-stair set and I can't fathom how Ash has the guts to kickflip it. I'm not alone, though, because neither do Dezzy and Matt. Logan attempts a few ollies, but he keeps bailing. When I say I'm surprised he's not hurt, he shrugs and says, "Well, it *does* hurt. Sometimes it hurts like a bitch. But you learn to roll it off."

We watch Ash land a few ollies. Then she tries a kickflip and lands all messed up, swearing up a storm. At least she falls smart—tucks in a ball, goes limp, and rolls off.

I shoot from the base of the staircase, but when it's clear Ash won't land the kickflip for a while, Dezzy offers to take over, which I'm grateful for because my arms are starting to cramp from holding the camera up.

I walk over to where Matt and Logan are rubbing wax all over a curb. Then they start grinding it, and the sound their trucks make is so satisfying. It looks easy—they're not even ollieing—so I try to join them. But the moment I get close to the curb, I freak out, bail, and smash up my shins.

"Hmm, maybe you should try a nose stall first," Logan says. He throws down, rides up, and raises his nose onto the curb. Digs in, leans forward, and rides out. It looks simple—keyword being "looks"—but it takes me a few times to get used to such a wide stance and several more tries to do the stall part correctly. Eventually, I figure out that I need to pretty much slam myself into the curb to lock into the stall and get my back wheels off the ground. The first time I get my wheels up, Matt and Logan drum their boards and fist-bump me, even though it's a stretch to even call it a trick and I know I look super sketchy doing it.

Ash is getting frustrated with the kickflip, so she joins us at the curb. I film her for a while, showing off my following and foot-braking skills, but to be honest I'm starting to get tired. I look at my watch. To my surprise, I've been skating for almost two hours straight.

"I'm going for a snack run!" Matt announces. "Anyone want anything?"

"Can I come with?" I say, suddenly dreaming of sugary liquid.

Matt nods and grins. I like him. He's shorter than me, with a deep, genuine laugh.

"Nothing for me," Ash says.

Logan hands me five bucks. "Get me a Slurpee?"

Dezzy gives me two dollars. "Whatever chocolate bar you can get with that. Surprise me."

As Matt and I cross the street, I ask him, "So how did you guys all meet?"

"Elementary school, around Grade 5 or something?" Matt says. "I was getting the crap bullied out of me because I was a weird kid."

"Yikes. Sorry to hear."

He shrugs. "All I did was draw during recess, which was considered too girly, apparently. The only boys who didn't make fun of me or try to lock me in the bathroom were Logan and Dezzy. And then I met Ash through them."

"Did you skate before?"

"Nope! I didn't even skate with them at first because I have asthma and I hated gym class and anything resembling sports. In fact, if you ask Logan, he'll tell you it took them quite a while to convince me to be friends with them. At first, I'd just sit on the ground and doodle in a corner while they skated. Logan thought I was being too cool or whatever, but hey, I like to draw." He shrugs. "But skateboarding's fun. You can stop and take breaks whenever you like."

We get our snacks. Matt holds the drinks while I hold the food, and we walk back to the parking lot.

Ash is trying the stairs again. Everyone grabs their food and Matt sits under a tree to enjoy his. I sit down next to him because I'm wiped, too. "So, what do you draw?"

"Cartoons, mostly." He takes out his phone and shows me a few blurry pictures. But even with the poor quality, it's clear Matt isn't just a kid who doodles on the edges of his math homework. He draws with confident, dynamic lines and a bold, distinct style. He isn't afraid to draw *loud*, which is interesting, considering he's not a particularly loud person.

"Sheesh," I breathe. "This stuff is *legit*."

"That's a character I made up," Matt says, pointing to a figure with intense eyes poking out of a hood. "Been drawing Hero since I was a kid. Hero can turn into a man or a woman based on the parameters of the mission."

"Like Orlando," I say.

"Who?"

"Oh, this character in this book Ash and I are reading for our English class," I say. "How long have you been drawing?"

"All my life." Matt takes his phone back even though I'm not done looking through his pictures. I get it, though; not all sketches are meant to be seen. Yet. "Well, it was more before I started skateboarding. I used to wish for rainy days because that meant I could stay inside to draw during recess."

I light up. "Me too! Ha, we could've been friends."

Matt says, "Who says we can't be friends now?"

Suddenly, we hear yelling and screaming. Ash is running around and bashing her board against things in triumph. Dezzy, cradling the camera, shouts at us, "She finally landed it! We got the shot!" He plays it back for Matt and me, and it's a sick shot. Although, if it was me shooting I would have favored a slightly lower angle. But whatever, it's a banger.

Ash wipes sweat off her face using the bottom of her shirt. I can see her stomach and it takes me a few seconds to realize that and look away. "All right, boys," Ash says, fist-bumping all of us. "I need to go." There's been so much fist-bumping today my knuckles are sore.

"Going to see Blake?" Logan says, and the other guys snicker.

Ash rolls her eyes. She says, "Shut up," then, "oh shit," when she sees the bus coming. Thankfully, she's got her skateboard and has zero trouble on cracked bumpy sidewalks. We drum our boards when she successfully catches the bus.

"So, what's this Blake guy like?" Dezzy asks me when the bus rolls away.

"He has a hipster 'stache," I say, "and he's in a band. They call themselves, what was it, 'punk revival.'" I make dramatic air quotes.

Dezzy snickers. "Sounds like you don't like him much."

"He sounds pretentious," says Matt.

"What do you know? You only listen to teenyboppers," Logan scoffs.

Matt glares at him. "Demi Lovato is *not* a teenybopper."

I turn to Dezzy. "Don't you know Blake? I thought he went to your school."

Dezzy shakes his head.

"Blake's a creep," Logan says, making a face. "He's, what, like, twenty?"

"Nineteen," I say, but to be honest, something about Blake creeps me out, too.

Dezzy says, "Logan's just bitter because he and Ash fooled around in Grade 10."

Logan swears at Dezzy, and Matt collapses into laughter.

"So Ash has dated guys before?" I ask.

Dezzy gives me a look and I see his shoulders relax. "Oh. So you know about it."

I stare at them. "Know about what?"

Dezzy's shoulders scrunch up again.

Matt says, "I wouldn't call what Ash and Logan did *dating*."

"Wait, what do I know about?" I say.

Dezzy and Matt exchange a glance. "Never mind," Dezzy says.

"No. Seriously. What are you guys talking about?"

Dezzy clears his throat and skates away with Logan. I stare after them before turning to Matt. He avoids my eyes. "No, you're right. Blake is Ash's first boyfriend, first anything," he says.

. . .

Ash's kickflip is a fantastic ender for our video. The day before the contest submission deadline, we sit together to watch it on Mr. Hussein's computer, and my body is humming with excitement as I press play. The video opens with a shot of Ash doing a huge tre flip off a skate park kicker, which I shot from underneath. The shot starts off at full speed then it slo-mos during the flip before ramping back up to real time again, the *brrr* sound of rising speed and pitch matching the crescendo in the song I chose to play over the action. Shooting that had scared me shit-less, but I'd trusted Ash, and we'd pulled that shot off in one afternoon.

I opted for a chiller vibe than Ash's first video. Folksy indie music, washed-out colors, and trick shots interspersed with random frames of the city. Telephone-poled laneways behind our houses. The mountains after the first snowfall. Gastown at sunset. Matt and the guys chilling under a tree while Ash 5-0s a curb in the foreground. I was worried about the lighting during the varial flip off a ledge at our school, but it turned out okay. I also included some of Ash's simpler tricks, like no-comply and caveman variations and her sweet little Gastown line, even though she told me they weren't gnarly enough to be included. But I thought that they were so, so stylish and I just couldn't resist.

It's only about ninety seconds of video, but it took weeks of work and even more weeks of practice. As I sit back and watch, everything feels fried, from my dry eyes and sore quads to the roughed-up skin of my thumb where it rubs against the grip tape when I'm carrying my board. I'm tired, but in a good way, like when you've been active all day and know you're going to have the best sleep that night.

Ash, on the other hand, watches on the literal edge of her seat, arms crossed over her chest, knees drawn up onto the chair. Her leg is jiggling up and down the way it does when she speaks in English class. When the edit ends with that kickflip banger, she finally stops moving and sits back. She's quiet.

"Well?" I breathe.

She looks at me, expression neutral and unreadable for a full three seconds, and then a grin slowly spreads across her face. She shakes her head. "God damn it, J.W. You did it, man."

"Yeah?" I say.

"Fuck yeah." She high-fives me so hard my hand stings. We submit the video to the Guild right then and there.

Skating home that afternoon is a party of stoke. Ash throws kickflips and shove-its and even tre flips all over the street. Even I feel extra confident pumping over uneven cracks. When we get to my house, she's all sweaty and panting, but she gives me a swinging high five and says, "Dude. I'm *so glad* I met you."

My face is sore from grinning. "Likewise."

"We should celebrate. Smoke a joint or something."

"Hmm." Then I remember something. "You should come to Whistler with us."

Ash laughs. "What?"

I nod. "Yeah. We don't have enough people in band interested in the ski trip to qualify for a school rate, so Ms. Hudson's holding a raffle for anyone in the school to join us. You should do it. We leave the last Friday of school before the holidays."

Ash scowls. "I'd still have to pay, though, right? What is it, a hundred bucks? Two hundred?"

I shrug. "It's two days of lodging, transportation, lift ticket, rentals, a lesson . . ." Ski band trips have always seemed like a good deal to me, but from the drawn-out line of Ash's mouth, I'm not sure she feels the same. Still, she says, "Yeah, I'll put my name in."

I nod. We kick around on our skateboards for a bit. I'm still so stoked about the video, I feel as if going home will ruin the magic. Then I realize something. "Hey, where exactly is your house?"

Ash gestures vaguely down the street. "That one."

"The Vancouver Special?" Vancouver Specials are notoriously ugly houses that are clones of each other.

Ash nods.

"Can I come over sometime?" I ask. "To play all those video games you and Logan talk about."

She snorts. "I play them at his house. Hey, don't you have to go home and, like, show your mom your homework?"

It's my turn to snort. "I bet your room has Violent Femmes posters everywhere and the walls are black," I say.

"Nah, it's just messy and my parents—well, they don't like visitors." She chuckles uneasily, which is a new sound for her.

I have the creeping feeling that maybe I've overstepped.

"And I don't *just* like punk music. I'm not the same person as Blake."

"Right. Yeah." I feel awkward, so I give Ash a short hug. "I'll see you tomorrow."

"Yeah," she says. "See you."

I walk through my gate, and Ash just stands there, a scrawny figure outlined in leftover sunlight. When I get up the stairs of the back porch, my hand on the door, I look over my shoulder. She's walking down the laneway, blowing out a smoke ring, and I crane my neck to follow her. She keeps walking, and then I hear the squeak of a gate. I can't see her anymore, but I know my block well enough to know that it's not the Vancouver Special.

CHAPTER 5

As if the skateboarding gods decided to reward us for an edit well done, Ash is one of five students who get picked to go to Whistler on the band trip. I'm instantly excited, but she tells me she needs to chat with the counselor first. "Chat" is a verb I hear adults use with each other when they have something business-y to discuss, so I'm not sure what she means.

I wait for Ash in the admin room outside Ms. Watanabe's office. Bored, I flip through a don't-do-drugs pamphlet I find sitting alongside a bowl of condoms on the table next to me. It's a collection of dramatic stories allegedly written by teens about accidental overdoses, bad trips, and dangerous drug combos. Through the thin walls of the office, I hear Ms. Watanabe talk slowly on the phone with someone. She repeats a bunch of questions and Ash interjects with Cantonese translations. I can't hear everything, but I think it's money-related.

Finally, Ash jumps out of the office with a big smile. "I'm in!"

"Awesome!" I say.

"We're sharing a room, right?"

"Yeah, we're sharing one with Min and Sophie."

"They won't mind?" Ash murmurs.

"I mean, I'm already sharing a room with them." It had just sort of happened. Kind of the default choice now, since my best friend is now best friends with them.

Ash says, "You know, now might be the time for me to admit that I've never skied or snowboarded in my life."

I laugh. "Me neither. Well, not snowboarding. I learned to ski on the last few trips. But this time I'm snowboarding."

Ash smiles. "Cool. We'll fail together then."

. . .

The day of the ski trip, we all get to the school parking lot at the crack of dawn to board the bus. Ash must have stayed over at Blake's the night before because she comes to school with him. I see them about a block away, holding hands. Ash turns her body into Blake's, making them both stop in their tracks. She tucks a strand of hair behind her ear. Blake says something, Ash laughs, and he pulls her face up to kiss her.

I'm suddenly aware of how much of a creep I am, watching them kiss from across the street. But I can't tear my eyes away. Then I feel a sharp pulse between my legs and I force myself to turn around. I decide my random flash of creepiness is due to sleep deprivation.

Ash greets me with a sleepy fist bump. "Dude, what's up with Min?" She gestures at Min, standing miserably next to Sophie and the rest of the woodwinds section, carrying a bike helmet and elbow and knee pads.

I snicker. "It was the only way her mom would let her come on this trip."

"A *bike* helmet?"

"Yeah. They're technically FOBs. I'm not surprised they don't know anything about skiing." Ash gives me a look. "Fresh off the boat," I clarify. "Min got here in grade nine. That's why she has an accent."

"I know that." Ash crosses her arms. "But there's nothing wrong with having an accent. There's no such thing as 'right' English, to quote Mr. Hussein."

I shrug. "But don't you find the FOBs . . ." I trail off, suddenly wishing there was a way to backspace my words.

"What?"

My body feels all tense and my eyes dart around to focus on anything else. Randomly having the image of Ash and Blake flashing in my head doesn't help. "Well, the FOBs at our school. Like, they're so loud and flashy and they only stick to themselves."

Ash tilts her head at Min, who's struggling to hold her helmet and pads in one arm while putting on her backpack with the other. "Is Min like that?"

"I didn't say *all* FOBs."

Ash nods toward the bus. "Let's just get on. I wanna take a nap."

I follow her, relieved to be spared further conversation on this topic.

Ash and I grab a seat at the back of the bus and wait for everyone else to trail on. Sophie and Min sit in front of us. David isn't coming because band is the one thing he's *not* involved in. Dude finished all his piano exams before he graduated from elementary school and now wants as little to do with music as possible.

The bus weaves through downtown, passes Stanley Park, and crosses Lion's Gate Bridge to the North Shore where it accelerates onto the Sea to Sky Highway. The drive is arguably my favorite part of our annual ski trip up to Whistler. On our right, the road hugs steep cliffs of loose rock held back by concrete and mesh. On my left—the side I'd made sure we sat on—you're treated to a spectacular view of the sea and the hilly little island-pods that float on the turquoise water. In the early morning mist, everything is painted a heavenly robin's-egg blue.

"Hey." Ash nudges me with her elbow. "Can I, um, talk to you about something?"

"Sure." I'd thought she was asleep.

Her earbuds are hanging down her shirtfront and she's frowning at her MP3 player. Her voice is low and small. "You've never had sex, right?"

I stiffen. "Wow. Presumptuous much?"

Ash shoves me playfully. "I never said it's a bad thing. It's actually kinda cute."

I sit up taller to peek over the seat at Sophie and Min, but they both have headphones on and look unconscious. "Fine. No, I've never had sex before."

"Well, I have," Ash says. "So why does the thought of doing it with Blake feel so . . . weird?"

"Wait, when did you lose your virginity? If you're okay sharing that," I add quickly.

"In Grade 10 when Logan and I were tipsy and curious. It lasted, like, two seconds." She laughs.

"Maybe you're nervous because Blake's more experienced," I say.

She scoffs. "Doubt it."

"Well, maybe Blake means more to you so you're nervous because he's your boyfriend." I pause. "Does he?"

Ash shrugs. "Maybe."

A few moments of silence, and then she says, "I don't know. I mean, I think so? I like hanging out with him. We have good chemistry and our conversations are hilarious. And he kisses better than Logan. Like, *a lot* better."

I imagine Logan fuming at this. "You can just, like, keep kissing him and *not* have sex with him," I suggest.

"I guess. But . . ." She smirks. "You don't know this since you're a virgin, but sex is fun."

"Was it fun with Logan?"

Ash scowls at me. I snicker. "Well, it's *supposed* to be fun," she says.

I grunt. Everyone says sex is the most amazing thing on earth. Every song, every movie is about sex. But I, for one, am skeptical. I can't say I don't want to have sex—I'm curious at the very least—but I doubt it's the best thing ever. Surely it can't be better than David's mom's jap chae, hitting the upload button when a video's ready to publish, or getting a higher mark than Wendy on a music theory exam. (Which happened once. Wendy cried for three days.)

Ash says, "Thanks, Jay."

"For what?"

She shrugs. "Listening, I guess."

I just nod.

She says, "It's nice, you know, having a girl to talk about this stuff with."

"Because all your friends from Mackenzie were guys?"

She shrugs. I want to ask her about what the guys were hinting at that day I met them for the first time, after she left to see Blake. But I stop myself. It doesn't feel right.

Ash hands me an earbud. I push it in and the soaring vocals and thumping electric tones make me want to run and jump into the water below us. I get the profound, rumbling feeling that something epic is about to happen.

. . .

Over many band trips, I have become a somewhat decent skier. But snowboarding is an entirely new beast. We pick it up faster than Celeste and Hannah (they're in the flute section and one of them came in *jeans*) and the other girls we share a lesson with. Snowboarding is nothing like skateboarding, but being used to standing sideways and knowing that we're goofy-footed helps. We nail skidding down on our edges in no time.

Our instructor is a big Australian guy named Alex. Every time he's busy holding someone's hand or picking them up off the snow, the other girls in the group giggle about how hot his accent is.

"I wonder if Alex can do a cab three stalefish," Ash murmurs as we wait for the rest of the class to slowly shimmy down the hill.

"Ask him," I say.

She cups her hands around her mouth and yells, "Yo, Alex! Do a cab three stalefish off the XL rail!"

Alex looks up and only loses focus for a second, but the girl whose hands he's holding falls over with a shriek. Ash and I collapse into giggles.

After lunch, seeing how bored we are, Alex lets us take the chairlift up the bunny hill by ourselves with the strict instruction that we return to the chalet by four. On the chairlift, human sounds fall away below us, replaced by howling wind. It lashes at our cheeks. We're freezing cold now that we're sitting still. Ash and I cuddle up close like penguins, our faces tucked under the collars of our jackets. Ash murmurs something.

"What?" I can't hear her.

"This has been a kickass day," she says. "Thanks for asking me to come."

"Don't thank me," I say, "thank the losers who chose not to come."

The chairlift hums its way up the mountain. The boys in front of us bang their ski poles against each passing chairlift tower. I twist around, trying to catch a good view, but Ash stays quiet and huddled, as if too cold to move.

Suddenly, the hum cuts and the chairlift stops. As we hang there, my front foot starts feeling numb from the snowboard strapped to it. "Some kid probably fell while getting off the lift," I say through my clattering teeth.

"I went down on Blake," Ash says. "Does that count?"

The chairlift hums back up. I feel like I momentarily lose my voice. I clear my throat and say, "What?"

Ash shrugs. "You know. Oral. Does that count as sex?"

"Uh..." I shuffle lower into my jacket. "I guess that's up to you, right?"

"Right." Ash sits there, staring at the safety bar. "See, I *wanted* to have sex. I was all stoked to do it. But the moment the main course was supposed to happen, I just... froze. Blake got all freaked out and so did I because it was like my body didn't work."

"Oh." I lick my chapped lips. "I'm... sorry?"

Ash sniffs loudly. Both our noses are runny in the cold.

"Is Blake okay with you, y'know, not wanting to?" From the TV shows I've seen and the Internet forums I've read, boys being pushy about sex seems like the norm.

At this, Ash loosens up. "Yeah! Actually, he was *so cool* with it. He said he likes me for my mind and personality, not my body. He's not like other guys. I had a feeling as soon as he sat down with us. That's why I went out with him. He's an artist, a *brain person*." She tosses me a smile. I politely smile back. I'm glad Ash didn't get forced into anything, but I'm also lost as to why she thinks Blake is so awesome. Maybe since I'm not the one dating him, I just can't see it.

We get to the top of the hill. Getting off the lift in skis is easy because all you do is stand up. But on a snowboard, you have to stand up at an angle. I lean forward, reminding myself to commit. It works and I don't fall—for the first five seconds. The moment I try to turn, I keel over. Ash does too, and we collapse into a tangled puddle of boards, legs, laughter, and cuss words.

Once we gather our dignity, I strap in faster than Ash then watch her struggle and swear at her bindings. She catches me. "What?"

"You okay?"

"Yeah." She grunts and gestures at the run. "Let's do this."

The bunny hill is steeper and longer than I'd expected. With every turn, I wince at the possibility of skidding out and toppling into other people. Ash lets herself go faster, which just means she falls harder and more frequently. When we finally get to the bottom after what feels like ages, we're exhausted beyond comprehension and super relieved.

• • •

That night, we fall asleep the moment our bodies hit the mattress. Ash gets to sleep in the following day, but Sophie, Min, and I have a master-class in one of the conference rooms. We spend five hours getting taught by an eccentric "guest conductor." He has a lovely singing voice, which he uses to yell at teenagers for ruining the sanctity of music. As luck would have it, I fall asleep against my bass drum after lunch and miss a crucial measure. I'm woken up sharply by a shout: "You! In the percussion section! Yes, you! Don't think just because you get to hit something once every ten measures, you can sleep! Percussion demands perfection! *Percussion demands perfection!*" He enunciates everything, the p's in particular, and the poor clarinet section is in the splash zone.

When we get back to our hotel room, Ash is sitting in bed watching *Buffy* reruns. She looks delicate in an oversized hoodie and leggings, and I feel this weird urge to hug her. The urge intensifies when I see that her eyes are wet and swollen. When she notices me, she quickly wipes her face with the back of her sleeve. When I open my mouth, she just shakes her head and slaps on a forced smile.

We're not sure what to do, but we're sore, hungry, and cheap. So we eat dinner at what my dad calls a jaap sui buffet—that is, cheap, oily Chinese food made for Westerners. I wolf down as much self-serve ice cream as I humanly can because Ma Mi's not here to tsk at me. And Ash has no problem piling up her plate with a mountain of deep-fried goodness. Sophie seems impressed; Min looks terrified. When Sophie asks if she can even finish her meal, Ash says what my mom always says: of course, it's a buffet, and you better get your money's worth.

When Ash and I get back from our second dessert run, Min is restless, cradling her head in her hands.

"What's up?" I say, sliding in next to her.

"Her mom just called and yelled at her for not calling back fast enough," Sophie says. "Classic Min's mom, honestly."

"She called me eight time within the last half hour, while I was getting food," says Min. "Said that I'll worry her into an early death and blamed herself for letting me go on this trip."

"Your mom sounds like a control freak."

We all turn to Ash, who's scarfing down a mountain of cake, Jell-O, and ice cream. It's not that I don't agree with her, I'm just shocked she has the nerve to say it out loud.

"I mean, she's not a *freak*," Min says unconvincingly.

"I think she wants to keep you dependent on her," Sophie says, jumping on Ash's boldness. "That's why she won't let you take driving lessons or cook."

"She says I'll just mess everything up and make even more work for her," Min says quietly. "That since I'm going to the local university anyway, it's not like I need to learn how to do those things."

Ash shakes her head. "Which is why you need to go far away. Like Montreal or Toronto."

"But I can't just *abandon* my mother," Min says, frowning even harder.

"My dad is in China most of the year. I'm all she has."

"Sounds like she needs to make friends," Ash says. I shoot her a look. She mouths "What?" at me then says to Min, "Look, I get where you're coming from. My dad's a piece of work, and I decided ages ago that he doesn't deserve my time. I'm moving out as soon as I can. As soon as I graduate, actually."

Min stares quietly at the saltshaker.

"Wow," says Sophie. "Have you got a lot saved up?"

Ash nods. "I've been washing dishes at my friend Simon's restaurant since Grade 10. Of course, my dad wants half of my pay, but I just lie to him about what I make. Last year he banned me from working because he wanted me to focus on school, but I still grab a shift here and there. Cash-only sort of thing."

"So, are you planning to, like, get an apartment after you graduate?" Sophie has her chin in her hand and seems genuinely fascinated.

"That's the idea," Ash says. "If not, I'll crash on a friend's couch. *Anything* to get away."

Sophie shifts awkwardly in her seat.

Min shakes her head. "I can't just *leave*," she mutters.

Ash stops eating for a moment and looks straight at her. "Yes. Yes, you can."

When we return to our room, it's too early to go to bed on a night without parents. Sophie suggests that we go to Celeste and Hannah's room to play card games. "But we can play cards *anytime*," I say, yawning.

Min shrugs, but Ash smirks. "I have a proposal," she says slyly.

"Ash has a proposal!" I repeat, but Min and Sophie don't seem as excited.

Ash fishes into her backpack and pulls out a prescription pill bottle. Inside are narrow, tubular things. We all squint through the orange plastic. Then Sophie says, "Are those . . . is that *weed*?"

Ash grins, but Min quickly turns around with an audible swish of her clothes. "Nope, nope, nope, I'm not a part of this!"

Sophie just chuckles. "Thanks, but no thanks." But the way she looks at me, it's like she's a little impressed.

I turn to Ash. "Let's do it."

Ash tells me to act natural and not walk too fast. My heart pounds as we go past the front desk toward the hotel's rotating doors. But the front-desk people don't so much as look up from their computer monitors.

It's December, so it's pitch-black outside even though it's barely past seven. I feel like I'm sneaking out at midnight. My skin is tingling everywhere and there's a steady pounding in my chest. Ash seems to pick up on my tension because she looks over her shoulder and says, "You okay?"

"'Course I am." I watch where I step because the drop in temperature has made the ground icy. "Why wouldn't I be?"

I wonder what David would think of this. See, if you get paired with David for a project, you'll ace it. If you say you can't hang out because you need to study, he'll understand. And if you invite him over to your house, there's no awkwardness because your parents will like him right away. Not so much with Ash. With David, there's a sense of safety. With Ash—well, I wouldn't say doing stuff with Ash feels *dangerous*. Just . . . *uncertain*. You might get in trouble, or you might not. The question is: do you care?

I follow Ash through the Village, down a side path, then another side path, and then we go off-trail and into the woods, stepping over snowy underbrush with our arms outstretched for balance. The lights of civilization fade behind us and the snow muffles all noise, erasing any evidence that there are other humans close by.

We break into a clearing and when we stop walking, it's majestically silent. We're surrounded by pine trees wearing downy snow jackets. They look like gnarled monsters in frozen conversation, edges coolly illuminated by moonlight.

Ash lights her joint. "Dude, I'm still sore from yesterday." She hands me the joint. "Some natural painkiller, m'lady?"

I accept her offer with a fancy bow and we take turns puffing off the joint. As we do, time starts to drag.

"Dude," Ash says, "This is a j. Like you, Jay. You were, like, born to smoke weed." She giggles. I giggle too, and it takes us an absurdly long time to stop.

I feel a familiar heaviness and sleepiness, so I pull my jacket down over my butt and sit on the driest part of a fallen tree I can find. Ash does the same. In silence, we watch wisps of smoke snake their way up through the treetops. Just as my eyelids start to droop, Ash says, "Jay. I don't think I like boys."

"Wha'?" My eyes snap open. "What do you mean?"

Ash blinks and her eyelashes glisten with a peppering of snowflakes. "You know how in the movies, when people fall in love, there's this, like, euphoria? Like suddenly you're high off your own hormones? I've never felt that way about a guy. I've only felt high when I'm, y'know, high." She starts giggling again.

I laugh too. "I've never felt it either. Wendy says I just haven't met the right guy yet. So maybe you haven't met the right guy yet. Maybe Blake's not it."

"Maybe," Ash says. "Or maybe the movies are lying to us."

"Maybe."

The forest ripples around us in waves. I squint and remind myself to breathe as the silence between us stretches. I start to shiver again, but the last thing I want to do is move. I don't want to leave this little place in the trees. I don't want to return to the real world, school, my family, the unfinished university applications on my desk. *Please, can I please just stay here?* I think.

"Can we listen to the song you played for me on the bus?" I ask Ash, and my voice feels echoey and far away.

"Sure. It's a Kiwi band called the Naked and Famous," Ash says, and we each plug in an earbud. I close my eyes, lean back against the tree, and let the soundwaves caress me. Geometric patterns pulse through the backs of my eyelids, and I watch it all with a huge smile on my face. I must look ridiculous, but I don't care. I don't care much for the pot either, not really. I just love that there's no one else here, no one else but Ash. Ash and me and snow and time.

I must have fallen asleep because the next thing I know, Ash is shaking me awake. "It's getting late. Let's go back."

I feel like everyone is watching us when we get back to the hotel, but when I actually look, no one is staring, it just feels like they are. When we get to our room, Min and Sophie aren't even back yet. Our mouths are as dry as sandpaper though, so we stumble out to the hallway to hunt for drinks.

I'm clumsily inserting loonies and quarters into the vending machine when Ash hisses at me and points to the room next to the vending machine. "Yo, isn't this Ms. Hudson's room?" I shrug and she knocks on the door.

My eyes widen and she grabs me and practically tackles me behind the corner. We crouch there, her hot breath beating against my collarbone. "Who is it?" the all-too-familiar irritated voice of the band teacher calls from behind the door. We wait a few long seconds then Ash reaches around and knocks on the door again.

Steps thump toward the door. Ms. Hudson waddles out in her hotel-issued bathrobe and slippers. "Who is it?" she demands. When she's met by silence, I hear her swear under her breath and go back inside.

When we get back to our room, we can't stop laughing. We flop onto the bed and it's like we have the hiccups. Our bodies are out of control.

When we finally calm down, Ash says, "What now?"

"I think I'm still high."

"No shit." Ash sits up and plops the hotel phone into her lap.

"What are you doing?"

She hushes me with a finger and calls the front desk, putting the phone on speaker so I can hear. She asks—in a businesslike voice I don't recognize at all—to be patched through to Ms. Hudson's room. My jaw drops, but she shoots me a look that shuts me up. The concierge must be bored out of her mind because magically, she patches us through, no questions asked. Hudson answers the phone, her voice as gritty as always. "Hello?"

"Hello." Ash drops her voice an octave. It's now smoky, sultry, like what you'd expect from a burlesque dancer in a black-and-white movie. "Good evening, madam. I am the . . . *sexual experience therapist* you ordered?"

"Excuse me? Who the hell is this?"

Ash clears her throat. "You had scheduled an appointment with us, ma'am? I promise you, we *will not* disappoint."

"I never—!"

Before I can think it through, I clear my throat and try to make my voice as low as Ash's. "We can give you your pick, ma'am. How would you like a stately gentleman, tall, dark, and handsome?"

"Who is this? Is this one of my students? Are you the one who knocked on my door? This isn't funny; it's harassment. I demand you tell—"

"Or perhaps you are more interested in a more rugged fellow—"

Ash slams down the phone. "Oookay, I think we're done for now."

She's right. A sudden heavy wave of sleepiness washes over me and it takes all my residual energy to put on my pajamas. We figure we won't die from it, so we don't even bother brushing our teeth, instead tucking ourselves straight under the covers. There's a skylight above us and it's raining gently now, so we lie in the quiet and listen to the calming plips and plops. I'm riding a high tide of sleep now, but I manage to murmur, "Ash?"

"Mm?"

"I'm glad you came with."

"Mm. Me too."

"Good night," I say.

She murmurs, "Good night."

Min and Sophie come back a few minutes later. I listen to them dutifully brush their teeth and change their clothes. Sophie even takes a shower. Then it all goes black.

. . .

The next morning, when I wake up, Ash is sitting up with a bleary-eyed look, saying, "Huh, Sophie and Min must've already left for breakfast." I must have slept through my phone alarm.

When we get to the breakfast room, most of our bandmates are almost done eating. I'm not high anymore, but my eyes and mouth are still dry and I'm super self-conscious about it. We're nosing around the breakfast buffet when Ms. Hudson power walks over out of nowhere. "Jessica. Ashley. My table. *Now.*" She gestures to her table in the corner, where Mr. Hussein is also sitting with breakfast and a newspaper.

"Shiiiit," Ash mutters, and I feel a sharp zap down my spine that makes all my hair stand on end.

We shuffle to the staff table, aware that the entire breakfast room is staring at us. Mr. Hussein's eyes shimmer with something more like annoyance than anger, as if we've intruded upon the sanctity of his coffee and waffles.

Ms. Hudson sits down, crosses her arms, and gestures for us to take the chairs opposite her. "We know it was you girls who played those nasty, inappropriate pranks last night." She looks almost triumphant. The blood drains from my face and a ball of anxiety starts to grow in my stomach. Ms. Hudson continues, "Now, I understand these trips are a rich opportunity for you youngsters to escape your parents and do whatever you want, but there are limits. And consequences. I talked to the concierge this morning and he traced that phone call to your room. Hannah and Celeste corroborated that Sophie and Min were in their room last night at the time of the call. Which naturally leaves the two of you."

I look at Ash, but her face is completely blank, almost calm. Meanwhile, I feel like a kettle about to boil over. "I'm sorry!" I burst out. My life flashes before my eyes—if this gets bad, no more Europe, no more leaving home. Is everything ruined? "We didn't mean it. I'm sorry. It was terrible. It won't happen again." I'm suddenly aware that everyone, including Ash and all the other kids, is staring at me. I shrivel up, slouch over, and flop my bangs over my face as much as possible. I can't stop muttering, "I'm sorry, I'm sorry . . ."

Ms. Hudson rubs her temples and sighs. "Miss Wong, you've always been a model student. What happened?" The only response I can manage is a quivering lip. Ms. Hudson looks over to Mr. Hussein, who folds his arms and keeps chewing. "And Ms. Chan," Ms. Hudson says, addressing Ash, who's staring at the table, silent. "Given your history, you really should have known better." She waits for Ash to say something, anything, but Ash is a statue, still and silent. "I'll let Ms. Watanabe know of this incident. She'll want to speak to you the first day back. Both of you will have detention in the new year, and your parents will be notified." I swallow. *Fuck.* I've never had detention . . . ever. Hudson looks at her watch and sighs, like we're the biggest inconvenience to her existence. "And in addition to being pranksters, the two of you are also incredibly tardy. I don't think either of you will have time for breakfast, so I suggest you grab some granola bars, go pack up, and eat on the bus. Run along now."

We robotically get up from the table, trying to ignore the everyone else's looks after us. I make brief eye contact with Sophie and Min. I half-expect them to smirk at us, but they just look uncomfortable. I wish David were here.

Ash and I go to our room in silence and pack our things, also in silence. Ash finishes first. She zips up her backpack and flops onto our bed. "So. I'm staying with Blake over the holidays."

I look up from my suitcase, my head pounding. "But I thought— honestly, I thought you were going to break up with him. You said you don't like boys."

She startles a little. Did she forget she told me that? Maybe she just hoped I would forget. "Well, people are more than just 'boys' and 'girls,'" she says quickly, fiddling with her backpack zipper. "And we *just* started dating, you know? I don't think I've given him a fair chance. That whole thing about falling in love instantly, that when you know, you just know—that's bullshit. Relationships take work." She sighs. "Anyway, his family has a cabin on the Island. They don't have Internet, so—"

"Really? What kind of people don't have Internet these days?"

She shrugs.

"I thought Blake doesn't talk to his family," I mutter.

Ash looks away. "It's . . . complicated."

First detention, now this. "So, I won't hear from you at all during the holidays?"

"I guess." She looks me in the eye finally. "Hey, I had fun this weekend, no matter what happened."

I shrug. "Could be worse, I guess." I try to smile. "I mean, it's nice to be away from our parents, right?"

Ash looks away. "At least you have parents."

"What does that mean?"

Ash gets up. "Think I forgot my toothbrush."

I call after her, "Hey, Ash? What happened at your old school? What was Hudson talking about when she said 'history'?"

"Nothing," Ash says from the bathroom.

But for once, I'm not satisfied. "Come on. Something obviously happened. Why won't you tell me? We're friends."

She comes out of the bathroom. "I don't have to tell you shit just because we're friends," she snaps, so sharply I physically flinch. "And why does everyone think I 'obviously' did something? It wasn't just me, you know. Just like last night wasn't just me." I notice she's clutching some hair ties but no toothbrush. "And I have a date with the counselor; you don't."

Heat rises in my cheeks. "Well, knocking and prank-calling were both your ideas."

"Dude. If you didn't butt into the phone call, she may not have realized it was us. I bet you she put two and two together when she heard both our voices, and you barely even disguised yours." She scoffs. "If you wanna be punk, Jay, at least be good at it."

I scowl and throw my last pieces of clothing into my suitcase, hard.

Ash shoulders her backpack. "I'm starving. I'm gonna grab one of those fancy protein bar things. I'll see you on the bus. But"—she pauses and looks away—"I'm sitting alone."

On the bus, Ash sits in the very back row, feet propped up on the seat in front of her. Earbuds in, hood up. Sophie asks if I'm okay, and I mutter an unconvincing "yeah" before taking the seat behind her and Min. I curl up next to the window and put on some music myself, but I can't pay attention to it. I text David a long paragraph about what happened. He responds, *oh shit that sucks* and *you pretended to be a gigolo, seriously?!?* but I sense he has no idea how to help me feel better. I don't think either of us have been in this much trouble before.

I can't even enjoy the Sea to Sky view outside or the rather delicious granola bar I'd picked out because all I can think about is how mad my parents will be. I feel the sobs coming, so I hide my face under my hoodie. Then, someone sits down next to me. I rub my eyes dry and look up. It's Mr. Hussein.

He's got his arms crossed and he's regarding me curiously, like I'm an interesting animal at the zoo. "You've never been in trouble, have you?"

I give a nervous laugh. "Honestly? No. I'm a bit of a goodie two-shoes."

"Don't get me wrong; getting in trouble isn't cool," he says. "But don't beat yourself up over it. One day, you'll look back on this and laugh at how big of a deal you thought it was. Trust me." For the first time ever, I see him smile. Just barely. He puts a paper on my lap. "You got an A on this," he says. "Not bad. Just wanted to give you some good news."

I hold the paper with both hands. "Thank you."

CHAPTER 6

Of course, Ma Mi eviscerates me when I get home from Whistler. De Di and Wendy hide in their bedrooms while she paces up and down the living room calling my intelligence into question. "How can you jeopardize your chances of a good education like this? You're *this* close to finishing high school, and you're just going to throw it all away? Did all those years of hard work mean *nothing* to you? And for what? To look 'cool' in front of your friends?!"

Her lip does that twitching thing that happens when she's angry. At least my parents don't know I've tried pot. I don't think Ma Mi or De Di have ever been drunk their entire lives. Whenever the marijuana legalization debate comes on the news, De Di shakes his head, sighs, and goes on a rant about how British opium ruined China.

"Why can't you be more like your sister?" my mom says. "She has friends. She's popular. *And* she does so well in school. Jessica. Jessica, are you even listening to me? Wong See Kar!"

Oh shit, I've been Chinese-named. I force my eyes up. "Yeah, I'm listening."

Ma Mi shakes her head at me. "You're not allowed to see your friends until school starts."

I sigh. It's not like I can see Ash anyway, and David is too busy with applications.

"And I'm keeping your skateboard between now and the end of your detention."

This grabs my attention. "You can't do that!"

"Don't question me, or your computer is going next."

That shuts me up. With no computer to watch or edit videos with, it would be a long, long winter holiday.

. . .

Helpfully, Ma Mi and Wendy get into an even bigger fight the day after.

Ma Mi had bought Hainanese chicken on the way home from work. As we eat, she places chicken pieces in everyone's rice bowls without asking (which is expected). But when her chopsticks get close to my sister, Wendy jerks back her bowl and shakes her head. Ma Mi looks so surprised, I almost burst out laughing.

"I've decided to go vegetarian once a week," Wendy announces.

"Why?" De Di stares at her as if she's just offered to pay extra taxes or something equally ridiculous.

"It's better for the environment," Wendy mumbles.

Ma Mi scowls. "You need protein wor. You need to eat *some* meat."

Wendy shakes her head. "I'll just eat tofu next time." Then, sensing that she has our attention, she puts down her bowl and chopsticks and laces her fingers together on the table. "By the way, I want to skip the violin recital this weekend," she says, staring down at the table. "There's a climate protest at city hall and a bunch of my friends in the Conservation Club are going." Her words tumble out in a rush.

"I didn't know you were in the Conservation Club," Ma Mi says. "I thought you wanted to focus on orchestra and Model UN this year."

"I'm not in the Conservation Club. My friends are." There's no Conservation Club at George Van. There's the Environmental Club, but all they do is pick up litter. They don't go to protests. I wonder if this has something to do with Justin and his school.

"Then you don't have to go la," Ma Mi says.

"But I *want* to go."

"But you have the recital."

"I can skip it."

"For a protest?" Ma Mi continues eating now that she's decided Wendy's idea isn't worth her full attention. "I saw plenty of those in Hong Kong. People yelling, holding up signs, and blocking traffic. They made commuting to work a pain. That's why we immigrated, to escape the handover chaos."

"Well, I prefer *not* to run away from problems." Wendy squirms in her chair. "If world leaders don't divest from fossil fuels within the next few years, we'll be past the point of no return. The planet will warm, the ice caps will melt, and there will be extreme weather, mass extinctions, and human civilization as we know it will cease to exist."

"You make it sound like the zombie apocalypse," I mutter.

Wendy turns on me sharply. "Because it *will* be an apocalypse."

Ma Mi shovels chicken broth rice into her mouth. "But Ah Mui, this is a very important recital wor. You go every year. It's a masterclass for all the advanced students and you always leave having learned something."

"It's fine. My teacher can catch me up during our next lesson. I also missed an endangered species conference last summer for an orchestra concert. I'm not missing this."

Ma Mi lets out a familiar you're-too-young-and-shortsighted sigh. "Why the sudden interest in protests? It's not like climate change will only happen if you, Wendy, don't show up. Besides, protests are dangerous. Your father almost got trampled at a June Fourth memorial when we were in university." She looks at De Di, who gives a single nod. "He had to go to hospital. What if someone throws an explosive into the crowd? What if you get arrested? If you get arrested, you won't get to go to medical school." She puts her bowl and chopsticks down with a decisive clang and wipes her mouth. "You know what, don't think about it. You can't go to the protest. It's too dangerous."

Another clang as Wendy puts down her own bowl. "You can't keep me from going!"

"Of course I can. I'm your mother."

"You're threatening my freedom of speech! You're threatening democracy!"

De Di chuckles. "Democracy in this country barely works anyway."

Wendy whirls toward him. "Because the first-past-the-post system benefits conservative voters. Like you."

De Di's face freezes. "Don't talk back."

"You can't go to the protest," Ma Mi says firmly. "Go to your recital."

"Unnngh!" Wendy kicks back her chair and stomps up to her room.

I hear Wendy crying later that night, her whistle-like sobs accompanied by De Di's low voice as he tries to calm her down. Man, she must really be in love with this Justin guy. She eventually agrees to go to the recital, but she grumbles for days that we eat too much meat and dairy.

. . .

The holidays are boring. In true Vancouver fashion, it rains almost every single day and never snows. Which is the worst. I spend the long, dark days holed up inside, either designing made-up skate decks or plodding through *Orlando*. When it comes to *Orlando*, the language is so flowery that I feel like I'm wading through concrete. I wonder if people actually talked like this in 1920s England. Must have been a huge effort just to have a conversation.

I'm forbidden from seeing anyone, but it's not like anyone's around anyway. Ash is on the Island dancing naked with internetless hippies (because I can only imagine Blake's internetless family are nudist hippies). Min is visiting family in Hangzhou. Sophie is skiing in the Alps with her parents. David is the only one in town and he's drowning in scholarship applications. I send him random links of things I find—K-pop videos of his favorite idols, anime clips, the odd YouTube skit I think he'll relate to—but he only ever responds with "lol" or "niiiice." I miss actual conversations with people.

Ma Mi pokes her head into my bedroom one day and says, "I need your help."

I drop *Orlando* onto my lap. "Huh? For what?"

Ma Mi frowns at my unmade sheets as she walks over to me, flicks away a discarded sock, and sits down on my bed. "I can't deal with your mui right now. Every time we talk, we argue." She sighs. "I need to deliver a few pies to Auntie Agnes at the country club and I need you to help me carry them." Ma Mi has been making pies nonstop this week because she wants to bake the perfect pie for her church's Christmas potluck. Everyone brings either Chinese food or sushi platters, so bringing Western food will make her the coolest person there. Ma Mi has half a dozen pies sitting around that our family can't possibly finish. Luckily, a rich church friend is willing to take some off her hands and give them to her rich country club friends.

"Can I drive?" I ask. "I need the practice."

Ma Mi is too tired to argue.

A few hours later, I'm standing in the parking lot of the swanky country club. Ma Mi's still inside gossiping with Auntie Agnes and I'm twiddling my thumbs when, to my surprise, I see David. I jump up and start waving.

David doesn't see me at first. His dad's busy yelling at him—well, I'm too far to hear them but it definitely looks like he's yelling at him. Holding a tennis racket in an iron grip, he points to his wrists then makes aggressive backhand and forehand swings. I wait for one of the swings to smack the back of David's head, but the poor guy just stares at the ground and nods and nods. His two sisters and mother are also there. They quietly walk past the men to their car as if they're afraid they'll get whacked by the tennis racket themselves.

Finally, David sees me and excuses himself from his dad, who shuts up and nods awkwardly at me before shuffling away. "Jay? I thought you were grounded." He's wearing a polo and track pants he grew out of a long time ago.

I gesture at the club. "My mom's here to see someone. I didn't know you played tennis here."

He sighs. "My dad drags me here on Sundays. Says boys shouldn't sit at desks all day, that I need to 'learn how to use my body.' How gross is that?" To be fair, David's dad has a point. David has no physical coordination whatsoever. Ever since he got cut from the Grade 6 basketball team, his dad has been forcing sports on him to "man him up." He doesn't seem to care that David is always at the top of the class or that he'll likely go to university for free on a full-ride scholarship. He's just not "well-rounded" enough because when you throw a ball at him, he runs away, arms flapping.

"Parents suck, eh?" I say.

He shrugs. "Your dad seems chill."

I grunt. "Have you talked to Min or Sophie?"

"Min is stuck behind the Great Firewall of China and Sophie's awake when we're asleep," he says. "But hey, about Whistler. Man. I have to say,

I'm impressed." He crosses his arms and rocks on his heels, looking at me like I'm a new person.

"It really wasn't a big deal," I say. "It was just a prank."

"Yeah, if anything, Hudson deserved it. She's such a tightass." David smirks and I smirk back.

My mom comes out of the country club. She takes one look at David and immediately brightens up like a set of Christmas lights. "Oh my, David! How tall and handsome you've grown! How are you? How is school? Have you picked a university yet?"

"Oh, no, still waiting on some scholarships," he says with a polite smile and a bow of his head. I roll my eyes so far back, I hope they get stuck in my skull so I don't have to see my mother's reaction.

"Oh? What scholarships are you applying for?"

"Well, this morning I was working on one from the City—"

"The City has scholarships? Jessica, you never mentioned that."

"David's doing one based on social involvement because he's in Student Council," I explain. "I'm not."

She scowls at me. "And who's fault is that? I *told* you to try for Student Council." She turns back to David and smiles, shaking her head. "David, you *have* to convince her to do better. She'll never survive university with her work ethic."

David grins and does another mini-bow. "I'll try."

"I need to put these back in the car," Ma Mi says, indicating her armful of empty containers. When she passes me, she whispers into my ear in rapid Cantonese, "I know his family and ours don't speak the same language, but don't you think he'd be a *brilliant* boyfriend—"

"Mom!"

Ma Mi giggles and walks away.

"Ugh, I can't wait to not live with her," I grumble.

David snorts. "Boy, if I have to live with my dad for another year . . ."

His voice dribbles off. "You know." David's hands are in his pockets and he stares at the ground, kicking at some leaves. "We should hang out sometime. I feel like it's been ages."

"You're always busy," I say.

"You too," he shoots back. "With Ash and all that skateboarding stuff."

"Well let's do something, then," I say. There was a time when I'd go to David's house almost every week. We would play with Lego and Hot Wheels and eat jap chae. His mom has always liked me because he has all sisters but I did "boy stuff" with him.

"Come to a movie night at Sophie's house," he says. "Her place is incredible. They have a home theater with surround sound and a giant projector. We were thinking of doing a Studio Ghibli marathon. I know you love Studio Ghibli."

"With Sophie and Min?" He nods. "Why don't we hang out, just the two of us?"

"I rarely have a day free," David says, "so when I do, I want to hang out with everyone all at once."

I shrug. "Why don't you come with me to the skate park sometime? Your dad wants you to do more sports anyway."

David makes a face. "I don't think that would count."

We stand there in silence, shivering in the cold with our hands stuffed into our pockets. Then I hear my mother yell my name from the car. I see David's dad is staring at us too, both hands on the steering wheel.

"I should probably go," David says.

"Me too," I say.

. . .

Ash and I have one text conversation over the entirety of winter break. It goes like this:

Me: *yo u started reading orlando yet? it's sooooo slow.*
Ash: *yeah it's slow at first but you'll get used to it.*
Me: *how?!?! this is more obnoxious than shakespeare.*
Ash: *pfff it's not obnoxious it's beautiful. u just gotta get used to it.*
Me: *>__>*
Ash: *trust me.*
Me: *how's the island?*

She never gets back to me, but she's right. *Orlando* gets easier the further into it I get. It's like, my Cantonese is pretty awful when I'm in Canada, but a few years ago when we visited relatives in Hong Kong, it improved exponentially because I was surrounded by the stuff. So about a week in, I start to appreciate the language in *Orlando*. I love how every sentence is a carefully crafted melody, each word choice intentional. I won't lie, it takes *effort* to appreciate, but the first time I saw skateboarding I didn't fully appreciate it either, not until I tried it myself.

I read voraciously about the book online. Both Virginia and Vita were married to men, but they wrote hundreds of love letters to each other and their careers peaked when they were together. I marvel at the guts you would have needed to pull off a homosexual relationship in their era. I don't think I could handle being openly gay *now*.

I'm enjoying some coffee and reading one day when Ma Mi comes home and berates me for not doing anything "productive."

"I'm reading this book," I say, holding up *Orlando*. "It's for AP English."

"But your English assignment isn't due until the end of year," Ma Mi says. "I think you should study ahead in biology. You always say your biology teacher goes too fast. Maybe read ahead in the textbook."

"Ma Mi, it's the holidays. I'm not reading a *textbook* over the *holidays*."

"Look at your sister. She's working so hard."

I snort. "Isn't comparing children the first thing they tell you *not* to do in Parenting 101?"

Ma Mi sighs. "When I was your age, if I talked to my mother like that . . ." She shakes her head and massages the bridge of her nose. She's had a long day at work. I really shouldn't rile her up like this, but I can't help it. She probably thinks she's enlightened by letting me pursue art at university, but sometimes, she nails all the Chinese mom stereotypes. "I just mean she's a good example," she says, quieter but firmer. "She works so hard. She's willing to give up fun, like she did with the protest. Ah Nui, you're so smart. If you worked a little harder, you could be so successful."

That night, De Di and I do the dishes while Ma Mi picks Wendy up from a late recital. It seems like Wendy is even busier during the holidays because she has so many recitals and Christmas concerts. Her orchestra even did an overnight trip in the Interior. For the most part, I don't mind being the chill one while everyone hustles Wendy from one thing to another, but I do sometimes fantasize about it going the other way. Maybe Wendy and my parents will have to attend a gallery opening for me someday.

"De Di," I say, "why don't we ever use the dishwasher?"

De Di frowns. "It's a waste."

"A waste of what?"

"Water."

"We're using water right now."

"Energy, then."

I guess the reason why we don't use dishwashers will remain a mystery.

De Di says, "If you want Ma Mi to worry less, you can open up a textbook when you're around her."

"I don't want to study during the holidays. It's *the holidays.*"

"I know. She just wants you to succeed, that's all. You know she cares about you, right?"

I grumble.

De Di lowers his voice. "Don't mention this, but your mother is worried about work. They've been hiring a lot of new people. Young people. Your mom gets self-conscious about her English. The Hong Kong accent isn't a nice-sounding accent, you know that. She's worried she'll be let go in favor of someone younger and local. Someone who's better with computers."

"Is that why she's working late all the time?"

De Di rinses our wok. "Well, all those young people take a lot of sick days,'" he says. "Your mother has never taken a sick day in her life."

It's true. My mother goes to work even when she's sniffling. I'm just not sure that's something to be praised. I pick up the wok with one hand and dry it with the other, straining under the weight. "That sucks, but she still shouldn't take it out on me."

De Di takes over drying the heavy wok for me, and I shake my arms out in relief. "Your mother wasn't as lucky as you when she was your age. She worked to put her siblings through school. Neither of us had even been on a plane until we immigrated."

I grunt. I admit I feel a little bad. But it's not like by studying I can go back in time and make my mom's childhood better.

De Di turns to me thoughtfully. "Ma Mi is going to the church potluck alone this year because I need to pick up Wendy that night. Why don't you go with her? It will make her happy, I'm sure."

"De Di, I haven't gone to church in years," I say. Wendy and I grew up going to Sunday school, which doubled as Chinese language school, but as we got older and busier (well, Wendy at least), we stopped. For a while we still went to the special functions, but now only Ma Mi and De Di do that. My mom isn't diehard religious, but a friend had introduced her to a Cantonese-speaking church and I think she just likes having other Cantonese-speaking middle-aged women to talk to. Hanging out with all those aunties doesn't sound like my idea of a Christmas party, but maybe it'll help get Ma Mi off my back. "Fine, I'll do it," I say.

Ma Mi is absolutely delighted at the news and for a few days, she seems extra nice to me. When, on the day of the potluck, we get to the multipurpose room in the church basement, there are multiple sushi party trays, plates of marinated meat, and at least five tubs of fried noodles and fried rice.

"None of these things make sense with apple pie," I mutter, but Ma Mi makes me put her pies at the head of the table anyway.

Within a few seconds of being free of the pies, I am accosted by middle-aged ladies I barely remember. "Cecilia! Your daughter has gotten *so tall.*" "Is this your eldest or your youngest? The one who plays concertmaster?" "How is your husband doing? I haven't seen him in a while." "Jessica's in Grade 12, isn't she! What is she doing after high school?"

"Jessica, you remember to greet your aunties." It's good manners to call your elders Auntie or Uncle when you see them, and Ma Mi doesn't let me get food until I greet everyone.

"It's *so nice* to see you again!" says a lady I call Auntie Fanny. "Jessica, you should join our youth group on Saturdays. You'll make so many friends there." Gradually, the memories come back—I did not like Auntie Fanny one bit back in Sunday school. Her son stole my crayons and drew dicks on my Jesus coloring pages, and his mother had—has— the fakest voice.

"That's okay. I'm very busy," I say. "You know. Grade 12. University applications and all that."

"Of course!" Auntie Fanny pouts, feigning empathy. "My Jordan is writing essays every day. He's already won a full ride to Toronto, but he's still applying to more because he wants a better deal." She looks around at the other moms, who "ooh" and "mm" politely. "But he still makes time to lead bible study. Jessica, if you go to any of the big Canadian universities, they should have a fellowship club for Chinese students."

"Actually, I'm going abroad to study," I say.

A cloud of *ahh*s from the moms.

"It's not set in stone," Ma Mi says briskly. "She still needs to get into one of her schools."

"Oh, she will! The way you talk about her, she sounds *so* smart." Auntie Fanny's grin is stretched so hard across her face, I think her head might crack open.

We get a temporary reprieve at the buffet, but when my mom and I sit back down, she's accosted with questions. Where am I applying to? What will I study? What kinds of jobs will I do after graduating with an art degree? I wonder if Ma Mi regrets bringing me. She's brought the wrong daughter, the one with the vague dreams. The one who looks more like a son.

"Ladies, change of topic." Auntie Fanny returns to the table after doing a lap around the room, no doubt to gossip. "I found the strangest handout in my son's things the other day. It was about homosexuality and transgender people, about how those things are totally normal and should be accepted. There was even . . ." She coughs. "Well, they even mentioned how two men . . ." She makes agitated gestures. "How frightening is that?"

A few moms nod in agreement, some saying they had found similar handouts and homework assignments. They don't seem as bothered, and I wonder if they hadn't looked up all the unfamiliar words. One says she saw her kids read a story about a kid with two moms.

"Don't you think that's inappropriate?" Auntie Fanny says. "It's going to give children the wrong ideas. I'm already uncomfortable with them teaching about birth control and abortion in these classes. Now this? Maggie," she says to the mom who mentioned the two-moms book, "take Michelle out of Sex Education class. I'm taking Bosco and Jordan out too. We have the right." She crosses her arms. "I can't believe the Canadian government sometimes."

I jam food into my mouth to keep myself from talking. Then, a slightly younger mom I've never met, likely a new member, says, "Maybe they just want to prevent bullying."

A few nods from the other moms, including my own. I'm suddenly optimistic until one of the older women vigorously shakes her head. "It's the Western way," she grumbles. "We Asians, we're disciplined. We have values. Westerners—they divorce more, drink, do drugs. Don't you notice more of their kids have ADHD, are gay? I know it's not politically correct to say this, but it's true. You know it's true."

More nods around the table. I look at Ma Mi, and she nods along with a blank expression. I can't tell if she agrees or is just being polite. She's told me she doesn't agree with everything the church says, but she doesn't want to offend anyone.

Ma Mi lets me drive the car home. She usually gets anxious when I drive, so I think she must be in a good mood. I watch the windshield wipers flick rain back and forth, take a deep breath, and ask her, "Ma Mi, are you going to pull me out of Sex Ed, too?"

She chuckles. "You're already in Grade 12. Too late la!"

"Good," I say. "Auntie Fanny is a bigot."

I can feel her tense beside me, but I don't know if it's because of what I said or that I just pulled a right turn that was a little too wide. "Don't talk about Auntie Fanny like that. She's got a good heart. She started that program for inner-city immigrant children."

"Yeah," I say with a snort, "to indoctrinate them."

"She helped your father and I *a lot* when we first immigrated. Explained to us how everything works. Told us which neighborhoods had the best schools. You wouldn't have your friends if it wasn't for her."

"Still, she's close-minded."

"Each person has their own beliefs," Ma Mi says, "and we need to respect that."

"Sure. Unless they're bigots and homophobes." I grip the steering wheel with white knuckles. "Ma Mi."

"Yes?"

"What if—say, *hypothetically*—Wendy was gay. What would you do?"

Her head snaps toward me, but I keep my eyes on the road. "Wendy is gay?"

"No. Just hypothetically. What if she was? What would you do?"

"Jessica, if Wendy told you she's gay—"

"Oh my god, I made that up. I'm asking you what you would do in that *hypothetical* scenario."

Her body deflates as she sighs. "Don't scare me like that."

I shrug. "It's not *scary*."

She sighs again. "I don't know. Maybe I'd talk to her teachers? A school counselor? To be honest, I've never considered it. You're both well-adjusted kids."

"What does being well-adjusted have to do with anything?"

Ma Mi shrugs. "I'm not saying that homosexuality is a choice—"

"What *are* you saying, then?" My voice is strung like a taut wire.

"I don't know. Maybe some people are more likely to be gay because of unfortunate circumstances, and maybe those circumstances can be changed."

"Ma Mi! Lots of famous, successful people are gay." My face feels hot. Maybe it's because I ate way too much at the potluck, but my stomach starts to cramp. "Doctors. Politicians. Scientists. *Christians*."

Ma Mi rubs her eyes. It's clear she wants this conversation to end. "Look, I don't know, Jessica. If Wendy was gay . . . I don't know."

. . .

Christmas day is busy. Wendy has a city hall concert in the morning and another in the afternoon, so I get to sit through two performances of *The Nutcracker Suite*. That night, at De Di's urging, I keep Ma Mi company at the midnight mass. Wendy is too tired from her day of concerts and De Di has an online meeting with clients in China who don't observe Christmas.

Throughout the entire service, I wish I could tape my eyelids open. But I must admit that the music department has improved dramatically.

On the drive home, Ma Mi is all warm and fuzzy, humming the hymns. "I just love church music," she says. "I wanted singing lessons when I was little. But your grandparents couldn't afford lessons for all five kids; it would only be fair for all of us to learn something, after all. I'm so happy Wendy gets to play violin! And Jessica, if you ever want to go back to piano. . . You had real potential for music, you know."

I yawn. "I think percussion in band is more than enough for now, thanks."

On Boxing Day, the whole family wakes up early to take advantage of the big sales at the mall. It's a long day of standing in lineups and carrying heavy bags. "We should have gone to Washington," De Di grumbles all day as we sip mall bubble tea, which is just syrup and tapioca. "More stuff at the outlet malls."

"Then we'd have to pay for motels and pay to eat out every day. All that greasy American food," Ma Mi says.

But our parents give Wendy and me each $100 of Christmas lai see, so that's nice. I buy new skate shoes because mine have holes from ollie-ing. They cost $50, so I save the rest. I expect Wendy to spend her cash on makeup or clothes, but she follows me into the skate store instead, peering at the plethora of gear in the glass cases with her arms crossed.

"Aren't you getting anything?" I ask.

"No. I'm putting $70 into my college fund, giving $20 to charity, and I'll use the remaining $10 for bubble tea with my friends."

"Wow, seriously?" Wendy spent all her lai see last year on makeup alone and when she couldn't afford a certain brush, Ma Mi had bought that for her, too.

"We're an overcapitalistic consumerist society," she says in that godawful tone of hers. "Capitalism is a direct contributor to income inequality, waste, and environmental degradation. Everything here was made by kids paid twelve cents an hour, you do know that, right?"

I sigh. "Then why did you follow me instead of shopping with Mom and Dad?"

"Because I don't want to waste time explaining this to them." She wrinkles her nose. "They're from Hong Kong, the most capitalist place in the world. They won't get it."

I laugh. "That's all they care about, eh? Work and money."

Wendy rolls her eyes. "And they eat *so much meat*!"

We look at each other and smirk.

Over the next few days, I text Ash a few times and send her photos of my new shoes in case she happens to get reception somewhere. She doesn't answer. Then, on the day after New Year's, Ma Mi puts something in front of my toast at breakfast: a big manila envelope. She's all jittery and excited and *proud*. Which freaks me out a little because she's never that way around me. "Looks important," she says. "From *England*."

"Wow!" Wendy exclaims sarcastically. She has massive dark circles under eyes, which means her default setting is cynical.

De Di glares at her and puts a hand on my shoulder as he stands behind me. "Open it," he says.

My hands are shaking as I hold the envelope. It's an early admission response from a university in the UK. It was a freaking extensive application, and I had to chase down several teachers for reference letters, which

I'd hated doing. Ma Mi gives me a letter opener and I slowly tear open the envelope, afraid of ripping apart what could be a coveted acceptance letter. The ripping sound is as loud as thunder.

"Well?" Ma Mi says after I've scanned the first few lines of the letter.

My hands drop to my lap with the letter. "I didn't get in."

Wendy quietly returns to her jok, her spoon clinking against her ceramic bowl. De Di sits next to me and pats my shoulder. Ma Mi sits across from me with folded arms. "Did you proofread your personal essay? Three times, like I told you to?"

"Yes."

"Did you mention you wrote for Journalism Club?"

"Yes."

"That you've been on the honor roll every term since Grade 8?"

"Yes."

"That you won second place in that district art competition in Grade 10?"

"Yes, yes, Ma Mi, I did!"

"Well . . ." Ma Mi uncrosses her arms and crosses them again. "Have you applied to any of the local universities?"

"I plan to."

"Which programs?"

"Art."

Her shoulders droop. "Have you considered anything else? Aren't you doing well in AP English? You know, an English degree can be very versatile—"

"I don't want to do English, Mom. I want to do art."

She sighs. "Look, Ah Nui, it doesn't hurt to have a backup plan."

"I want to go to school in Europe," I say, "and I'll get a scholarship. I will."

Wendy snorts. "You know you have to get *in* to a university to even use a scholarship. Maybe your portfolio wasn't strong enough."

De Di gives her a look and I feel my body vibrate with heat. "Shut up." I say it under my breath and I'm not sure if she hears it, but I tell everyone, "I don't want to talk about this. You guys don't know anything about art anyway."

I leave my half-eaten toast on the table and snatch up my mug of coffee as I stand. My family stares after me. I only catch their faces for a second before I storm off to my room, but while De Di and Wendy look shocked more than anything, Ma Mi looks sad. Or maybe she's just tired.

. . .

I'm sitting in a giant lecture hall. Mr. Hussein is giving a welcoming speech at the podium in a British accent. I feel nothing but relief. I'm in, I've made it. Then my eyes flicker open and there are globs of rainwater sliding across my window. Damn it, I'm still in fucking Raincouver.

I get up and turn on my laptop and start reading the long list of instructions for my next application: a hefty scholarship to an institute in Amsterdam. It has a later due date, but it's even more extensive, and there are hints all over the place that you need a strong digital portfolio.

I plug in my new external hard drive—the thing had cost me several birthdays' worth of savings, but you can practically store two computers on it—and look through our video clip slush pile. Sure, this stuff might not be skateboarding-competition worthy, but hey, maybe it's art-school-portfolio worthy. There are so many random clips here, of Ash just chilling, smoking, staring through her fingers at trees after having a joint. And there are clips of me, too, stumbling over my no complys and landing primo on my kickflip attempts, bailing and laughing and at times cursing at the sky.

I gather a few clips and smush them into iMovie. Then I get to editing.

I try not to think about whether the edit will make for a good portfolio piece, I just think about what will make it a good edit. The next time I look at the clock it's almost four. I'm not tired, though. In fact, I don't remember the last time I had this much energy.

I think people like things like sex, music, drugs, parties, and even skateboarding because they make you *feel* something. And shit, I like those things too. Well, maybe not the sex part because I haven't tried that yet. But the feeling I got from weed was similar to the feeling I get sketching, and drawing, and editing videos—which are better than weed, honestly. You get this, like, tunnel vision. Everything else disappears like the black part of a vignette and suddenly, two hours have whipped by and your mother's calling you for dinner and you're suddenly aware of how much you have to pee. You can argue that being in "the zone" or whatever you call it is the *lack* of feeling, I guess, but to me, I care more about creating something beautiful than feeling. Everything, everything to me is making something beautiful come to life that's never existed before.

My video runs to three minutes. I play it back and think this is a good length to stop. Just one more thing: I add a black screen at the beginning and type the words "This is a video where nothing happens and everything happens."

It's a little cheesy, but I like it.

You can ride through the city for years and only notice concrete.

January 2011

CHAPTER 7

The first day back from winter break, I'm told to report to the gym after school for detention. I haven't seen Ash all day, and when she walks in a few minutes after me, our eyes briefly meet before she leaps up the bleachers two at a time to sit several rows away.

Mr. Acosta, our gym teacher and detention supervisor, slaps down a pile of lined paper. "Here's how it's going to work. I will assign you a two-page essay each day and you can leave at quarter to four. Capiche?"

"Capito." That was a reflex response, but I feel Ash staring at me like I'm the biggest dork ever.

"Your essay topic today is the dangers of binge drinking," Mr. Acosta says huffily. "I'll be in my office. Don't try any funny business."

Ash takes a sheet of paper without making any eye contact. I take out my stationery and stare at the blank page. Then I start writing: *Binge drinking is harmful to health. It causes vomiting and bad decisions.*

And then I'm stuck. I covertly watch Ash through my bangs. She's writing away, her pen never stopping. I wonder what she's bullshitting. Ash looks different: her red streaks have faded to a dark orange, and I think she's done something different with her eyes. Her eyelashes are thicker, so maybe she finally figured out how to use mascara (she had ranted about her shitty eyelash curler before). She pushes her hair off her forehead and the orange flows messily up and over before falling back down. She sniffs. The concentration in her expression pushes out a slight dimple on her right cheek.

And then it happens again: that unspeakable pulse—an ever so slight contraction of tissues that don't normally contract. I quickly pull my focus back to my essay, my face on fire. But also, I'm surprisingly grateful that I'm not a guy.

I write another line: *Making bad decisions is harmful to young people because we have a future ahead of us, and we should be focused on school.* I feel like I'm channeling my mother.

The forty-five minutes are agonizing, but somehow, I survive them. Ash and I stand up, stretch, and go straight outside where the sun's already setting.

I break the silence first. "How was your Christmas?"

"Tolerable." She cups a shivery hand around her cigarette to light it. "Yours?"

"Tolerable," I say.

Maybe it's just me, but she seems almost . . . shy. Like she wants to tell me something but can't quite work up to it. I wait, shivering in my jacket. Ash takes a long drag then lets out an even longer exhale, and then she says, "I passed the second round of the skate contest. I'm going to Kelowna."

"Holy shit," I breathe. "Congratulations!" I want to hug her, but she's holding a burning cigarette and something tells me she's not quite in the mood for a hug.

"Thanks." Ash pauses for a few blinks. "It was all thanks to you, you know. Your camera, your editing, your . . ." She coughs. "Thank you."

We get to the end of the school road. I turn left in the direction of our houses, but Ash stays planted. "I'm going to Blake's," she says.

"Oh." I guess that makes sense. "I'll see you tomorrow, then?"

She gives me another small twinkle of a smile. "I'll see you."

The next day, our essay topic is "Why is plagiarism never okay?" I really don't know how to fill two whole pages about the importance of citing your sources. When detention is over (and I have just one page to hand in), I ask Ash how she wrote hers. She scoffs and says, "Dude. No one's gonna read it. I just wrote *Naruto* fanfiction."

I laugh.

The next day, we're told to report to Mr. Hussein's classroom instead. When we get there, Mr. Hussein is leaning against the chalk shelf with his arms crossed and a subtle smirk half-hidden in his beard. "Mr. Acosta can no longer supervise you," he says. "So today's your lucky day! Unfortunately, that means no more writing about the hidden passion between one Uchiha Sasuke and Uzumaki Naruto." Ash freezes, and is it just me or is she turning red? I stifle a chuckle because I don't remember ever seeing Ash embarrassed before. "I'll actually read your essays," says Mr. Hussein, giving us a knowing stare before turning around to write on the chalkboard. "Today's topic: your best friend just told you they're pregnant. They're scared of getting in trouble with their parents and they want your help. What do you do?"

Ash groans, but I like this topic more than Mr. Acosta's.

After detention, it's rainy and dark and Ash forgot her umbrella, so we squeeze under mine until we get to the end of the road. "What did you write?" I ask her. "I said I'd encourage the friend to talk to a counselor."

Ash shakes her head. "The counselor would just tell the parents."

"The parents will have to know eventually," I counter. "And *shouldn't* they know?"

Ash frowns. "If someone is scared of telling their parents they're pregnant, it's probably for a good reason. The friend's not gonna want to tell them. It won't be safe."

"But you can't *hide* being pregnant. Sooner or later—"

"Then it's up to the friend when and how to tell the parents, not up to some counselor. Not all parents are like the ones in *Juno*, you know."

I turn left at the road and Ash follows me, tucking into the umbrella even more. When she looks at me, I feel her warm breath on my cheek. "Going home today. Finally," she says. "Haven't been in like a week."

"A week? You've been at Blake's for *a week*?"

"I was actually, uh, I was actually at his place all winter break," Ash mutters, staring at the ground. "I didn't go to the Island. Sorry. I lied."

I scowl, but I'm confused more than anything. "Why?"

She sighs hard. "When my dad got the memo about Whistler, he completely blew his top. Insulted me with every name in the book. I learned some new Chinese vocab that day." Another big, hard sigh. "I told you I'd be at Blake's because I knew shit was gonna go down with my dad, that I'd maybe have to leave. And I did. I lived with Blake and his roommates in New West for two weeks. Then my mom called me on New Year's Eve saying she'd convinced my dad to let me back in. The house was a mess when I got back, so I spent the rest of the holiday being my parents' maid. Then we had another fight just before school started so I left for Blake's again."

"But why didn't you just say you'd be at Blake's all winter break?" I ask. "Why did you make up the Island thing?"

Ash looks at the ground. "I don't know. I just wanted some time alone, I guess."

"But you were with Blake."

Ash is quiet.

I say, "You could have come over, you know. You can come over anytime."

Ash shrugs. "I didn't want to intrude."

She has a point there. The thought of explaining all this to my parents makes me squirm. "You could've stayed at Matt's," I say, hoping she forgets what I said about her coming over anytime. "Or Logan's, or Dezzy's."

Ash shakes her head. "Blake's my boyfriend."

I don't see how that explains anything, but whatever. "Well, did you guys do anything fun over the holidays?" To be honest, I'm not interested at all in what Ash and Blake did, but it feels polite to ask.

"Mostly movies, and cake, and bong rips," says Ash. "Well, a little making out and some, uh, hand stuff." I try not to cringe. "I figured I'd work myself up, you know?" she says with a nod.

"How's that going?" I force myself to sound supportive.

Ash avoids the question, much to my relief. "Blake wants me to move in," she says. "Even offered to pay my share of rent. But I can't let him do that. He'd *own* me, you know? We got into a small fight over *that*, so in a way I was happy when my mom called." She laughs sarcastically. "Everywhere, men like to pick fights with me."

I grunt. "Blake sounds like a possessive jerk. Your dad's a jerk too, but at least he's your dad. What's so cool about Blake anyway?"

Ash examines the dirt underneath her nails. "He has a job, he's in a band, and he *knows* things."

"Like what?" It's not like his punk revival band is making millions.

"Life things. He's seen shit."

I stare at the ground. "I, uh, I didn't get my UK scholarship."

"Oh." Ash clears her throat. "Shit. I'm sorry. I know that meant a lot to you. What did you put in your portfolio?"

"The deck designs I showed you. And your competition video."

"That video was a banger and artsy as hell. Did it not help?"

I shrug. "They probably wanted something more—I dunno, something that *says* something?" I make a face.

"And skateboarding doesn't?" Ash laughs, and I laugh too, but I think this is something people who don't skate just don't get.

She touches my arm. "I hope you get the next scholarship. They're shitheads for not accepting you."

"Thanks." I smile.

We keep walking. We walk and we talk. About music, movies, *Buffy, Orlando,* skateboarding. Ash tells me she finished *Orlando* over the holidays. I ask her what she thinks of it.

"Orlando is a little insufferable at times," is her answer, which surprises me, but I guess we all have our own interpretations. "I went down a fascinating gender rabbit hole on the Internet, though. Have you heard the quote, 'one is not born, but rather becomes, a woman'?" I shake my head. "Simone de Beauvoir," Ash says, as if I should know who that is.

I'm not sure what that quote means, but the rain falls harder and the talking gets easier. We left on awkward terms after Whistler, but by the time we get to my gate, the rain has washed away any weirdness. Ash says bye to me and I watch her walk down the laneway with her hood pulled over her head, hands in her pockets.

The rain doesn't stop for several days. Fantasizing about university is what keeps me from falling asleep as I shuffle from class to class. I calculate budgets in my notebook margins and think about all the ways I can save so I can splurge on what matters—galleries, museums, live concerts, clubs. I don't need decadent food, I want *experiences.* Too bad it was Blake who gave me this idea.

Of course, I don't expect Europe to be a total cakewalk. Ma Mi and De Di will nag me. About not returning their calls, about being in debt, and *wouldn't it be so much easier if I lived at home and saved money and spoke the language?*

But what I want to prove most to them is that I can take care of myself, that I don't need De Di cooking dinner for me or Ma Mi reminding me not to forget my umbrella when I leave the house. So, after school, after I've done all my assignments, I watch YouTube endlessly. I learn how to cook pasta with white wine, different ways to unclog a drain, even how to make a bong out of a water bottle. Then, when I've learned enough party tricks and drinking games to impress people during frosh week, I watch skateboarding videos until I fall asleep.

. . .

"How's detention?" David asks me in Friday's geography class. His eyes are red. If it wasn't for his well-known nerdiness, you'd think he was a stoner.

"It's actually not that bad," I say. "Today's my last day. The worst part was getting yelled at by my mom. But that's over and done with."

David whistles. "Man, if I got detention . . ." He shudders. "So what happens?"

"Not much. We just write essays."

"Can you do homework?"

"Nope."

He scowls. "So, it's basically really boring and a waste of time?" I nod.

But detention really isn't that bad. Mr. Hussein has been giving us interesting topics. Yesterday's was "Should swearing be banned in schools?" Today, we get "What would you do if your parents are against you pursuing your dream job?" Which hits me hard. I write: *I'm dealing with this problem right now! My mom wants me to study something practical at a local university, but I want to go abroad and study art. I'm not sure what I should do. I just know I want to show my mom that I can make these decisions on my own and that it's my life and I can do what I want with it. But she thinks I'm too young to understand how life works and she thinks I'm going to be miserable. But she doesn't get that I'll be miserable if I do what SHE wants.* I end up spending the rest of that detention period venting on paper and hand in five pages. I think I was even out of breath by the end of it.

Mr. Hussein quietly hands back my essay the following week while we're writing reading responses in AP English. I see that he's given me a note: *It's normal for parents and children to not understand each other, especially if they grew up in different cultural environments. Not to mention a lot has changed within a generation. But I think your mom has your best interests at heart, even if she may be wrong. Remember that your parents are people, just like you. They have their biases, and so do you. Your parents may also change their mind over time. You're a smart kid and I'm confident that you will figure out how to live your best life.*

Mr. Hussein's note gives me an unexpected spurt of motivation. I had been in an art rut with Mr. Templeton's second-term project because I've never been awfully inspired to do public art. But by the end of that week, I come up with an incredible idea. Who says skateboarding has no meaning? No meaning, my ass. Mr. Templeton is iffy about my pitch at first, but we come to a compromise for it to count toward my grade.

I spend every lunch hour in either the art room planning my project or at Mr. Hussein's iMac updating my CV (I'm going all-out and using InDesign instead of MS Word this time). Ash joins me because it's too rainy outside to practice tre flips. She often ends up eating my lunch because I forget to eat and she never has a lunch with her anyway.

One day, Ash comes in and starts bouncing a tennis ball against the wall. "Yo, do you realize five months from now we'll be out of this shit heap?" she says. "Then it's no more school for the rest of our lives!"

I grunt. Ash seems to have forgotten that I have university in September. And after that, my mom will likely bug me about grad school.

Ash keeps tossing the ball. It's loud and a little obnoxious, but so is a question I've had knocking around in my head since that last morning in Whistler. "Hey Ash," I venture, "can I ask you something?"

"Sup?"

"You don't have to answer it if you don't want to. I'm just curious."

This must intrigue her because she throws the ball and then lets it dribble onto the floor and roll into the corner. "I'm listening."

I say, "Why did you leave your old school?"

Ash blinks then gets up to retrieve the ball.

"Like I said, you don't have to talk about it if you don't want to," I say again, quickly.

She plunks the ball onto the desk she's sitting at. "I got kicked out."

So there it is. She's confirmed the suspicions I've had. Finally. I can't help but shift a little uncomfortably in my seat. I've never been friends with someone who's gotten expelled or even suspended. And this includes friends I've made at summer camps and Sunday school. I realize I've never rehearsed what to say in this scenario, so I just say, "Oh."

"You want the juicy, scandalous details?" Ash asks. "They found out I went to this party when I was in Grade 10 where there was underage drinking and drugs. I didn't even touch anything there."

I scowl. "You got expelled for going to a party? What about Grade 11?"

"Well, I also had a horrific attendance record," she says, shrugging. "But it was a win-win, in a way. People at Mackenzie sucked. Well, other than Matt and Dezzy and Logan. So there was the party thing, and then Grade 11 was shitty for me, so the counselor and my parents made a mutual decision to move me here."

"So, you weren't expelled. Just . . . transferred," I say, kind of relieved.

She shrugs. "They didn't want me there. Whatever. It doesn't matter.

I left that place in my dust and I'm happy I did. Now all I gotta do is graduate."

All I gotta do is graduate. Ash repeats this all the time. When she gets a bad but passing grade, she mutters to herself that all she has to do is graduate. When I ask her what plans she has after graduation, she just shrugs and says she'll figure it out when she gets there. For now, all she has to do is graduate. If my biggest goal in life was to graduate from high school, my parents would a) burst out laughing; and b) send me to the academic equivalent of military school or something. De Di always jokes about how American movies make high school graduation a big deal. In families like mine (and David's, and Min's, and Sophie's probably), graduating from high school is a default expectation, not an achievement worth awarding.

That weekend, I tell my parents I have a group project meeting and take the bus to Ash's usual park in East Van. I have my skateboard back and know the bus routes like the back of my hand now. And even though lying to my parents still makes my palms sweaty, I try to embody Ash's attitude: if you want to be independent, you gotta take the first step.

I get to the park early and I'm nervous because it's a little busy. There are kids on scooters zipping around and twentysomething legit dudes throwing slides and grinds. I try to remind myself that my parents pay taxes, and so will I, and this is a public space funded by taxes, so I have the right to be here. With that in mind, I warm up around the periphery of the park, careful to avoid eye contact. When I'm a little more warmed up, I try some ollies and shove-its. Then I go to the transition section, gear myself up for a rock to fakie . . . and promptly smash myself into the quarterpipe.

I'm red in the face as I get up, terrified that everyone's gonna laugh at me, but I hear someone stomping their board instead. It's a shirtless guy with long hair, smoking on a bench with his skate buddies. "You almost got it!" he says. "Just a little more speed!"

I nod. Almost obediently, I run back to the other side of the park and throw down again. I skid out this time, but less violently. "Almost there!" the guy yells. I try again. This time, I land it. The guy whoops, and even his buddies drum their boards in applause. Maybe older skate bros are nicer than I thought. This guy isn't hiding behind a keyboard typing sexist comments. He's here, actually skating.

A few minutes later, Matt rides in all laid back, a can of pop in one hand. His eyes widen and he jumps off his board with open arms when he notices me. "Hey! Haven't seen you in ages. I didn't know you were coming here."

I side-hug him. "Been busy. Grade 12. Applications. You know."

He grins. "Well, I'm glad you survived snowboarding and the subsequent detentioning."

I laugh and punch him in the arm. We skate around for a bit, just the two of us, when I decide to ask, "Hey, Matt, what was Ash like when you guys went to the same school?"

Matt shoots up the side of a pipe and kicks his board up into his hand with a grace I can only admire. Turns around and drops in. "Snarky. Swore a lot. Pain in the ass. Not that different from now. Why?"

"Just wondering," I mutter. "She said she didn't like her old school much. Except you guys," I quickly add.

"Right." Matt brushes the sweat from his forehead with his shirt. I wait for more, but he doesn't volunteer it.

I trip over my board when I try to do a kickturn on the ramp. I go back to the bottom and try it again. Better this time. "I heard Ash went to a party."

Matt drops his head and scratches the back of his neck. "Yeah."

"What happened?" I ask.

"She didn't tell you?"

"She said she got kicked out for going to a party."

"Yeah, sounds about right."

"Did something happen there?"

"I wasn't at the party." Matt drops in again. He rides regular stanced, left foot forward, his back toward me. "Is Ash okay? Did something happen?"

"No, she's fine," I say. Then, in an effort to change the subject, I ask, "Hey, is dropping in hard?"

"You've never dropped in before?" Matt laughs. "Oh, it's scary for sure. But once you do it, it feels amazing."

We cruise around the bowls, Matt carving tightly around the corners, me failing to get more than a foot up the bowl. Ash arrives ten minutes later with Dezzy and Logan and we do a round of fist bumps. I'm already sweaty and high on endorphins.

"Hey guys," Matt says, "Jay has never dropped in before." I shoot him a look, but he just sticks his tongue out at me like a toddler.

Dezzy gasps. "Well, shit! We gotta make you then."

I squirm at the word "make," but he and Matt are already shoving me to the top of a small ramp. I look over the edge and my stomach swirls. What looked like a simple two-foot drop is now a ten-foot tidal wave. If I squint, I can make out every possible crack in the concrete I could wipe out on.

Matt teaches me how to anchor the tail of my board against the coping and put my back foot on it. My front foot is supposed to step forward on the nose bolts and into the ramp, but it's shaking when I put it there. The guys shout tips from the sidelines.

"Don't lean back," Dezzy says. "It's your instinct to lean back, but fight it. Leaning back will make you eat it."

"Just remember one word," Logan says. "Commit."

I close my eyes, open them again, and to hell with it, I step forward.

The ground below me rushes forward and there's a roaring *fwuuummm* sound I may or may not have imagined in my head. Just like Dezzy predicted, I instinctively lean back. My board teeters, squeals, and shoots out from beneath me. My ass hits the ground and I slide down the rest of the way, heart thumping and cheeks burning.

But the guys thump their boards in applause. Matt pulls me up. "I'll give you a hand this time."

I nod, climb back to the top of the ramp, and diligently align my board into position. Ash is smoking underneath a big tree, watching me. Matt stands on the bank with his hands outstretched. I step down while holding his hands, focused on putting my weight forward. I smack the landing, Matt lets go, and I ride away. Matt, Dezzy, and Logan roar their support. When I slow down, I 180-kickturn back, which I've already warmed up with. I look for Ash. She's smiling big beneath the tree.

We spend the rest of the hour skating. Dezzy teaches me how to carve the bowls and Matt gives me ollie pointers. I'm really effing stoked. The guys and Ash chat about video games, sports, and gossip from Mackenzie. They make plans for the following week and I'm surprised at how much free time they have. No lessons, no clubs, not even tests to study for, it seems.

I take out my camera and grab a few shots. Mostly bails, but still stuff I could use for my own edits. Matt crouches down next to me and explains what Ash and the guys are attempting, enlightening me on some skate terminology in the process. "That's a front board she's trying. Frontside because she's goofy and facing the rail. If she was pivoting the other way, that'd be backside."

"What's the difference between a boardslide and a lipslide, then?"

"Board is when your front trucks go over the rail; lip is when the back trucks do."

"Damn, I want to be able to nail a back lip at some point. They look so stylish."

"They do. Ash can do them on flat bars. They took her forever to learn but last summer she stomped 'em. Now she wants to do them on handrails, like the pros."

There are more people in the park now, lots of little kids riding their scooters with no spatial awareness. Ash is 5-0ing a hubba ledge but keeps having to bail because kids keep cutting her off. When it happens for the fifth time, Logan swears and marches toward the kid. For a terrifying moment I think he's going to sock him, but instead he crouches down on one knee to talk to the kid. I see the kid nod then point at Logan's board. Logan shrugs and holds the scooter while the kid tries out his board. He ekes out a baby ollie and Logan fist-bumps him. The kid then loudly talks about how his mom won't let him get a skateboard so Logan tells him he can use his for ten minutes while he takes a smoke break. The kid goes to a corner and tic-tacs around, giving Ash ample space to 5-0 wherever the hell she likes.

Pink and orange streaks smear across the sky as early as four o'clock. Tired now, I sit back from the park and lean on my elbows as I wait for the sweat on my skin to dry. Matt plops down next to me and throws me a can of pop. "Hey, great job on the video."

"Thanks." Ash spins out on a flip trick and swears when her board body-slams her. Logan whoops and drums his board against the ground, laughing. I'm starting to buy into skating with friends over skating alone. Friends cheer you on, even when you fall. *Especially* when you fall. And if you see a friend do something scary and survive it, like dropping in, you really want to do it, too.

Plus, no one seems to care that I suck. Everyone is stoked that I'm stoked. I'm starting to think that's the only requirement: to be stoked. I'm thinking about how long I can stay when Ash jogs toward us. "Jay,

I'm going home."

"What? This early?"

"Yeah. Gotta take a shower and, uh, change before I meet up with Blake."

Logan boos her from the top of a ramp. Ash laughs, fist-bumps Matt, slaps me on the shoulder, and rolls off. When she's out of earshot, Logan says, "I can't believe they're still together."

"Me too," I mutter.

"Hey, at least this time, someone likes Ash back and she's not crooning after her like a wounded puppy," Dezzy says. "Hated watching that."

The guys all nod, but my ears perk up. Did Dezzy say "her"? I stand there frozen for a moment before Matt skates past and says, "What are you, rebooting?!" He makes robot noises. I shake myself out and join him at the top of the ramp. The moment has passed, and I need to practice my drop ins.

· · ·

One rainy evening, the doorbell rings in the middle of hotpot night. We all look at each other around the table. Ma Mi gets the door. "Uhhh . . . Jessica?" she says a few seconds later. "Your friend is here."

I wipe soy sauce from my face as I follow her into the living room and almost drop my napkin when I see Ash soaked through in the doorway.

I clear my throat. "Um, hi Ash?"

"Hey." Her eyes dart to me then to my mom and then back to me. The three of us stand in an awkward triangle for a moment before my mom mutters something about making sure the hot pot soup doesn't boil over and walks away.

Ash steps in and wipes her feet on the doormat. "Hey. So. Do you think I can get some dinner? I'm starving."

"What?" I stare at her, wondering if she's having issues with her dad again.

She rubs her hands together. "I forgot to salt the sidewalk and my dad accused me of trying to murder him, no joke. So he kicked me out for the night."

Yep. "Oh, shit." I blink, thinking fast. How the hell am I supposed to explain this to my parents? But I can't let Ash starve. "Okay, wait a sec." I close the door behind Ash and go to the dining room where my parents and Wendy immediately look at me, expecting answers. "Uh," I start, "can Ash join us for dinner?"

Ma Mi scowls, but De Di says, "Sure. We do have too much food for four people. But why?"

"There was a, uh, a mix-up," I say. "Her parents are out of town and they thought they left her food but it, um, went bad." Ma Mi looks at De Di, but he just shrugs.

Thirty seconds later, we all sit in silence and watch as Ash guzzles down rice, soup, tofu, bok choy, enoki, fish balls, and—my favorite, which she eats *a lot* of—pork neck. She heaps rice into her bowl and dumps a whole side dish of soy sauce into it. White rice mixed with soy sauce, eaten like a toddler. She doesn't speak until she eats the equivalent of a full meal then finally says, in Cantonese, "This is delicious. I don't normally eat vegetables, but Auntie" —she swallows and switches to English— "this is *the shit*."

Ma Mi winces but De Di chuckles. "Actually, *I* do the cooking here. But really, this is just a soup mix I bought at the Chinese supermarket."

"It's still delicious," Ash says. "My parents never make stuff like this. Thank you, Uncle." Her leg is jiggling up and down a thousand miles a minute, which is something that De Di *hates*. If it was me, he would have yelled at me three times by now.

"Your Chinese is very good," De Di says.

"My parents don't speak much English," Ash says, her mouth full. De Di is right: Ash does speak well in Cantonese. She doesn't stutter or do the thing Wendy and I do where we start a sentence in Cantonese, give up halfway, and end it in English. There was a time when De Di refused to acknowledge us unless we spoke Cantonese. He'd pretend he didn't understand English. But Wendy and I refused to cooperate and he eventually gave up doing that. Now I wish he'd never stopped.

"So." Ma Mi pulls me back to the present. She's wearing her polite-stranger smile, the one she uses to ask store clerks to double-check discounts. "Your parents are out of town?"

"Yes," I say, before Ash can answer, and I shoot her a glance which I hope she understands. "They're just out tonight."

Ash says, "I really appreciate this. Truly. I was starving!"

After hot pot, Ma Mi and De Di tell us kids to eat fruit while they wash the dishes, no doubt to gossip about the strange new friend their kid never talks about. Wendy pretends to be focused on peeling and slicing her apple, but I catch her eyes flicking curiously toward Ash every few seconds. "I told them your parents were out of town and there was a mix-up," I tell Ash. "Sorry. It just seemed, well, easier."

She nods. "Makes sense." She catches Wendy looking at her and says, "My dad and I got into a fight. I said 'fuck you' to him and he shoved me out the door." Wendy's eyes go wide and she puts a hand to her mouth, as if she's about to choke on her apple. Ash turns to me and grins. "Anyway, I remember you said I could come over any time."

I guess I did say that. I just wish Ash had, you know, given me a call first. Like a normal person. But it's too late now.

"So, can I stay over tonight? I just don't wanna deal with my dad," Ash says.

Crap, another awkward ask. I drag my feet to the kitchen where my parents are murmuring to each other over the running water and knock on the wall. "Hey, uh, can Ash stay over tonight? Since, you know, she's already here and won't have breakfast in the morning."

Ma Mi hesitates, but De Di gives her a reassuring glance. "That's okay," he says to me. "Just don't stay up too late and don't be too loud, okay?" I nod and slip out of the room.

I look for spare clothes for Ash that she can wear to bed, but everything I own is too big, so I just give her my old school P.E. set. When she ducks into the shower, I hear her singing Green Day from the other side of the wall. While she does, Ma Mi comes into my room with her forehead knotted in worry. "Jessica . . ."

I spin around on my desk chair. "Yeah?"

"Is this—is this the friend you went to Whistler with? The one you skateboard with?"

I spin back to my computer and aimlessly click around. "Yeah."

"This is the first time I'm seeing her."

I shrug. "I know a lot of people, Mom. I can't introduce you to every person I know."

"But you two seem so close."

I pretend to be engrossed in my computer. I don't talk about Ash at home because I don't want my parents to judge her, judge someone I know they will never understand, someone so wildly different from David, Min, Sophie, even me.

"Your father and I think we should call her parents," Ma Mi continues. "Just to make sure they know where she is."

"I don't think they care," I say.

"What kind of parent doesn't care where their child is? Ask if her parents have a cell phone with them or what hotel they're staying at."

Surprisingly, Ash isn't fazed by my mother wanting to call hers. She dials her home number on our phone and gives it to my mother, who introduces herself in her double-check-the-discount voice. She explains that Ash is safe at our house and then, after a few uh-huhs, clicks off without saying goodbye. "She just hung up," she says, bewildered.

"That's my mother," Ash says breezily.

All things considered, it's a chill night in with Ash. I show her the skate deck sketches I had done over the winter break and she gushes over them. She's seen me digitize my favorite ones in the art room, but I think she loves the sketches even more. Then I finish my homework while she watches skateboarding videos on the computer. De Di comes up at some point with two bowls of tofu pudding and Ash squeals, "Oh my god, is that dou fu fa? I haven't had that in *years*!"

We prop my laptop up on a stack of books, turn on the fairy lights strung around my bed, and snuggle under the covers to watch *Shrek* while we eat our dessert. I know, I know, it's a kids' movie, but it's been a while since I've seen it and Ash isn't in the mood for something with explosions or spies or a complicated plot. "Besides, sometimes it's nice to be a kid, you know?" she says.

When (spoiler alert) Donkey discovers that Fiona is an ogress, I turn to Ash, yawning, and notice a smudge of leftover eyeliner on the bottom edge of her eye. "Hey, are you okay?"

She laughs, full-bellied and deep. "Jeez, Jay, it's just a kids' movie and she falls in love with Shrek anyway."

"I don't mean the movie. I mean the stuff with your parents."

Ash sighs loudly. Then she rolls over onto her side to face me and hugs my big bread loaf stuffie to her chest. She pets it as she talks, her voice low and unusually velvety, as if the conversation is being softened by all the pillows and duvets and stuffed animals around us. "So. My por por died when I was ten, but she practically raised me by herself because my parents were always working. I think I've mentioned this, but she'd take me to the community center to skateboard while she read a book in the park. She bought me my first board. I still have it, even though it's plastic and in three pieces."

I don't know why Ash is telling me about her grandmother. We haven't discussed our grandparents much. I'd sort of forgotten that her por por was the one who introduced her to skating and had assumed her grandparents were in Hong Kong or Shenzhen or Guangzhou or somewhere equally far away like mine. Old people who send us lai see in the mail with four-word greetings on birthdays and Lunar New Year. I shift to my side and listen attentively. *Shrek* keeps playing in the background, but we've both seen the movie and don't need to pay attention.

"Por Por believed that kids should be kids, that they should have fun while they can," Ash continues. "She grew up during the war and didn't finish school. Could barely read. Saw her neighbors get bayoneted by Japanese soldiers, so she never got to enjoy her childhood." Her face tightens then relaxes. "She was always a badass, perhaps *too much* of a badass, because she never told anyone she was in pain and by the time she did, it was too late. Not that she trusted Western medicine, anyway.

"My mom has always been a bit of a mess, but she really fell off the wagon when Por Por died. Got fired from everything. Practically ran out of Chinese supermarkets to work for. Then she started sleeping for days and refused to get out of bed. So, I did the cleaning and cooking and translated stuff for my dad. And, of course, I had to ace school.

"My dad ruled the house like a dictator. I wasn't allowed to do *anything* but school, chores, and homework. Came home straight after school every day to make dinner, study, rinse and repeat. One day, I just decided not to give a fuck. I went out after school, stayed over at boys' houses without my dad's permission, failed tests, skipped class, the works."

She looks away. "Since then, my dad's pretty much given up on me. For as long as I can remember, he's wanted a son. I'm a disappointment by default—and then some." Her voice wavers, and she clears her throat to steady it. When she speaks, it's guttural and crackly. "He'd never have done it because it makes him look like a failure, but he probably wanted to give me up for adoption years ago."

Silence. Ash's eyes drift up to the ceiling. I feel her tense. She's hugging my stuffie so hard I think it'll burst. Her cheeks redden slightly and she squeezes her eyes shut. "God. I can't believe I just unloaded all that shit onto you. I'm so sorry."

"It's okay." I'm not sure what else to say. I feel a slight burn in the back of my nose, like I'm about to tear up. I want to reach out and hug her, but I'm not sure if she wants that. So I just repeat, "It's okay."

"No, seriously. I haven't even told Blake this shit."

I'm secretly jubilant that she hasn't. "Hey," I say. "Your dad can sit on a cactus." Ash laughs. "You're smart and talented and you don't need him," I add.

Ash reaches under the duvet and squeezes my hand. I feel the squeeze in my fingers, wrist, forearm, shoulders. "Thank you." She doesn't let go.

"You know," I say quietly, "you can tell me anything. Anything."

Ash nods. "I know."

I wait, tracing the patterns on my pillowcase with the tip of my finger. I close my eyes, suddenly enormously tired. I drum my mind for something to say when I'm interrupted by a rumbling snore. I open my eyes. Ash is asleep, her mouth slightly open and her eyelids twitching. The last faint shreds of reddish orange in her hair are splashed against the pillow like delicate, sunny tendrils. I reach over her to turn off the fairy lights, my other hand still tightly clutched in hers.

CHAPTER 8

One Friday, AP English class is canceled because we have a special sexual health presentation in the auditorium. All Grade 12s have to attend—all Grade 12s whose parents haven't kicked up a fuss, that is. I remember the church aunties incident and I'm weirdly grateful for being allowed to feel awkward for the next hour.

Ash and I take a seat near the back and I hear a guy behind me say, "Why do they need to teach us sex ed? It's not like we don't know how to put condoms on by now."

"They always do this right before Valentine's Day. Like they think we're getting it on or something."

"Whatever. It's not like I haven't had sex."

"Stop bragging, you pervert."

"Shut up, virgin."

Our guest speaker is a skittish-looking, lanky young woman in a unicorn T-shirt, her spiky hair combed sideways. Her name is Dee, and she represents an organization with way too many letters in its acronym. It takes a while for the class to calm down before she speaks. We go through the basics: the pros and cons of different types of birth control, how to cut open a condom to make a dental dam, and so on. My mind drifts for most of it because it's not like I plan to have sex anytime soon. Then we're told to write down questions about sex, and Dee passes a basket around the room to collect them. I see some of the boys in the back look through the questions and snicker. I decide not to put anything in.

I'm visualizing ways to improve my shove-its when Dee starts writing words on the chalkboard: *gay, straight,* and *bisexual* I know. *Pansexual* is new and apparently doesn't reference cookware. *Genderqueer* and *Two-Spirit* are also new and quite interesting. I quietly wish we could talk more about these words, especially "pansexual" and "genderqueer," but Dee seems to hurry through them as if terrified that we'll ask too many questions.

When it's time for the sex questions, the first few are simple enough. Mostly anatomy stuff. I learn that blue balls technically exist, you just don't need to have sex to relieve them. Then Dee picks a question out of the hat that takes everything up several notches of awkward. "How do lesbians have sex . . ." The words tumble out of her mouth before she can stop them. The boys in the back start howling with laughter and Dee turns bright red. Mr. Hussein stands up and tells the laughing guys to shut up. I can see pit stains on Dee's T-shirt. Mr. Hussein walks up to her and says something in her ear. She nods vigorously and Mr. Hussein takes over.

"Aaaaall right, settle down, people." He clears his throat. "It's simple. Two women have sex the same way anyone else does."

A girl raises her hand—one of the honors biology students. "But how does it . . . work? Like, what are the mechanics?"

The girl behind me mutters, "Oh, wouldn't you like to know." I admit the biology girl has balls.

But Mr. Hussein is unfazed. "Sex isn't just about penetration. There's the clitoris." Some of the boys are trying so hard to stifle their laughter, it's a choking hazard back there. "There's oral sex," Mr. Hussein says. "There's digital sex. For a lot of people, sex is about pleasure. It's a joint activity to feel good, and yeah, sometimes it's for making babies. But even straight men and women don't have sex just to have babies."

A few girls giggle, but I notice others nodding thoughtfully. We did learn something new today. I glance at Ash and even she seems interested, sitting still instead of her usual fidgeting.

At the end of the class, Dee gives us a stack of pamphlets with information. Free confidential sexual health clinics. Tips and tricks on how to come out to your parents. Places to go if your homophobic parents kick you out. By lunchtime, I see heaps of these pamphlets in the school recycling bins.

I keep my pamphlets. I figure they'll be entertaining toilet reads at worst, and I hate the idea of throwing stuff away before I've read it. I try to explain this to David when he sees me at lunch with them, but he just scoffs.

"I don't get why we need so many fancy words for every possible sexuality. It's not rocket science. You either like the opposite gender or you don't."

"Or you can like both. In different ways, maybe?" I shrug.

David pushes the peas around in his lunch tray. "So hey, did Ash really show up at your house in the middle of the night?" I had casually texted him about it, not thinking much of it.

"It wasn't the middle of the night," I say.

David makes a face. "Still. That's so weird."

I shrug. "Her home life is . . . complicated."

David snorts. "Same here. But when have I ever showed up randomly to eat your food?"

"You don't live down the street." *And your parents feed you,* I think.

. . .

I'm in Mr. Hussein's classroom nearly every day for the rest of the month to finish my public space project. Even though I technically don't need the computer for it, I like the quiet here.

I tell David to join me when he's not in Student Council, but he usually can't make it because he needs to use lunchtime to commute. The guy skipped so many math grades, he's literally run out of classes to take and has to go to the community college. So Ash is my only company. She watches me between piles of cardstock as I cut stencils with a scalpel, my nose inches from the table.

"Is that a—I can't tell. What are you making?" she asks with a genuine lilt of intrigue, her mouth otherwise full of my sandwich.

"They all fit together to make the same scene. It's gonna be a kitchen."

"How about this one?"

"Oh, that's my favorite." I arrange the stencils on the table so she can see the entire image of a girl in martial arts robes wielding a menacing sword.

"Graffiti-ing male-dominated spaces with feminine subjects . . ." Ash whistles. "This is *so cool.*"

I smile. I've never had anyone as excited about my work as her, not even my own family. Wendy can't draw a stick figure to save her life, Ma Mi doesn't understand art unless it's hyper-realistic Michelangelo stuff, and De Di would rather buy me art supplies than touch a paintbrush himself. "Too bad I can't actually graffiti them," I say.

Ash frowns. "What do you mean?"

"Mr. Templeton got me to call city hall a few times, but no one was willing to give me a license or whatever."

"Wait—then how are you doing the project?"

"Templeton really liked the idea, but he didn't want to be liable for anything," I explain, "so I'm spraying these on cardboard to show the final product, and using my"—I make air quotes—"'handy-dandy graphic design' skills, as he says, to superimpose the designs on photographs of the skate parks I want to paint. To show how they would look *in theory*."

"That fucking sucks." Ash scrunches her nose. "'Cause this is *sick*. You can't not do this for real."

"If I wanted to do this for real, I'd have to sneak out in the middle of the night."

She gives me a familiar look, serious and focused yet playful and cunning at the same time. "Then let's do it."

I laugh. "What?"

"Let's do it," she says. "Let's graffiti these motherfuckers in the middle of the night. I mean, you already have all the materials." She's right. Asking my parents to buy me art supplies to do crime had been awkward, but they'd given in when I said it'd be "fake." Ash says, "I'll ask Blake to drive us." She takes out her phone and starts texting.

"But—" My heart scampers into my throat and my mind goes a mile a minute. "What if we get in trouble? What if we get arrested?"

Ash scoffs. "Dude. It's a *skate park*. Skate parks are full of graffiti already. Sure, the parks board people might officially tell you you're not allowed, but do you think they actually care? I bet they would even like it. It adds *character* to the city. Isn't that what old people talk about all the time? That we need more *character* in this city?"

She has a point there. I mean, I'm scared of skateboarding on roads because I'm terrified of dying and cursing someone with being responsible for my death. But this is different. It's not like I'm drawing hate symbols or gang signs. Like, I wouldn't actually be *hurting* anyone, right?

Ash shows me the text she's about to send Blake. "I think it'll be fun, but it's up to you."

We stare at each for a moment, Ash holding her phone, me going through everything in my head. I technically already have all the materials—my parents had even bought me a respirator to spray-paint cardboard. So, before I can stop myself, I say, "Sure. Let's do it."

Ash grins. "All right! And you should totally make a skate deck out of one of these, too. I'd buy it."

We plan for Sunday night. Sneaking out of the house is easy because my parents are asleep by eleven on school nights, and if Wendy's up late studying, she's way too engrossed to care about me wandering around the house. All I have to do is disable the alarm.

I see Blake's car in the laneway, where I've already stashed my box of art stuff between a bush and the garage. Ash waves at me from the passenger seat next to an unsmiling, clearly grumpy-to-be-awake Blake. She's wearing all black, like me. Blake smokes out the window while Ash helps me load my paint, stencils, gloves, respirator, and tape into the trunk. Then I slide into the back seat and say hi to Blake. He grunts. Ash hands me a coffee.

"Okay, let's get this over with," Blake says. "First stop?"

Blake drives like a fiend, starting and stopping so abruptly I want to throw up within five minutes. When I spill my coffee, he growls at me for ruining his car, which is an old shit heap anyway. "See? I told you not to get her coffee," Blake mumbles to Ash.

The first park I want to paint is near an area that's notorious for being dangerous for women walking alone at night. Stories of assault are why my parents want Wendy and me home by dinnertime even though we're almost adults. Funny enough, Wendy is more upset about this than I am even though she never goes out at night. Recently, when a police officer in Toronto suggested women avoid dressing "slutty" to avoid being assaulted, Wendy and De Di had a days-long screaming match. De Di argued the police officer "had a point, just badly phrased" while Wendy accused him of being sexist.

In one of the bowls, I do a detailed spray of my wuxia lady. It takes several layers, and while I wait for the paint to dry, I spray a simpler stencil on a ramp that reads, "Men are afraid that women will laugh at them. Women are afraid that men will kill them. —Margaret Atwood." I try to avoid the art that's already there because I did some online research that you gotta respect those who've been in the game longer.

Blake snorts when he sees the quote. "Men have to be afraid of getting killed too, you know," he says.

"More women than men get assaulted," I say.

Blake playfully elbows Ash and says, "I, for one, wouldn't mind making a girl laugh." He laughs at his own joke and Ash gives him a halfhearted chuckle.

Later, I paint the kitchen scene on one of the wider ramps in Ash's favorite East Van skate park. It takes a long time because although the image is simple, I'm using many small stencils designed to be stitched together. It's a lot of physical work, crouching, shaking cans, and contorting my body into weird angles. I'm glad Ash brought her skateboard to keep herself occupied while I work. Blake just smokes cigarette after cigarette in a corner. When I'm done, I stand back with a satisfied sigh and throw up my arms.

"Ha. 'Odd-looking kitchen,'" Ash chuckles from close behind me. She rests her chin on my shoulder, admiring my work.

Blake sidles up to us and throws an arm around Ash, effectively scooping her off my shoulder. "Didn't Carlos Garcia have a retro fridge like that?"

I feel Ash stiffen beside me. "You've been to Carlos's house? Were you—"

"No, I wasn't at the Donna party. I told you that." He plays with a lock of Ash's hair. Her body is tense and her eyes stare straight ahead, unblinking. I wonder if this is *that* party, the one that got Ash pulled out of school. Then Ash mumbles that we should head out because the sun's about to rise. Blake steers her back to the car, his arm around her waist. I stand there alone for a few moments, wondering if they'd notice if I didn't move. Then I snap out of it because I don't want to find out.

The edges of the sky glow with a faint grayish-pink when we get back to our neighborhood. I manage to push out the words "thanks for driving me" to Blake. He makes a grunt-snort sound in return.

"He's just sleepy," Ash says, stroking his hair. Then she says to me, "Next time you're in this car, we'll be going to Kelowna!"

I grin. I'm honored that Ash wants me to go with her to Kelowna for the invitational, but I'm pretty sure my parents won't be cool with it. I'm about to say that but I save it for later; I'm in a stoked mood right now and I don't want to ruin it.

So, here's to a night of smashing the patriarchy. I hold my breath as I quietly close the back door behind me, but it's as if I never left the house. I tiptoe to my room and slump into my desk chair. The sun rises over the garages in the laneway outside my bedroom window. I'm awake thanks to the coffee, so I open my laptop and log on to Facebook. I don't like the idea of stalking people on social media, but at the same time, who *doesn't* stalk people on social media? When Ash and I first friended each other, I'd scrolled through some of her photos. She made a comment on a profile picture *I'd* uploaded a few years ago, so I'm pretty sure she stalked me. Still, I feel weird about filtering people by hometown or school, so I just type "Carlos Garcia" in the search bar and see what comes up.

Pretty quickly, I find a Carlos Garcia who graduated from Mackenzie Secondary last year. He's got a thousand friends, including Blake, Simon, and even Dezzy. I search his friends list for a Donna and I find two: a middle-aged woman who's probably his aunt and a Donna Nguyen.

Donna Nguyen doesn't have much of a Facebook presence. Her profile picture is a bichon frisé and her photos are 75 percent bichon frisés, 20 percent landscapes, and 5 percent blurry pictures of people I'm pretty sure aren't her. I lean back in my chair, my brain whirring. I close my eyes and try to organize my thoughts.

Dezzy said "she" when he talked about Ash liking someone who didn't like her back. But Ash has never mentioned this person to me and neither has she mentioned a Donna in her old life at Mackenzie. I feel uneasy, like I'm walking in the dark. I also feel—well, not exactly *angry*, but like I've been purposely disinvited from something. Because it's clear that Blake knows something I don't.

But I also know stuff that he doesn't. Important stuff. I think back to the night Ash stayed over. It had felt so close and so real. It *was* close and real. She had reached out and held my hand, so why does it feel like I'm grasping at air?

. . .

I walk through the week with held breath, paranoid that my parents will find out about the graffiti trip. But they don't. Instead, Wendy steals the spotlight again.

She comes home just before dinner on a rainy orchestra day, steaming with emotional heat. Goes straight to her room, slams the door shut, and starts screaming and ripping and throwing things.

We all stand in the hallway as De Di jiggles the locked doorknob to no avail. He smacks the door with the palm of his hand. "Ah Mui! What is going on?!"

"I-I-I . . ." The sound of Wendy blubbering into a tissue, and then she screams, "I got a C+ on my physics exam!"

My parents and I all look at each other. Wendy has never, ever gotten anything lower than a B. *Ever.* She once joked—only to be scolded by our mother for joking about such things—that she'd rather get pregnant than get a C.

De Di clears his throat and leans against the door. "What was it, a small pop quiz?"

"No! A unit test!"

"But you studied, didn't you? How did that happen?" Ma Mi says.

"Go eat dinner," De Di tells us. "I'll talk to her."

Ma Mi and I pick at our food while De Di talks to Wendy through the door, pleading with her to stop throwing books against the wall.

"I wonder what happened," Ma Mi mutters. "She's always in that room of hers, studying and studying, never letting us in. Do you think she's faking? Maybe she's playing computer games or talking to her friends?"

I wonder if she's been spending more time with Justin.

"Aaiii, she's always been so sensitive," Ma Mi continues. "Blows up at the littlest thing."

"She's afraid of disappointing you and De Di," I say.

A nervous laugh from Ma Mi. "But we've never laid a hand on either of you. We're not the type of parents who will disown you for bringing home a bad grade."

"Maybe." I drown my gai lan in oyster sauce, ignoring my mom's disapproving glare. "But Wendy believes she must be perfect in everything. Or else."

"Or else what?"

I shrug. De Di comes downstairs sighing and shaking his head. He grabs a bowl and heaps rice and gai lan into it. He's about to add barbeque pork when I remind him it's Wendy's vegetarian day. De Di nods and adds tomato egg instead. He brings the bowl and Wendy's favorite pair of chopsticks from when she was little—a pink-and-white Hello Kitty set that is honestly too short for her fingers now—up to my sister's room. When he returns, he flops down at the table with a heavy sigh.

Ma Mi shakes her head. "I told her not to go with us to that dinner with the Chius. She probably didn't have enough time to study."

De Di's voice is low and gravelly. "She's very stressed. Don't scold her."

"She didn't look stressed last weekend."

De Di stirs tomato egg into his rice. "Stress can show up in a number of ways."

Ma Mi speaks into her rice. "Right. Like every time I ask you whether you've found any salaried jobs and you say you're too 'stressed' to. All you do is sit in that office . . ."

De Di sighs. "I'm working on—"

"So why haven't you gotten a new contract in months?" Ma Mi's chopsticks clang loudly against everything she touches as she dumps tomato egg into my bowl. "Maybe if you did, we could send our eldest to an overseas university like the Chius. I asked you to take that job with city hall, but no, government pensions aren't worth the paycheck of a private firm, and—"

"Be quiet!" It wasn't a yell, but it was loud. Louder than De Di expected because he looks surprised at the volume of his own voice. His mouth stiffens, and then he pushes away the rest of his food and walks out of the dining room. Seconds later, I hear the clang of dishes being done in the kitchen.

Ma Mi sighs. "Here. You need to eat more vegetables."

She gives me more gai lan. There's so much food in my bowl, I think it's going to topple over. "Um," I say, my voice tiny, "I can get a job. Kids at school work at the McDonald's. I'm sure I could get a few shifts. You know, just to pay for my own tuition—"

"No," Ma Mi snaps. "That's not your job. Your job, as the child, is to do well in school. Our job, as the parents, is to earn money. Focus on your own job, nothing else."

I chew on a piece of egg. "I can help with the dishes."

"No. You go study."

. . .

We do a belated Lunar New Year's dinner the first weekend in March with members of our extended family who have also immigrated here. Kou Fu, my mom's younger brother, spends the whole dinner talking stocks with Suk Suk—my dad's younger brother—and Uncle Terry, who is my Ah Yee's husband—Ah Yee being my mother's younger sister. (Yes, Chinese names for family members are super complicated.) I think De Di was supposed to be part of the "manly" stock conversation, but he just nods and barely participates. He doesn't eat much, and I get his share of sago pudding.

Meanwhile, Ma Mi, Ah Yee, and Kou Fu's wife Auntie Kathleen chat endlessly about their kids. My cousins look up to Wendy like a star, and one of them is an up-and-coming concert pianist herself. "Oh, and Jessica. Jessica has her hopes set on going to Europe for university," I catch Ma Mi say as an afterthought.

"Why, that's fabulous!" says Auntie Kathleen. To me, she asks, "What are you studying?"

"Art," I say shortly.

"Art? That's interesting."

"Well, she's always been good at it," Ah Yee says. "It's not surprising at all." She winks at me.

"What are you doing afterward, then?" Auntie Kathleen asks. "What kind of jobs do people do with art degrees?"

I roll my eyes internally but feel my mom's gaze on me. "I'm keeping my options open, but I might go into cinematography or graphic design."

"Interesting!" Auntie Kathleen nods politely. She turns to Ma Mi.

"You must have so much confidence in your kids! Having a career in art isn't easy, you know."

Ma Mi sighs. "That's what I keep telling her."

"Well, the world will always need artists. Someone designed your clothes, and even the dishes we're eating on needed an artist to make them," Ah Yee says. "Jessica is smart. She'll figure it out. I'm certain." I've always looked forward to dinners with Ah Yee. She and my mother are so different, I often wonder how they came from the same uterus. Ah Yee married early, divorced early, doesn't have kids, and doesn't seem bothered by any of that. With no one to spend money on, she often vacations in random and unusual places by herself and Ma Mi will scold her for not being cautious of her own safety. I secretly think she's a rock star.

After dinner, I sit on my bed and count my lai see: almost $300 combined from all my relatives. I put aside $50 to buy a camera caddy (the DIY version that Ash built hasn't fallen apart *yet*, but it gives me anxiety every time we use it). The rest of the money I save for Europe. Not that $250 will make a dent in the tens of thousands of Euros I'll need, but you gotta start somewhere.

. . .

That night, Wendy plays violin in her room, Ma Mi watches TV in the living room, and De Di does whatever he does in his study.

I'm bored. So I look through my old sketchbooks. I do this sometimes—to entertain myself more than anything—and there are usually more cringes than smiles. When I open a notebook from circa Grade 5, an old shopping catalog falls out. It's a bra catalog, and I'm confused for a full three seconds before the memories topple over me like a tower of bricks: I used to pinch underwear catalogs from the mail to "practice drawing anatomy."

A woman power-poses with the kind of confidence you have when you have a waist that small and hair that luscious. Delicate collar bones jut out above her breasts. The faint outlines of her ribcage are visible right beneath. She's skinny but not too skinny, and I can make out the soft contours of every muscle in her body. It's a good photograph, really.

And then I feel it again: a thin layer of heat on my skin, a tumble-and-squeeze in my lower belly, that godawful stir in my crotch. I realize that this isn't a new sensation—I've had it since the time I drew these sketches. I used to ignore it, toss it away as some weird puberty thing like smelly armpits and forehead pimples. But I've since found an antiperspirant that works, and my forehead has cleared up. Yet this feeling hasn't changed. If anything, it's gotten stronger.

I quickly stuff my sketches into the back of my desk drawer. I get on my computer and google "am I gay." Turns out there are tons of quizzes you can take online that will tell you whether you're gay or not. Most of them are for guys, so I type "am I a lesbian" and do the first quiz. There are questions like whether you liked dolls or action figures as a kid (I liked neither) and whether you like pants or dresses (pants, all the way). I get results like "You might be gay. You should think about it!" Fat lot of use that is.

I remember Dee teaching us about Two-Spirit people in Indigenous cultures, and I wonder if something similar exists in Chinese culture. I figure it's unlikely—my impression of traditional Chinese values is that they're conservative and strict; I don't think I've even seen my parents kiss. But apparently, I'm wrong. After a brief Wikipedia dive, I see that homosexuality was definitely a thing in ancient China. There's even a famous story about an emperor who cut his sleeve rather than wake his male lover sleeping next to him. I wonder if my Christian mom knows about this story at all.

All this distraction, and the feeling hasn't left. It's pulsing just under the surface of my skin. I stare at my desk for a few seconds, and then I give in. I dig the catalogs back out, get under the covers of my bed, and stick my hand between my legs. When I'm done, my sheets are soaked with sweat and the entire room feels muggy, but at least the feeling is gone.

CHAPTER 9

With spring break approaching, the Grade 12s are getting restless. People have been passing around the word *senioritis*. Many of us have received answers from our universities, and even for those who are still waiting, there's not much to do other than be anxious. People skip class here and there, and the teachers seem to give us a pass because it's not like we'll give them trouble next year.

I'm still too nervous to skip, but I've developed a liking for taking long bathroom breaks and walking outside. Breathing in the crisp, early spring air is like hitting the refresh button in my brain. I do a lap around the school and then return to class, rubbing my tummy so it looks like I had a legitimate reason to take a ten-minute shit.

On one of my walks during a particularly mind-numbing math class, everything is going to plan until I catch the stench of cigarette smoke. I round the corner and my jaw nearly drops on the floor.

David huddles against the wall just outside the gym, sucking on a cigarette. He sees me and turns into a statue.

"David?" I gasp.

"Shit." He drops his cigarette and stomps it out, hard. "Heeeyyy . . . Jay."

"Hey, Dave. Why—why are you smoking?"

He scowls. "Ash smokes. Why do you care?"

"I don't, dude. I'm just asking," I say, bristling at his bristling.

David sighs. "Back when I was deep in those uni applications, I was super stressed out. So I jacked one of my dad's cigarettes and tried one and, uh, they're surprisingly . . . well—"

"Not as gross to smoke as they are to smell," I say, nodding.

He nods back. "Yeah." Then, after a pause, he says quickly, "Don't tell anyone, okay?"

"Of course." That's a promise from me.

"Aren't you supposed to be in class?"

"Math was making me physically ill so I'm 'having diarrhea.'" I make air quotes. He snickers, and I suddenly flash back to when we were kids, reading toilet humor jokebooks in the library when we were supposed to be doing research for a project. His snicker hasn't changed. "Aren't you supposed to be at your fancy college math class?"

"I usually get back ten, fifteen minutes early. So . . ." He waves his box of cigarettes halfheartedly.

We let the awkward silence hang for a bit. Then I ask him, "So how's uni math with uni kids?"

"It's fine. Oh!" he lights up. "One of my classmates—the guy who gets me cigarettes—went to Mackenzie. You know, Ash's school." His voice drops. "Said it was a super sketchy place."

"I'm friends with Mac people," I say. "They're all right."

"At his after-prom, some Grade 10 girl overdosed on tainted drugs and this other girl got expelled over it."

A hot arrow pierces through me. "Who was it?"

He shrugs, surprised that I would care. "No idea."

I shake the shiver out of my body. "Well, people from Mac are all right," I say again. "You shouldn't assume everyone from the same school is the same way. It's like we learn in social studies class: you shouldn't generalize an entire country or race or culture."

"Hey, it wasn't me, it was this guy in my class," says David.

"Maybe he's a nerd," I say with a chuckle. "An uptight nerd."

David makes a face. "Aren't *we* nerds?"

The question hangs between us. "I don't *feel* like a nerd," I say. "Like, my grades are good, but I'm not *just* a nerd. I'm not, like, Min. Or Sophie."

David rolls his eyes. "Min and Sophie aren't 'just' nerds either. I don't get why—"

"Well, I don't mean—"

"—you have such a problem with them—"

"—who says I have a problem with them? I—"

"You're just—you don't seem to like them." David kicks at the ground.

"Just because they're your friends doesn't mean they have to be my friends, too," I say.

"I guess." David shrugs. "But they're really all right. I know Min seems uptight, but that's just 'cause she's shy around new people. Once you get to know her, you might be surprised. And Sophie . . ." He looks at the wall. "Sophie gets me."

"What do you mean?" Is David about to confess that he has a crush on Sophie? Because that is *not* the vibe I've picked up from them.

"Her parents are professors, like mine. And her brother might drop out of film school, so she feels like she needs to make up for him. It's kinda the opposite of me but also kinda the same. Everyone in my family is so smart; I need to be just as smart if not smarter."

I just nod. There's that silence again, but this time it's not awkward so much as . . . depressing. Then I realize how cold my hands are. "Let's go inside, yeah?" I say to David. He nods, stuffing his stiff hands into his hoodie pockets like me.

. . .

That night, I sit in front of the computer staring at Donna Nguyen's Facebook profile. Then my phone buzzes and I almost jump straight out of my chair. It's Ash: *yo jw, there's a party in your neighborhood this friday. right before spring break.* For some reason, Ash calls our area "my" neighborhood even though she lives here too. *free beer and weed for your birthday too let's goooo.*

I suddenly flash back to a conversation Wendy and I had with our dad years ago, when I was just entering high school. "You're going to meet a lot of people as you grow up, people from all walks of life," he'd told us. "But not everyone will be good for you, so be very careful who you choose as friends." I remember thinking, *Why would this affect me? My best friend is the biggest nerd in school.* But since September, I've lied to my parents, gone to a party with questionable substances, and pranked a teacher so badly I got detention for the first time ever. I even snuck out in the middle of the night to do property damage. All things I wouldn't have dreamed of doing when I was in Grade 8 yawning at my dad's lecture.

And I did all these things after I met Ash.

Ash doesn't look like who Grade 8 me imagined a "bad influence" would be. Sure, she skateboards (something "bad" kids do), has dyed hair, and dresses like what my parents would call a fay nui—literally "fly girl," meaning delinquent. But she's never teased me or bullied me into doing something I didn't want to do. Everything I've done—the party, the sneaking out, the weed—*I* chose to do. And I don't regret any of it. Well, except prank-calling Ms. Hudson. She's not my favorite teacher, but she doesn't deserve being sexually harassed over the phone. I've since said sorry to her one-on-one.

Still, I can't help but feel unsettled. I wonder if Ash was at the party I've been hearing about, if she had anything to do with the drugs. The thought of Ash being involved with an overdose makes me taste metal. I don't think I even want to know.

. . .

I can't shake off wondering about what might have happened at that party, and the more I try to tell myself it's probably not a big deal, the more it latches onto my brain. It rattles between my ears as I go from class to class. And it plays in the background when Ash finds me sketching in Mr. Hussein's room one lunch hour.

"Wanna go skate?" she says, leaning against the table. "I know you didn't bring your board, but we can take turns. C'mon, it's not raining today."

My art project is done and I have no excuse, but I tell her, "Nah, I wanna try out a few things on the computer." Ash blinks at me, shrugs, and heads off.

That night, I stare at Donna Nguyen's bichon frisé. Again. My cursor hovers over the messenger icon. I wait as long as it takes for Wendy to finish playing her scales in the other room then I click and start writing: *hey, you probably don't know me. my name's jay. i go to school with Ash Chan. george van. you might know her from mac?*

My finger quivers on the mouse, the cursor hovering over the send button. I feel like I'm about to commit some sort of crime, but if I don't get some clarity, what if *I* end up committing a crime? Well, I technically already have, I tell myself, and the sky hasn't fallen.

But what if I'm playing with fire? I smash the send button. I'm not friends with Donna, so this will just end up in her "other" inbox. She might not even see it. She *probably* won't see it.

Twenty minutes later, I'm watching YouTube videos trying not to think about this when I get a notification. I all but jump out of my chair. Donna has replied to me; *yeah.*

I think about totally abandoning ship, but it might be more suspicious if I don't say anything. I type: *hi! mind if i ask u something?*

She replies almost immediately: *depends. but sure.*

I sit up straight at my desk, my brain humming. It takes me a minute to think of something that makes sense. I end up typing: *i'm planning an after-prom party. it's gonna be rad but i heard some sketchy stuff went down with ash at mac and i'm not sure if it's true.*

She replies: *what sketchy stuff?*

i heard someone brought drugs to the party and someone overdosed? if it's true i wanna know so i can be careful about our party yenno?

She writes back: *yeah that's fair.* Then she takes a long time typing. I sweat my pits out watching the ellipses flash at the bottom of the chat box. I search for a song on YouTube to distract me and choose a punk playlist. One song finishes then the next. The ellipses stop flashing. Donna's still online according to the green circle next to her name, but she's stopped typing.

Then, I get a short message: *yeah ash brought drugs.* Cue flashing ellipses then: *they fucked me up. i had to go to the hospital.*

I manage to type: *omg i'm so sorry.*

I'm glad Donna and I are talking through text because I'm all sweaty and I probably don't smell great. *what kinda drugs?*

idk. it wasn't a lot but it still fucked me up.

That's weird because I clearly remember Ash telling me she's never touched anything other than weed and beer. Did Ash lie?

Then Donna writes: *you're right. you shouldn't trust ash.*

what do you mean?

she has zero friends so she does fucked up shit to look cool. she's desperate.

Well, that doesn't make sense. Ash has lots of friends.

oh and be careful. ash is les. she goes after girls.

I feel ice go down my back. I type: *thanks for letting me know. really appreciate it <3*

After a few more seconds, I type: *probably goes without saying, but let's keep this convo between us. is that cool?*

yeah ofc.

thanks again. super appreciate it.

Then Donna goes offline and I'm alone again, feeling like I'm looking at the world tipped over on its side.

. . .

De Di hasn't been around as much lately. He's always in his office, door closed. Things are so different from when Wendy and I were in elementary school. De Di was finishing his master's degree in engineering then. Ma Mi didn't get off work until five, so De Di would pick us up from school every day after he was done school himself. University housing was a dump, but there was a playground nearby and he'd take me there after dinner when the weather was good. We'd chuck a frisbee and he'd promise not to tell Ma Mi if I climbed trees. But I don't remember the last time he had a frisbee in his hands or stood next to a tree. Or wore something other than sweatpants, for that matter.

I make a pot of coffee and pour a cup for De Di. I knock on his door, hear him grunt, and leave the coffee outside.

Wendy's studying in the living room, so I offer her what's left in the pot. "You've been studying nonstop. Thought you might need a pick-me-up."

She wrinkles her nose. "I don't do drugs."

"Coffee isn't drugs."

"Caffeine is a drug. Besides"—she lifts her chin—"don't you know how exploitative the coffee industry is? If you want me to drink coffee, ask De Di to get the fair-trade stuff."

I narrow my eyes at her over the kitchen counter. "You're very slap-pable, you know that?"

I take my own coffee upstairs and settle down with some *Orlando*. I take a sip and read a sentence. Then another sip. And another sentence. Three sentences and sips in and I've forgotten everything and have to reread the paragraph. Focusing has been difficult lately. The graffiti night was one giant dopamine rush and I'm in withdrawal, looking for my next fix.

My phone buzzes, and I pick it up halfway through the second ring. It's Ash. "Hey. You never said no to the party so I'm outside waiting for you."

I look out the window, and sure enough, there's Ash standing there with one hand in her hoodie pocket, the other holding the phone to her ear.

"I never said yes," I say.

"Hey, are you good, dude? You've been, like, quiet lately."

I swallow. "I'm good. I'm just worried about my applications, you know? Still waiting on one thing and it's late."

"Then come blow off some steam with me," she says. "Please? I don't wanna go by myself, plus I thought we'd celebrate your 18th?"

She's right. I'm almost an adult. I've been waiting to be one for so long and parties are no big deal for eighteen-year-olds. "Whose party is it?"

"It's happening at Blake's friend's house."

"You want me to hang out with Blake and his friends for my birthday?"

A big sigh crackles over the phone. "Blake's playing a gig there and in order to be a good girlfriend, I have to go support him."

"And you want me to support you supporting him."

She laughs nervously. "I guess, yes. Please? Be my emotional support animal? Again, free beer and weed!"

I sigh. Ash resembles a begging puppy sometimes. I look at my book on my lap and think, *Fuck it.* "Yeah, sure," I say.

I tell De Di that David's in the area and wants to have dinner, and he says he'll pass the information on to Ma Mi.

A few minutes later, Ash and I arrive at a house I didn't know existed in my neighborhood because it's hidden behind a tall hedge. I feel like we're trespassing when we walk through the gate because the house is enormous. Slick, modern, asymmetrical architecture, the kind of style you see in university viewbooks. I'm wearing an old jacket of my dad's from when he was in engineering school. It looks boxy and stylishly oversized on me, but I haven't met anyone inside this house yet and I already feel out of place.

Blake greets us at the door with a crowd of his friends. His cologne makes me nauseous and he has way too much gel in his hair. He narrows his eyes when he sees me. "I didn't know you were coming."

I shrug. "I'm here for the big show." It sounds more sarcastic than I intend, but I let it sit like that.

"Nice jacket."

I can't tell if *he's* being sarcastic.

Ash says, "Where's the dad of the guy you said I should talk to? The one you said might be able to get me a summer job?"

Blake wrinkles his nose. "Dude's not here, I'm afraid." Ash groans but he just shrugs it off. "We're setting up in the backyard. You can get drinks there."

Ash and I walk through large rooms of immaculate, modern furniture to the backyard, and honestly? That's where the house *really* begins.

There's a freaking *pool*. And beside the pool?

There's a mini ramp.

Whoever's house this is, they're rich enough to have a freaking mini-ramp in the backyard next to a pool.

"Do you know anyone?" I ask Ash. I notice she's not her usual chill self. She shakes her head. This must not be her scene.

"Yo. Bestie." Blake chucks a beer at me and I barely catch it before it hits me in the face. He tosses me another. "Give that to Ash, yeah?" I turn to her, but she's already wandered over to the base of the quarter-pipe, staring at it like a kid mesmerized by fish in an aquarium.

I walk over and hand her the beer, but she shakes her head. She walks up to one of the guys on the pipe. "Hey, your board seems my size. Mind if I try it?"

The guy says, "You skate?"

"Oh, she's a pro," I say. "Going to an invitational and everything." But the look Ash gives me makes me shut up.

The guy tosses us his deck. "I need a beer break anyway." He jumps off the pipe. I think that's the end of that but then he yells at his friends, "Yo! Apparently this chick's a pro!"

A dozen pairs of eyes shoot toward us. Ash clears her throat and stiffly climbs up onto the mini ramp. Everyone moves aside. She didn't ask for an audience, I want to yell, but Ash's look earlier tells me I shouldn't interfere. So I just stand there, pulse racing. The talking has died down to the point where I can hear the music coming from the portable speakers near the pool.

Ash lines the tail of her board up with the coping and grinds her back foot into the back pocket. I realize she has no idea what the board setup feels like, nor does she have a feel for the ramp. She's going in blind and everyone is staring at her. She steps down—good, at least the drop in doesn't look sketchy. She does a few rock n rolls, an axle stall. Then I get a feeling she wants to throw a backside disaster.

I can tell from the moment she rides up the ramp that it won't turn out well. She has too much speed, her shoulders and hips are pointed all wrong, and the board shoots out from beneath her. Ash falls hard onto the flat bottom. It's loud and not flattering at all. Everyone watching groans and winces.

I step forward to help her but she jumps up before I can get close. The guy who lent Ash his board runs past us to get it, swearing.

"Let's go," Ash mutters to me, her face several shades redder than before. She stalks off, wiping her hands on her jeans and limping a little. I follow, conscious of strangers' eyes boring into the back of my head.

We go back to the porch where Blake is setting up. He's down on one knee, balancing what looks like a fancy hybrid electro-acoustic guitar on the other. A small group of guys sit on the banister around him drinking beers. Ash stomps up the stairs and kicks over a pyramid of empty cans. "Dude! Chill!" one guy yells while the others laugh.

Ash ignores them. Arms crossed, she walks up to where Blake is kneeling next to his guitar case. "Jay and I are leaving."

Blake scowls. "No, you're staying for my gig. You promised."

"I'm not in the mood for indie rock."

"How many times have I told you, that's not our genre—"

"Well then I'm not in the mood for atonal ambient experimental soundscapes."

The guys on the banister erupt into a round of laughter. I start chuckling too, but Blake glares at me and that, along with Ash's lack of amusement, keeps me quiet.

"Can you guys fuck off for a sec?" Blake tells the others. They peel themselves off the porch, muttering about how much better it is to be single. Once they're gone, Blake stands up, looming over Ash. "Look, I'm sorry you embarrassed yourself, babe, but you *promised* you'd be here."

"And you promised me you'd introduce me to that guy's dad."

"I can't control whether a guy shows up or not," Blake says. He drapes his arms around Ash's shoulders. "We've talked about this. It's no big deal. If you need money for a few months, just live with me. I'll take care of you while you find a job."

Ash shrugs him off. "I don't need you to *take care of me*. I can take care of myself."

Blake laughs, and it's such an ugly laugh. Like a cartoon witch. "You really think you can make it all by yourself? I've been doing everything for you. Buying you shit, feeding you, driving you places. Even your little friend." He throws his hand at me. "And what have *you* done? Entered some contest? Because from what just happened . . ." He nods toward the mini ramp with a smirk. "It doesn't look too good."

I stare at him. "Dude. What the *fuck*."

Blake ignores me. "You think you're so grown up. You think you've got it all figured out. But you're just a kid, Ash. You're just a kid."

Blood beats against my ears. I expect Ash to give Blake the finger, even punch him in the face. But she just stares at him while he steps away from her and continues to set up his gear. Her lip twitches and her eyes look shiny. Holy shit, she's actually *affected* by this.

"Ash?" I reach out for her, but Blake swats my hand away and stands between us. "You're staying," he says to her.

Ash says, "No." But she doesn't move. She's quivering, but she doesn't move.

"Yes." Blake's voice cuts through me like a knife.

I push between them, my shoulders rubbing against Blake's bony chest. "Let's go," I say to Ash. "We can grab pizza on the way home."

"Sounds like a good idea," Ash mutters, and to my relief, she takes a step back.

Blake laughs. "Wow, seriously? You just do whatever the dyke says?"

Ash freezes. I can feel a new energy radiating off her, something hot and strong. She turns around slowly. Her voice starts low then rises in pitch. "Don't you *ever* call her that." People start to stare at us and my stomach drops.

"Ash—" I start.

Ash stalks back up to Blake. "You apologize to her right now," she growls.

Blake laughs again. He turns to me. "Hey, Jay, I'm sorry that your art is so *derivative*."

For a moment I think Ash might kick him in the crotch. But she does something way worse. She snatches Blake's guitar off the ground and, before anyone can react, chucks it over the porch and into the pool.

Blake screams. Actually *screams*. I'm paralyzed by the noise until Ash grabs my wrist and yanks me forward into a run. We hurry through the house as Blake's f- and c-bombs volley after us like arrows. I can hear footsteps behind us, more than one set, but I don't dare look back.

We're flying. Through the house, out the front door, across the yard, into the safety of the public street.

We keep running, long after any sound of pursuit has disappeared. Finally, when it feels like I'm about to throw up, Ash stops and bends over to cough and breathe. I follow.

"Fuck!" Ash kicks a piece of cardboard out of her way, totters toward a hydro pole, leans against it, and lights a cigarette. That's when I notice we've run all the way back to our laneway. Ash sucks smoke like she's sucking in oxygen, and I try to get my own breathing under control. I stand next to her by the hydro pole and tuck my hands under my armpits. Ash puffs out big clouds of smoke while I puff out wispy lines of warm breath. Ash mutters something.

"Pardon?" I say.

She spits into a puddle. "You didn't have to do that."

"Do what?"

"That. Stand up for me or whatever."

I breathe hot air into my hands and rub them together. "But I'm your emotional support animal, remember?" Ash stares at the ground. "Sorry," I mutter.

"No. No, shut up," she says. "It's not your fault."

"Sorry," I blurt out again.

"It's fine. Shit. It's fine. You're a good person, Jay, you know that, right?" And out of nowhere, she implodes, folding and collapsing into herself. Her body crunches down onto the ground, vibrating with high-pitched noises. I'm not sure what to do or say, so I crouch next to her and put a tentative hand on her back.

"God," Ash says, her voice swimming in phlegm. "Why am I so fucked up?"

"You're not fucked up," I say.

"Yes, I am! I fucked *everything* up. Blake was supposed to drive me to Kelowna. He's obviously not going to now, so we're done. We're done, Jay. You were right, he's an asshole. I should've listened to you. Why am I so stupid? I should've listened to you."

"You're not stupid," I say. "We'll figure something out."

"I doubt it." She drags a sleeve across her nose and loudly snorts up some tears. "Why do you even like me? I'm fucked."

"No," I say, "you're not."

She stops sniffling and looks at me. A crow caws right above our heads. I look up then something warm touches my jaw. It's Ash's hand, pulling me toward her. Her eyes are all wet and sparkly. My mouth falls open to say something, but before I can speak, Ash's lips meet mine.

And it's as if someone has poured gunpowder all over my bones and lit me on fire.

I pull Ash by the waist into my body, and she pulls me into hers. I feel a hand on my face, pushing my hair behind my ear, and it's like every square centimeter of my skin that gets touched comes alive as its own being. The moment seems to last forever. But we need to breathe at some point, so we pull way at the same time.

As quickly as the world exploded, we're back here again, sitting against a hydro pole on damp grass in the laneway behind our houses.

Ash shuffles around, gets up, and stretches. My ass is cold, so I follow.

Ash turns to me and rubs the spot between her eyes. "I should probably get home," she says.

"Me too," I choke. Ma Mi will be calling me for an update soon.

We start walking down the laneway. Ash's hands are buried deep in her pockets, her shoulders hunched. My legs are shaking.

We get to my gate and she gently touches my shoulder. "I'll text you," she says with a flicker of a smile.

"Yeah." I watch the gate swing shut, and it takes everything in me to not go skipping and dancing and screaming back into my house.

I go straight to my room because I don't want anyone in my family to ask me why my face muscles have broken. I can't stop smiling. When Ma Mi barges into my room demanding I eat fruit, I have to hold *Orlando* over my face and pretend I'm reading.

It takes me a while to fall asleep. All I can think about is Ash and me walking down the hallway holding hands, the hip queer couple. Ash and me on vacation, skateboarding in California, her rich after a career of pro skateboarding, me rich after a career of filmmaking. Ash and me buying that ridiculous house behind the hedges, claiming the mini ramp as our own and draining out the pool to make bowls. We'll turn it into a park where it's impossible to feel embarrassed.

I must have finally fallen asleep because the next thing I know, I'm blinking through sunlight—I forgot to close my blinds. My alarm's going off and I've forgotten why. Then I open my door to see De Di, smiling and holding a big cup of coffee with a scoop of vanilla ice cream. I smile back at him and gratefully accept.

"Happy birthday." De Di hands me a small white box. "Hok yip jeun bo." May you progress in your studies. He adds, "Maan see yue yee." May all the dreams in your heart, ten thousand of them, come true.

"Thank you." I look inside the box. It's a brand-new iPod. With enough gigabytes to hold all my favorite videos.

"Engraved with your name." De Di smiles at me, and I want to cry.

"De Di! You shouldn't have. Isn't money tight?" My insides twinge. Ash's dad, based on what I've heard about him, would never do something like this. Even if he had the money.

He shrugs. "Your mother didn't approve at first. She wanted to just give you lai see. But I told her this may be one of the last birthdays we'll spend with you for a while. Might as well make it a big occasion."

Hot tears prick the edges of my eyes. "Thank you," I say again. I feel an urge to hug my dad, but our family doesn't do hugs. Besides, seeing him smile is enough.

He says, "Get dressed. We're taking you to Denny's."

Denny's is one of the few chances Wendy and I get to eat at a Western restaurant. My parents don't like going out to eat often, especially at Western restaurants because they're expensive, but they have a soft spot for the pancakes at Denny's.

It's the best Saturday ever. The sky is cloudlessly blue, the lineup to get seated doesn't take long, and the bottomless coffee makes me giddy after two and a half cups. I look around and it's like someone has pulled up the saturation slider on my eyes. Everything is bright, colorful, optimistic. I even tell my parents all about my art portfolio without sparing any details. Ma Mi listens intently, De Di's eyes twinkle with pride, and even Wendy nods along as I speak.

"So, what else is going on?" Ma Mi leans forward, taking this rare opportunity where I'm weirdly open about my life. "How are your friends? Graduation is coming up. Are you going to prom with a boy?"

Wendy scoffs. "Please."

I scoff back at her. "I could so get a date."

"What, some skater guy? Those guys are such deadbeats. Are you a deadbeat too now?"

"*Wendy.*" De Di uses his warning tone.

"About skateboarding . . ." Ma Mi frowns. "I saw a young man almost get run over by a bus the other day while skateboarding on the street. He came out of nowhere. You're not skateboarding on the road, are you?"

I groan and shake my head. "No, Ma—"

"I just don't want you to get into an accident before you go to Europe. You always wear a helmet, right?"

"She's eighteen," my dad says. "She can handle these things." Then he waves at the menu. "Has everyone decided?"

"I want chicken and waffles," I say.

"Me too," Wendy says.

Ma Mi tsks. "So heavy! Wendy, didn't you say you were planning to study physics this afternoon? Eating so much will make you tired and groggy. And Jessica"—she juts her chin at me as if to say I'm not off the hook—"how many coffees have you had? You drink way too much coffee."

De Di tsks at Ma Mi's tsking. "Aiya, it's her birthday. She's on holiday."

"It's not Wendy's birthday."

"Let her have a good time with her ga jie!"

"Wendy, we can split the chicken and waffles between the two of us and have a side salad," I say, feeling oddly diplomatic. Ma Mi is satisfied with this.

When our food arrives, I casually say, "You know, I got accepted into the local universities. It's not in the mail yet but I checked the portals yesterday."

De Di's eyes widen. "Why didn't you tell us?!"

"Because you all know I don't want to go to them. I want to go to school in Europe."

De Di says, "You know we'll be happy no matter which school you go to."

"Even if I change my mind?" I've kept it a secret, but I've been toying with the prospect of majoring in film. I'm afraid to tell my mother though; she might think film is even more useless than fine art.

"Even if you change your mind," De Di says.

"What if *I* change my mind about going to med school?" Wendy says.

Mom puts down her mug of hot water. "You don't want to go to med school?"

Wendy shrugs and looks to the side. "Just what if."

"I'd be surprised," Ma Mi says. "You've always wanted to go to med school. And you're good at science."

Wendy grunts and stuffs her face with fried chicken.

I haven't heard from Ash all morning, so I text her on the drive home. Since it's sunny out and I have permission to not study on my birthday, I practice my ollies and shove-its in the laneway. I text Ash to join me. I keep looking up the road to where her house is so I can spot her the moment she comes out, but she never makes an appearance. Even as the sky dims and the sun goes down.

She still hasn't responded by dinnertime, but there's a text when I get out of the shower. I'm giddy, but when I open the message, my heart drops.

seriously?! you talked to DONNA?!?! WHAT THE FUCK JW.

I drop my phone like it's a hot coal. Freeze. Then peer back down onto the screen. The text is still there, followed by: *she told me you messaged her. and matt says you talked to him too, asked him all sorts of weird intrusive questions. who the hell do you think you are?*

My hands are shaking as I call Ash. When she doesn't pick up, I call her again. And again. Finally:

"What."

"Ash, I'm sorry. I'm so sorry, I didn't mean to. I just wanted to know—"

"You *don't* know. You don't know anything about me."

Tears sting my nose, and I feel the room falling away from me. Everything is gray, all the stoke I'd felt on my birthday washed away in an instant. "Ash, I—"

"If you call me again, I'll throw your precious MacBook into the pool along with Blake's guitar." She hangs up.

CHAPTER 10

For the next couple of weeks, it's like a curse is following me everywhere I go. It's not that my life has gotten markedly worse, I just notice all the shitty things all of a sudden. Like when you go inside from the rain and your umbrella drips all over your leg. Or how the school toilet paper is never wide or thick enough to cover the toilet seat when you need to take a shit. And everyone is so *annoying,* talking about their interests that don't matter: Wendy with her antidairy crusade, David with his favorite idols' haircuts, and Ma Mi gushing about deals she gets at one of the new Asian malls.

I time myself to arrive at school right when first period starts so I don't bump into Ash at the grad lockers. And I think she's trying to avoid me, too. If I do catch a glimpse of her, she looks like she's in a hurry to leave. Hood up, backpack on, skateboard under her arm. I try to convince myself that it's all for practical reasons. Like, maybe she's grabbing more shifts from Simon to pay off Blake and get to Kelowna.

But I know she's punishing me because she hates me (for good reason).

I avoid the skate park, too. And skateboarding, for that matter. It reminds me too much of Ash. Of the YouTube channel I don't dare try logging into for fear that Ash has changed the password. Of the competition I'm probably never going to see.

I find it difficult to concentrate on my assignments, so I start watching *Buffy* reruns on television. Yeah, the show reminds me of Ash because she was the one who told me about it, but I'm starting to think everything fun reminds me of Ash anyway, so there's no point in avoiding it. Still, when I see Tara and Willow being cute, all I can think about is Ash. Then my dad walks in—because parents *always* walk in on the most awkward moments—so I shut off the television and run upstairs.

By now, I've received acceptance letters from most of the universities I've applied to. I know I should be proud of this, but there's still so much uncertainty about where I'm going next year. One day, I decide to work on a scholarship application I found for one of the local universities I got into. Yes, I'm adamant about going abroad, but after writing so many applications, I've gotten good at it, so I why not? Who knows, maybe if I get enough free money, it'll change my mind about Europe.

I work for two hours straight. It's hard work, but it takes my mind off Ash at least. My eyes sting and my brain hurts by the time I feel done enough to get up and go to the bathroom. The moment I step into the hallway though, Ma Mi's voice comes rattling through the walls of the house.

"Are you serious?! You spent *all of yesterday and today* on a social studies project due *next month*, when your English paper is due *tomorrow*, and you haven't started it?"

"Ma Mi, I forgot—"

"How can you forget something like that? Did you not write it down? Do they not hand out school agendas for free?"

Silence. Then she stutters, "I-I got it mixed up. I-I thought it was next—"

"How could you have put this off for so long? I thought you started essays *weeks* in advance!"

A sniffle. "I—" Wendy starts to cry. It's not an unfamiliar noise— Wendy cries sometimes late at night on the other side of my wall. Her eyes will be puffy and she'll look more tired the following morning. When I ask her she says it's a lower than expected grade or missing Justin or something a friend said. This time, it's a little different. It's louder, more desperate, and it's snotty and blubbery. Like a toddler.

And it makes me angry.

Before I have time to think, I storm down the stairs with heavy steps. Wendy has her face in her hands on the sofa. Ma Mi stands in front of Wendy on the other side of the coffee table, stiff as a board. She's still wearing her work blouse, a super restrictive, white lacy thing that makes me feel suffocated just looking at it. When she hears me, she whips around, surprised and frazzled. "Oh! Ga Jie. Sorry if we—"

"Jesus Christ, Mother," I say in English. "Lay off Wendy."

Her eyes widen and her mouth twitches. "Wong See Kar!" she finally manages to burst out. "How can you speak to me like that?"

"How can you talk to Wendy like *that*?" I shoot back, using her own words in Cantonese.

"This does not involve you."

I stand between her and the coffee table, shielding Wendy, who's a little quieter now but still shaking. "Yes, it does fucking involve me," I say in English, and it's satisfying to see my mother wince as the f-bomb lands. "I'm working on an important scholarship and you've ruined my focus. But that's not the point. Wendy's been slaving away her entire high school career. She never takes a break, not even in the summer when she takes courses to get ahead. Don't you think she deserves a little slack?"

De Di's office door slides open and he steps out in his bathrobe. "What's with all the commotion?"

"Your daughter is talking back and swearing," Ma Mi says.

De Di sighs and drags his eyes to me like it's the most labor-intensive action ever. "Jessica. We've talked about this so many times. Don't bok jui." My dad has a real pet peeve about kids talking back to their elders.

"I wasn't bok jui-ing, I was expressing legitimate criticism." In a brighter time, my parents would have gotten a good laugh out of my Chinglish, but today they just look tired and offended. "All I'm saying is Wendy doesn't deserve to be yelled at like this. She's already stressed. And honestly, I am, too," I add, just a little more quietly.

"Stressed about school?" I hear the touch of a scoff in De Di's voice. He likes to say that the Canadian school system is too chill, that we don't know what *real* stress feels like in a competitive place like Hong Kong where everyone fights to get into good schools. Which makes me mad. Really mad. Because while Wendy and I have never gone to school in Asia, it's not like he's gone to high school here either. "Yes, De Di! Do you not see that Wendy never has free time? You have no idea what you're talking about."

De Di freezes and avoids my gaze. Almost as if I'm not in the room.

Ma Mi groans and says, "Ah Mui, go write your essay and we'll bring you dinner." Then both my parents hustle out of the room, and it almost feels like I scared them away.

I sit down next to Wendy. "Don't worry. I'll get you coffee and dinner, and you just focus on your essay, okay?"

Wendy sniffles. "I don't like coffee."

"Well, you're gonna need it."

Later, at dinnertime, when I make Wendy's plate and Ma Mi tells me not to put too much sauce on the rice, I make a point of adding *a lot* of sauce. Wendy could use the sodium, I feel. I bring a tray to Wendy's room where she's busy typing away.

"How's the coffee?"

"Disgusting. But it works."

"Good." I turn around to leave.

"Ga Jie?"

"Yeah?"

She spins around at me but tilts her eyes to the side. "I'm sorry I called you a deadbeat on your birthday."

I shrug. "Well, you're kinda right."

After dinner, I help Ma Mi with the dishes because De Di has an interview with a Chinese company. It's quiet and awkward, just like dinner. When an argument happens, my parents' usual tactic is to skip to the part where we act like no one remembers. But I sense something different in Ma Mi today. Her forehead is knotted, her mouth is pursed into a straight line, and she's scrubbing the same part of the pot she's holding over and over even though there's nothing there.

"Ma Mi, I think that's clean," I say.

She sighs and turns on the faucet to rinse the soap off. "Wendy has too much on her mind, that's why she's forgetting things." She hands me the pot to dry off. "I don't understand. I told her she should slow down the clubs and focus on her grades. That's what will get her into med school."

"Maybe Wendy doesn't want to go to med school. Maybe she wants to become an environmental lawyer," I say. "Or a politician." I shrug. It changes week by week.

"She hasn't decided, though, has she? Ever since she was ten years old, when your Tai Gong died of colon cancer, she's wanted to become a doctor."

"Well, she was ten years old. She's not anymore."

"She's still taking all her science classes. I'm sure she's still interested."

"She's taking those classes because she wants to make you happy."

Ma Mi is quiet for a moment, and then she says, "She needs to eat meat. That's why she's so tired all the time. I don't understand you children, depriving yourselves for some idealistic reason. Humans *need* meat."

I read a news article the other day that says otherwise, but I'm not in the mood to argue.

"Sometimes you girls paint me in such a blackhearted light. You do know I just want the best for you two." I focus on drying a dish, bracing myself for a lecture. "But you're right."

I nearly drop the dish. "What?"

Ma Mi sighs and turns around to scrub the stovetop. "You aren't children anymore."

• • •

I have never felt so alone at school.

Sure, people talk to me, and I talk to people. Laugh sometimes, even. But it's like I black out during conversations because I don't remember them after. When people talk, it's like they're underwater.

I spend all my lunch hours in Mr. Hussein's room. Alone. I keep Adobe open, but it's all just to make it look like I'm doing something in front of Mr. Hussein. The truth is I've felt no motivation to do anything lately, not even sketching, never mind schoolwork. I don't even watch skateboarding edits before I sleep anymore because they remind me of shredding with Ash and the guys.

Mr. Hussein passes me on his way out one day, stops, and looks over his shoulder. "Hey. I haven't seen Ash in a while."

I stare at my blank canvas in Adobe. "Yeah." It's been three weeks since Ash yelled at me on the phone. I feel Mr. Hussein's gaze on me. I yawn, pretending I'm super tired so I don't have to make eye contact. "She's busy," I say.

"Oh." Mr. Hussein lingers at the door for a moment. "I saw the video you guys made."

This makes me look up. "What?"

"Yeah." He grins. "Ms. Watanabe showed me." Ash must have shown Ms. Watanabe; she's always in her office. "You guys have legitimate skills. Both of you," he adds. "I think the word is . . . sick? The video is *sick*?"

I can't help but smile. "Thanks."

Mr. Hussein nods, gives the apple he's holding a toss, and walks off down the hall, whistling. I think he can smell my loneliness from a mile away, but at least he likes my video.

On Friday, I hear Sophie and David talking about doing an overnight Studio Ghibli marathon. "You and Min can come over and we can study for biology then watch until we fall asleep and finish it in the morning," Sophie says.

I walk up and hover between them. I don't say anything, I just wait for one of them to notice me.

"Hey, Jay," David says finally, after a few awkward seconds. "What's up?"

"You guys watching *Castle in the Sky*?" That's my favorite after *Spirited Away*.

Sophie and David nod.

"Can I come?" I ask.

"Don't you have skateboarding stuff?" Sophie says.

"We're done the skateboarding stuff."

"You're not taking AP Bio," David says. "Wouldn't you get bored?"

"I can do something else while you guys study," I say. There's a sting in my nose and I try to keep my voice steady and my words few. Because if I even express my feelings a little bit, I'm afraid I might burst into tears.

David and Sophie exchange a glance and Sophie shrugs. "Yeah, sure, why not?"

I stop at the bubble tea café on the way to Sophie's and order four large bubble teas. David's bubble tea order—mango, green tea base, no toppings—hasn't changed since our parents started letting us go to the café after school, and I remember what Min and Sophie got in Whistler. Taro and pearls for Min. Matcha and pudding for Sophie. I opt for an original recipe with jelly. To my relief, the bubble teas make everyone very happy, though David does frown at his.

"Man, no toppings?"

I panic. "You don't like toppings . . ."

David laughs. "I don't. Yeah, just messing with you!"

I do English homework while they scrabble over proteins and enzymes, or at least I try to. Focusing is a grind. So I write something passable and doze on the couch instead. It's quiet. Safe. No catcalling dudes, no drugs, no asshole boyfriends who can't drive straight. I have nothing to worry about. It's peaceful. Easy.

David gets a phone call and disappears into the kitchen. I take a trip to the ground floor bathroom and stop by Sophie's mom's home library. Sophie's house is amazing. It's so big, and her parents have actually made an effort at interior design. Everything's in a consistent style that reminds me of the quirky secondhand stores in East Van. Meanwhile, my parents buy the cheapest functioning furniture possible and wrap the TV remote with plastic to "keep it clean."

I decide to get a glass of water from the kitchen and bump into David just as he turns off his phone and leans over the sink, swearing in Korean.

"Hey." I knock on the wall to announce my presence. "You okay?"

David groans. "That was my dad. We're on day three of an argument."

"Oh, shit. What about?"

"He thinks I should apply to more scholarships, but I have so much on my plate already. Student Council. Calculus. Training for this tennis tournament he put me in at the country club."

I scowl. "Tennis tournament?"

He nods, rolling his eyes. "It's all 'cause I'm his only son, you know? He didn't go to an American university which is, like, his biggest regret. So he wants me to do what he didn't, like I'm his shot at a second life." He clutches fistfuls of his hair and swears again. "Oh, and he thinks I need to get a girlfriend."

I laugh. "What?" That one I haven't heard. My parents have always discouraged Wendy and me from dating in high school because they don't want anything to distract us from our studies. I had assumed David's parents have the same philosophy. Though I guess we're older now, and almost done school, and Ma Mi *did* mention David being boyfriend material.

"Yeah." He rolls his eyes. "He thinks I'm too soft."

"So? How is getting a girlfriend supposed to help with that? What, does he think you're gay or something?" David shoots me a look. That was probably inappropriate. I look away.

"I just . . ." Through his teeth, David says, "Sometimes I wish I had never been born."

"Dude . . ." I'm not sure what to say. I finally settle on, "Do you . . . do you need help?"

He rolls his eyes. "Are you gonna tell on me to Ms. Watanabe?"

"No," I say, "but I'm glad you were born. And I'm sure your mom is, too." David's mother is the sweetest. The first time I went to David's house for dinner, I fell in love with her jap chae and, ever since, she makes jap chae every time I visit. I've seen her hug David a lot, each time coaxing the biggest smile out of him, but I've never seen them hug—or smile—in front of David's father. I'm pretty sure when David's dad gets home, everyone goes quiet. I often wonder how someone like David's mom could end up with a man like that.

"You know what I'm gonna do, Jay?" His eyes flash. "I'm gonna join an Ivy League frat and rub shoulders with rich dudes whose dads are Freemasons. I'll get a job on Wall Street and never come home. I'll get even richer than my dad and I'll give him none of it and write him out of my will. And I'll never speak to him again. Yeah, that'll show him who's a *fucking man*." He kicks the empty recycling bin next to the fridge.

I pour two glasses of water and give one to him. "You know, you kinda remind me of Ash," I say when he calms a little. "Not the Wall Street part, but the I-wanna-get-back-at-my-dad part." I take a sip. "I respect that," I add.

David drinks and frowns. "Hey, what's up with Ash anyway? I haven't seen her in ages. Is she even going to school?"

I shrug. "I don't know."

"Are you guys . . . okay?"

I shrug again. "I don't know. Why do you care?"

He looks at me. "Because we're friends?"

I cross my arms over my chest. "I'm glad you say so." I close my eyes. If I say this to his face, I'll just break down crying. "I'm really sorry, David. I feel like I haven't been a good friend to you. I didn't know all this crap was going on with your dad."

He shrugs. "It's not like I told you, I guess."

"Why didn't you?"

He looks away. "It's fine," I hear him mutter. "Sophie and Min have done a good job of—"

"But *I* should be there for you." I want to cry again, so I feign rubbing my eye and take a few slow breaths. Thankfully, my body seems to suck the tears back in. "Like, if you need to talk, seriously, I'm here. Seriously." I watch him, and to my relief, he gives the slightest of nods.

"I didn't know you and Ash were going through something either," he says. "Do *you* wanna talk about it?"

Flashbacks of Ash and me making out in the dark. Then her angry voice on the phone: *If you call me again, I'll throw your precious MacBook into the pool along with Blake's guitar.* No, I don't want to talk about it. Not yet, anyhow. "Maybe later," I say.

David says, "You know, what you said about those time capsules in Grade 8 . . . I've been thinking about that. Truth is, I couldn't think of anything to put in mine so I made it up. All my life, I've been told what to do by my dad. I don't even know who *I* am. Did I ever tell you I wanted to take tap-dancing lessons as a kid, but he never let me because he thought dancing was for girls?"

Huh, he's never told me that, but I'm glad he just did. "What *do* you want to do, then? If your dad wasn't here to boss you around?"

David groans. "I don't know. That's the problem. *I don't even know.* I just . . . I'm starting to see why you want to do something big and classic teenagery before we graduate."

We stand there in silence. Elsewhere in the house, I hear Sophie's dad whistling.

"Hey," I say, "if you ever want to try something new—and, assuming I'm still friends with her—you're welcome to hang with me and Ash and our skateboarding friends."

David's forehead scrunches as he contemplates this. Then he says, "Maybe."

CHAPTER 11

In AP English the next week, Mr. Hussein taps me on the shoulder during an in-class assignment and asks me to go into the hall with him. "Don't worry, I'll give you extra time for the assignment," he says when he shuts the classroom door behind us, "but I wanted to speak with you in private."

I stiffen. "What's wrong?"

He crosses his arms. "You've gotten Cs on your last three assignments. Granted, they're not major, but your performance until now was consistently strong, so this is quite a dramatic drop. I know Grade 12s tend to get senioritis, but you've always been conscientious. So, is there something else going on?"

I look down at my shoes. "No."

"You're not in trouble, Jay." His voice softens. "Is something going on at home? I may be able to give you an extension on assignments."

I whisper, "No, nothing's going on."

He uncrosses his arms with a sigh and tucks his hands into his cardigan pockets. "I can help you, Jay, but you need to talk to me."

"Nothing's going on," I repeat, staring at the holes in my shoes.

"Then why the sudden drop in grades? If it's to do with managing your time—"

"No. Shit. No, it's not that." And suddenly, the floodgates fling open. The tears that rush out of my eyes are as unstoppable as a nosebleed. I bury my face in my hands as my sinuses clog up and I start choking.

"Whoa, whoa. Shhh. Here." Mr. Hussein leads me down the hall to the admin office. He says something I can't hear to the receptionist, who says he needs to go to the copy room anyway. We're left alone in the admin waiting room, and Mr. Hussein sits me down, my legs shaking, and hands me a box of tissues. He patiently waits for me to blow my nose, and when I'm no longer hyperventilating like a dying person, he folds his hands in his lap and says, "Okay, start from the beginning."

"My best friend hates me," I say. "Ash hates me. I did something awful and now she won't even talk to me." I wipe my nose. "And it's not just that. I've been a shitty friend to David, too. I'm just the shittiest person ever."

"Surely that's an exaggeration. Why don't you tell me a little more?"

"Well, I became friends with Ash at the beginning of the year. Ash and I just—we just *click,* you know? Have you ever met someone and instantly clicked with them?" I meet his eyes, and something in them flickers. The words are tumbling out of my mouth nonstop and I think, *Surely I'll regret this later.* But whatever. "And they make you feel . . . like everything's new, and exciting, and different, and you're stoked, like, *all the time.* You never get creative blocks because when you're with them, you feel like you can make anything, and anything and everything you make will be beautiful. Just as beautiful as . . . them." I suck in air and a huge glob of snot goes down my throat. "It sounds so cheesy but—"

"Yes." Mr. Hussein gives a simple nod, and I see the beginnings of a smile crinkle his mustache. "I know exactly what you mean."

"But then I did something shitty. Like, really, really shitty. I went behind Ash's back and did something so freaking *gross*—" I snort as if on cue. Gosh, *I'm* gross. "I don't think she'll ever forgive me, and I don't know what to do."

"Well. First of all, before you ask Ash for forgiveness, I think you need to forgive yourself."

I stop sniffling. "What?"

"You obviously care a lot about Ash if offending her makes you this upset." Mr. Hussein draws himself up with a big inhale. "I've seen you two, and a relationship like that doesn't just go up in smoke over one mistake. Ash will come around. Just give her time. Meanwhile, is there anyone you can talk to about this? Someone you trust?"

"I talked to David," I say, "but he doesn't know everything. I don't want to tell him everything yet."

"Why?"

"I'm not ready, I don't think."

"Hmm." Mr. Hussein tilts his head. "Why don't you try explaining it to me? Just for practice."

Explain everything to Mr. Hussein. At first, the idea seems ridiculous. He's not my dad or anything. But it makes sense. He knows me enough to care about how I'm doing—it's why we're having this conversation—but he's also removed enough that I won't have to sit through awkward lunches and dinners with him.

I shuffle around in my seat so that I'm facing him. I feel his eyes on me, patient but anticipating. He's still, hands gently clasped in his lap. I wonder if he has a background in counseling. I take a few seconds to gather myself. When I'm finally ready, I say in the smallest voice possible, "I think Ash and I are . . . well, we're more than just friends."

"More than friends?" he echoes.

"Yeah." I swallow. "We, um, we kissed."

"Oh." Mr. Hussein sits back in his chair. "Oh. Wow, you're dealing with a lot, aren't you, Jay?"

I nod, and to my surprise, a little laugh comes out.

"I'm guessing this is new to you."

"Yeah." I wipe my eyes. "Kinda." I sniff. "I'm scared of coming out to my parents."

"There's no rush to come out to your parents, Jay. I didn't come out to my parents until I was in college in New York," he says. "That conversation ended up costing me my ticket home," he adds, "and I haven't seen my family in years."

I frown at him. "Way to cheer me up."

But he chuckles and his smile teases out little crow's feet around his eyes. "It's scary at first, I won't lie. But believe it or not, I'm happier now than I ever was. My family didn't accept me—so what? I moved and built a new family. I got married, we adopted two dogs, and every second Saturday I watch my husband sing at a bar in the West End and it's the highlight of my month. Truly, I've never been happier."

I wipe my nose. "Thanks, Mr. Hussein. That—that actually helps." The thought of coming out to my parents terrifies me so much I'm scared to even imagine the scene in my head. I'm glad I don't have to do it right away.

"I'll give you a chance to rewrite your *Much Ado* essay," Mr. Hussein continues. "I can't give you an A, but if you write A-level material, I can bump your C up to a B. How's that?"

"Sounds like a good deal," I say. And it really is. I'd completely butchered that essay.

"Here's a tip," Mr. Hussein says. "You like art, right?" I nod. "Go draw," he says. "It'll help with your anxiety. When you feel anxious, do something tactile. Like draw. Or skateboard. And then just focus on the sensations."

I nod.

"One more thing." Mr. Hussein leans forward on his fist with a thoughtful look. "At your age, someone like Ash will seem amazing. You may be head over heels for her, and I'm not trying to dissuade you, Jay, because it's a beautiful feeling that should be enjoyed. Just remember that Ash is a person like everyone else. She makes mistakes, she has flaws, and she can be mean to *you* in the same way that you can be mean to her. Just remember that, okay?"

I'm a little confused and my head hurts because I'm dehydrated from crying, but I nod. I look down at my lap and see a bouquet of dirty tissues there. Mr. Hussein tells me to clean myself up in the bathroom and meet him back in class.

I still feel shitty about pissing off Ash, but when I walk back to class, my feet feel a smidge lighter.

· · ·

That Friday, I commit myself to sketching for ten minutes. Anything. Mugs. Pencil cases. The rumples on my pillowcase. Just like Mr. Hussein prescribes. And it works. I listen to music and the minutes tick into hours.

Suddenly, my phone buzzes. The caller ID says it's Wendy. She's at an orchestra friend's house tonight. Maybe she's ready to get picked up, but why would she call me and not the home phone? "Hello?" I answer.

It's all distorted noise on the other side. "Is this Jessica?" A guy's voice, shaky and breathless.

I frown. "Yeah?"

"Uh, my name's Justin? I—"

"Wendy's boyfriend."

"Yeah." A slight breath of relief from his end. "Do you, um, do you think you can get to Kitsilano?"

I frown even harder. "What's going on?"

"W-Wendy's really, *really* drunk. Your parents can't see her like this. I think you have to pick her up."

"I . . ." My head is ablaze with questions. Wendy . . . *drunk?* What kind of alternative universe is this? "Uh, well, I only have a learner's permit. I can't drive," I say, trying to be as calm as possible.

"I dunno, can you just come?" Justin sounds like he's about to cry. "Just don't tell your parents and come? I'll give you the address. We're at Ellen Park's."

"Uh . . . okay." I write down the address, hang up, and sit in my chair for a full five seconds. Then I start moving.

My parents are in their room watching some sort of Hong Kong game show where celebrities do ridiculous and embarrassing challenges. I knock on the door frame. "Hey, what time are you guys picking up Wendy?"

De Di looks at the time. "When she calls. Probably in an hour?"

"Okay." I try to look as unanxious as possible. "I'm not feeling super well. I'm going to bed early. Can you turn the TV down and try to be quiet when you leave?"

Ma Mi frowns and straightens up. "You're not feeling well? What's going on?"

"Oh, it's nothing. Just a headache."

She sighs. "You don't drink enough water. Eat some fruit la."

De Di says, "You know where the ibuprofen is, right?"

"Yes," I say. "I'll get some." I leave them before they can ask more questions, go back to my room, get dressed, and turn off all the lights. Then I listen and wait. When my parents laugh extra loud at some game-show shenanigan, I slip out of my bedroom.

I disable the alarm, take petty cash from the sideboard, run to the main street, and call a cab. Thankfully, Kits isn't too far away.

The cab drops me off in front of—I can't believe it—a raging house party. Ellen Park's parents must be out of town. The entire house booms with something that is definitely not classical music, and drunk teenagers are hanging off the front porch slugging ciders and coolers.

I spot Justin and Wendy in the front yard right away. Wendy's ambling about in uneven circles and Justin is following her around like he's lost and Wendy is his broken compass. When he sees me, his shoulders sag with relief. I also see that he has what I'm certain is vomit on his chest pocket.

Wendy sees me and freezes. Puts a hand up to her eyes and squints. *"Ga Jie?!"* Her voice is hoarse and raw. "What the flippin' fuck are *you* doing here?"

I try to ignore the fact that Wendy just said "flippin' fuck" and reply, "I'm here to get you home."

"Holy shit, are Mom and Dad here?!"

"No, they're not."

"Oh, *thank fuck.*" Her body teeters. "Mom and Dad can *fuck off.*" She burps and gags. I take a step back just in case and exchange a glance with Justin. He shrugs, grimacing.

"Come on, let's get you home," I say, pulling her wrist and then pushing her by the shoulders.

"I don't want to go home!" Wendy screams.

Justin says to me, "Yeah, I think we need to sober her up first."

"Right." I sigh. "I saw a Denny's on the way here. We can go there, put some food in her."

Justin nods. So we start dragging Wendy down the sidewalk, each of us shouldering an arm. The whole walk, Wendy grumbles about how much she hates Model UN, orchestra, violin, even Justin's Conservation Club, because they're all "phonies." She calls our parents phonies, too. I wonder if she just read *The Catcher in the Rye* like I did in Grade 11. "And you, you're a phony!" Wendy growls at Justin. "I *told* you not to call anyone."

Justin stares at his shoes. "Hey," I say to Wendy briskly, "Justin did the right thing, so don't call him that. You can call me whatever you like, but don't call him that."

"You . . ." Wendy burps and stops walking. Justin looks at me with a panicked expression, and I swiftly point Wendy at a bush before she can throw up on us.

"I what?" I say when she's done ejecting her stomach's contents.

"You're lucky," she mutters. "Mom and Dad . . . go easy on you."

My stomach goes hot with disagreement, but I keep it in. Now is not the time to think about myself.

When we get to Denny's, I ask the server for five glasses of water, coffee, and the cheapest stack of pancakes they have. I wrap Wendy's hands around a glass of water, tell Justin to make sure she drinks as much as possible, and then head outside.

I call home on Wendy's phone. As kids we used to imitate each other all the time, and I can still sort of imitate Wendy's voice in short bursts. I call my parents and shout, "Wai? *Wai?!*" pretending the signal isn't strong before hanging up abruptly. And then I text De Di: *Bad signal. Movie marathon is happening and a bunch of us are staying over. Ellen's parents will drive me home in the morning.* I wait tensely for about thirty seconds, and then De Di answers: *Ok. Call us in the morning.* Easy. Maybe because it's Wendy.

I get back to our booth. Wendy has finished half her glass of water and some of the pancakes. She's dozing on Justin's shoulder, and he looks like he's been run over by a truck himself. I sit down and push the coffee and pancakes toward him, but he shakes his head. So I ask, "What happened?"

Justin scratches his neck. "She . . . she's been upset all week, honestly. She wasn't planning to come tonight, actually." Huh, that makes sense. Wendy only told our parents she was going to what she called an "orchestra event" two days ago, which is late for her. It had struck me as odd in the moment. "Basically, she's in 'fuck it' mode. The moment she got there she started drinking on an empty stomach and it's the worst I've seen it."

I narrow my eyes. "Wait, so this isn't the first time?"

Justin freezes. "I mean . . ."

"It's fine, I won't tell on her. It's not like I've never been drunk myself."

Justin takes off his glasses and polishes them. His eye bags are so deep he looks like an old man. "The first time was in November, during this Model UN conference we both went to. There was this kid—Norway— who had a reputation for sneaking in all sorts of stuff. This time, he brought his dad's whiskey or something. It was the last night of the conference, and we all snuck out to his room. Most of us just drank until we got sleepy, but Wendy kept going and going. Neither of us got any sleep because she was throwing up all night and I was holding her hair."

"Yikes." So Wendy's outdone me. Even at this. Who knew Model UNers partied so hard.

"Then at Christmas when we visited the Interior, Wendy was really stressed out about her concerto," Justin said. "Sometimes after a concert, the older musicians will slip us drinks. Or we buy our own because in our concertwear we look older. Thankfully, she didn't go as hard that time because we couldn't get that many drinks, but she did have a killer hangover the morning after and I figured she'd learned her lesson." He shrugs. "Guess I was wrong."

I sigh. "I'll talk to her."

Justin looks around nervously. "Look, I should probably get home . . . My parents will wonder where I am."

It looks like he feels bad, so I say, "Yes, go. I'll take care of her." He nods, gets up, carefully peeling Wendy off his shoulder, and I side-hug him, careful to avoid the vomit patch. "Hey, you did good. My sister found a good dude."

I drink my coffee. Wendy oscillates between drinking water, eating pancakes, cradling her head on the table, and groaning. Then she opens her eyes, looks at me, and burps.

"How you feelin'?" I ask.

"Like dirt." Wendy drinks half a glass of water in one go. Her voice is still sandy dry. "After tonight, I don't even want to look at a glass of wine."

"Do you wanna talk about it?"

Her bangs hide her face as she bends over her food. "It was a mistake."

"Justin says this wasn't the first time." Wendy goes still. I say quickly, "Don't worry, I won't tell Ma Mi and De Di about this. Swear to god, I'll take it to the grave." After her shoulders relax, I say, "Sounds like it's been rough."

Wendy rubs the spot on her nose bridge where her glasses sit. "Yeah. I guess. Academically. Musically. Everything. Grade 11 counts for university so I'm trying to be as competitive as I can."

"You know Ma Mi and De Di won't care if you end up at McGill instead of Columbia," I say. "De Di's always going on about how the States suck anyway."

She sighs again. "But they *do* care."

"I'm sure they'd rather have a healthy kid in a Canadian uni than an alcoholic in an Ivy League."

Wendy rubs her temples slowly. The way she moves, her head must weigh as much as a bowling ball. "You don't get it. That's what they say but it's not what they *mean*."

"Of course I get it, silly. In case you haven't noticed, we have the same pa—"

"No." Wendy looks up through her nest of oily hair and I finally see it—the resentment. It's not a raging fire, just a candle flicker behind her pupils. It makes my insides crumple. "We're different," she says, her voice rough. "You get to do your creative stuff because that's *your thing*. Me, I have to be a doctor or a lawyer or a business mogul—that's *my* thing. We each have to be good at our things. Well, it just so happens that becoming a doctor or a lawyer means you have to be perfect at everything, the absolute top of the top."

"You know you don't *have* to be a doctor," I say.

"But that was always the plan." Wendy shrugs and carefully lays her fork and knife aside. "I just want to make our parents proud because—" She pauses.

"Because at least one daughter has to make them proud?" I finish for her.

She looks away. "Well, I wasn't going to say *that*. But having a kid turn out to be a doctor is just . . . easier to be proud of, I guess. It's not my fault artists aren't known for making money."

"You know De Di was joking when he said they'll rely on you in their old age." I reach across the table and wrap my hands around Wendy's cold fingers as they grip her coffee mug. Wendy stiffens, but she doesn't shrink away. Our family never shows each other physical affection—I don't think we've hugged in years—but in this moment, I think it's worth it. "I won't sink the family by becoming an artist," I tell her. "If I have to take two barista jobs to bail our parents out of debt jail, I will. You won't be alone. You'll *never* be alone. I . . ." I sigh then say, "I don't always *like* you, but in general, I do *love* you."

She allows herself a crackly laugh. "Thanks."

"Seriously, cut yourself some slack."

We stay at the restaurant for another hour—until our parents' bedtime. When I'm confident that they'll be asleep when we get home, we take the bus. Then, we painstakingly and quietly sneak into the house. At the door of her bedroom, I whisper, "I'll wake you up in the morning. You'll put tonight's clothes back on and come in like you were just dropped off, okay? Just don't stand too close to Ma Mi. You're a little smelly."

Wendy blinks at me. "Have you done this before?"

"Sneak in and out of the house?" I shrug. "Maybe."

Wendy looks like she wants to ask me more questions, but she's so tired, she lies down and conks right out.

The next morning works out according to plan. I distract my parents in the kitchen with random questions about the game show they were watching. Meanwhile, Wendy sneaks outside in last night's clothes. Then she pretends to come in.

"Wow, you're back early!" Ma Mi exclaims when she walks into the kitchen, bleary-eyed but not nearly as fucked-up-looking as last night. "Lai la, lai la! Come, come! Have some jok and tea."

"Nah, I have a headache," Wendy mutters. "I think I'll take a nap." Who knew headaches would be so useful as excuses?

Ma Mi looks suspicious for a moment and I tense up, the wheels in my brain getting ready, but she lets it go.

I leave Wendy to sleep in for a few hours, and then I make her a cup of her favorite green tea and bring it up to her room. I knock on her door and her answering voice has more energy than I expect. When I get in, she's on her computer, yawning.

"Feeling better?" I set down the tea.

"Yeah." She taps the desk with two fingers, thanking me for the tea.

I sit on her bed. "What's that?" I point to her computer screen.

She spins back and forth on her desk chair, drinking tea. "I visited

Justin's school a few weeks ago. For Conservation Club. This guest speaker from this organization came and they have this, like, super cool youth internship program."

"I thought the people at Conservation Club were phonies," I say with a smirk.

She's not in a mood to sass me back. "Nah. With this program, you spend a year after high school traveling around the world, interviewing activists. But . . ." Her voice ebbs away. Ma Mi and De Di frown on gap years. Gap years are for indecisive Western kids with rich parents who can afford a year of gallivanting around Europe to "find" themselves. In our family, you don't waste time; you go straight from high school to university to a well-paying job.

"Damn," I say, "You're really into this environmental stuff, aren't you?"

"Not just the environment. There's so much that needs to change." She takes another sip of tea. "Like, take racism. No one ever talks about racism against Asian people. We still have white people playing us in movies and no one even bats an eye. Have you heard of the model minority myth?"

"No." I brace myself for a lecture.

"The stereotype that Asians are all high-achieving doctors and lawyers."

I scoff. "But isn't that true? I mean . . ." I wave a hand at my sister as the best example of this phenomenon, but she shakes her head.

"Not all the time. Sure, De Di is an engineer. But what about Mrs. Ly, who cuts our hair, whose accent is so thick we can barely understand her? Not everyone fits the stereotype." Ash comes to mind. I'm still not sure what her parents do, but looking at my parents, it's starting to make sense why she wouldn't want to tell me. "We get grouped into one narrow category, but we're a lot more diverse than that. It also pits us against other minorities because people start to assume that, well, if Asians do so well in math then other minorities just aren't trying hard enough. Ignoring that we're all super different, with different struggles to deal with."

"You should do it," I say. "The internship." Wendy scoffs, but I continue, "You'd be good at it. You have such a deep understanding of things. I wouldn't've thought of all that stuff you said."

"Well, you just have to do a little research—"

"Do it, Wendy. Become an activist. Or a journalist. Save the world. You're one of the few people who gives a damn, and you're fucking smart. Don't waste that on a career you don't like."

A tiny flicker of a smile. "Thank you. And thanks for not telling Ma Mi and De Di about this."

I shrug. "You're not the only one with secrets."

She snorts. "Where have *you* snuck out to?"

I look at the wall, and maybe I'm just tired, but I find myself saying, "It's not really that . . ."

Wendy's eyes twinkle with curiosity through the mug steam. "Wait, what do you mean?"

I think about Halloween, Whistler, the graffiti trip. But what comes out of my mouth—before I can stop it—is simple: "I think I'm gay."

My heart starts pounding. The words just materialized and I can't unsay them now. I look at Wendy—she blinks for two agonizing seconds before saying, "Oh." She straightens up, looks at me, looks away, looks at me again. Uncrosses her legs. Recrosses them. "Oh," she says again.

"Annnd . . ." I swallow, hesitating. But I've already popped the trick, I might as well commit to the landing. "And I think I'm in love with my best friend." I swallow. "Ash."

"Hmm." Wendy swings around in her chair. "Are you sure? How long have you known?"

Maybe I've timed this well. Maybe Wendy is too hungover to freak out. Unfortunately, I can't count on my parents to be in a similar state when the time comes.

"Pretty sure. I think I've known on some level all my life. Also, Ash and I kissed."

Wendy chokes on her tea. She coughs everywhere and for a moment I wonder if she's laughing, but she's not. When she finally calms down, she wipes tea off her desk and says, "Wow. Okay. Um. Are you gonna come out?"

I massage the area between my eyes where a real headache is brooding. "Maybe."

"I think our parents will be okay with it." Wendy shrugs, and I'm kind of impressed by how chill she is. "Maybe not right away—they might be surprised—but I doubt they'll, like, disown you."

"Yeah." I think about Ash and I can't even imagine how her dad might react to this. "Yeah, we lucked out with our parents," I say quietly.

"When will you do it?"

"I don't think I can," I say, "until I come out to Ash."

CHAPTER 12

A gray-and-black-striped hand warmer slams down on the paper I'm writing. I look up and my body clenches.

"So, when are we getting together to work on it?" Ash leans over my desk in AP English.

I swallow, for a moment wondering if I'm dreaming that she's talking to me. "Work on what?"

She sighs. "The *Orlando* presentation."

Oh. Right. I had totally forgotten about *Orlando*.

Ash narrows her eyes. "Don't tell me you haven't finished reading it."

I haven't finished reading it. "I'm almost done."

Ash huffs a long, dramatic sigh. "You wanna just go to your place after school and get it over with?"

"Sure." I don't see any other option.

"I'll meet you at your place."

When I get home that afternoon, Ash is already in front of my house. She's on her skateboard, using the sidewalk cracks to practice manuals, balancing on her back and front wheels. It occurs to me that her competition is coming up.

De Di is out grocery shopping, but we walk in on Wendy eating yogurt out of the fridge. She almost chokes when she sees us. Ash beelines to the bathroom and Wendy shuffles up to me in quiet excitement. "Oh my god, are you guys on a *date*?"

"Shut up, we just have an assignment."

She gives me a disturbingly salacious wink. "Right."

"First of all, never wink at me again." I push her face away with the palm of my hand. "And second, shut up and leave us alone."

Ash comes out of the bathroom, nods at Wendy, and goes upstairs. I follow.

"I'll give you *plenty* of privacy," Wendy whispers after me, giggling. "Use protection! Or . . . don't. Huh, I don't know how it works. Be safe!"

Upstairs, I shut my bedroom door. Ash dumps her bag on the floor and slumps into my desk chair with her arms crossed. "Your sister seems happy to see me for once."

I sit down on my bed. I want a wide swath of space between us. There's a montage in my head where I cross that room in two seconds and kiss her, but I fight it.

"So how far are you from finishing the book?" Ash peers at me like a cat half-interested in a bird out the window.

"About ten pages."

She takes the book from my desk and chucks it at me. I catch it. "Finish it, then. I'll wait."

I stay on my bed and start reading. Meanwhile, Ash dicks around on my computer. She opens my video editor and looks through my library of clips. "Hey," I say, "don't look at my stuff."

"Why not?"

"It's private."

She snorts. "They're all clips of me. How private can they be?"

I keep reading. A few paragraphs later, she plays a video and I recognize the music. "Can you not look at that?"

Ash ignores me, of course. She leans back in my desk chair and spins it to the beat of the Naked and Famous track. It's a video that contains a patchwork of aesthetics: softly colored summer haze, hypersaturated sunsets, wide off-center shots. She wouldn't know, but I always zoom in on Ash's expression after she lands. I like to capture that moment of pride in detail. Ash hasn't seen these shots because they get edited out of the final product, but I keep all my rough cuts.

Ash says, "I didn't know you were still making these."

"I like making videos," I say. "Can you please stop looking at them?"

"Why? You're being weird."

"I'm not being weird. I just don't like it when people see stuff of mine that's still in progress."

She grunts.

"You can go on Facebook or YouTube or whatever, but I would really appreciate it if you didn't go snooping around my stuff."

Ash spins away so that all I see is the back of the chair. "Would have loved it if you did the same."

"I'm sorry." The words catch in my throat and come out all awkward and hoarse.

"No." Still facing away from me, she holds up a gray-and-black-striped hand. "We're not doing this, not now. Just finish the damn book."

Against all odds, I finish the chapter within a half hour despite Ash's presence. When I'm done, I want to pee and have a snack, but Ash wants to finish the project right away. She sits cross-legged in my desk chair and drums on her lap with her hands. "So. What should we talk about?"

"Well, it's certainly an interesting commentary on gender," I say.

Ash rolls her eyes. "No freaking duh. Let's do something less obvious. C'mon, J.W., you're a creative person. Think."

I want to say I'm not creative at stuff like *this*, but I want to avoid conflict as much as possible. "Uh, okay, how about Vita's son's assertion that this is 'the longest and most charming love letter in literature'? Maybe we can talk about, I dunno, what *is* a love letter?"

I expect Ash to scoff at my idea, but she straightens up and uncrosses her legs. "Huh. That's interesting. Because frankly I don't think of this as a love letter. Not really."

I frown. "Why?"

"Well, it's a little creepy then, isn't it?" Ash tilts her head and thoughtfully flips her sheet of hair over her head. "Writing an entire fantastical novel based on a real person. Putting them on a pedestal. Making your lover a character when they're a real person."

"But it's obviously fiction," I say.

Ash nods slowly. "Okay. That's your argument then. I'll make up mine. Then we'll debate in front of the class."

It's an idea. "Sure. I guess."

"Cool. Then I'm off." Ash grabs her bag. When she opens the door, I manage to squeeze out an "um." She pauses.

"Do you want to hang out sometime?" I finally ask.

She's half-in, half-out the door. "Maybe later," she says.

When Ash is gone, Wendy knocks on my door and, when I open it, jumps in with two feet like a bunny rabbit. "You guys barely talked!" she giggles. "What the hell did you get up to?" I groan and shove her back out into the hall.

. . .

The day of the presentation, I keep wiping my palms against the front of my pants because they won't stop sweating. Meanwhile, Ash sits next to me cool as a cucumber, literally eating my leftover mini cucumbers.

She'd flopped down next to me and pointed at my uneaten lunch like she hadn't been avoiding me for a month. Meanwhile, I'm acutely aware of her body close to mine, emanating heat like a radiator and smelling like rain.

I'm also nervous because we've barely prepared. Well, I'm sure we've prepared enough by Ash's standards, but I'm used to having multiple meetings before a presentation and several rehearsals. If I'd done this project with David, we would have prepared a month ahead. David would have yelled at me to finish reading the book by Christmas.

Mr. Hussein walks in wearing his favorite matching plaid suit and burgundy bowtie. With his height, he looks like an oversized, bearded boy. "Settle down, folks. We have a lot of presentations today, presentations that make up a *third of this semester's grade.*" He makes sure to say this about once a month. "And, please, if I see one more of you texting under your desk, I'll confiscate all your phones. Just because I wear glasses doesn't mean I'm blind." Then, he turns in my direction and peers at Ash and me over his glasses. "And now, first up is a group I'm quite looking forward to. Ash and Jay with Virginia Woolf's *Orlando.* A wonderful book, a beautiful book, a *romantic* book." I feel my shirt sticking to my back with sweat. "Will you two be needing the projector? The whiteboard?"

"No, we've decided to do our presentation in a debate format," says Ash.

Mr. Hussein's right eyebrow arches up. "Oh? How unconventional indeed. Well, take it away." Chairs squeal against linoleum as Ash and I stand up to take his place in front of the class. Ash more or less shoves me to one side of the board and stands on the other. My pulse rattles between my ears as thirty pairs of eyes drill into me, waiting to be impressed.

Ash speaks first. "*Orlando* is a fictional biography of a nobleman named Orlando who transforms into a woman halfway through the book and lives through centuries of change, traveling through Europe." Good, at least she has the sense to summarize the book first. "Virginia Woolf based the character of Orlando on her lover, Vita Sackville-West, who—"

A guy in the back says to his friends, a little too loudly, "Wait, isn't Vita a girl's name? Isn't that kinda gay?"

"Patrick, homophobia will *not* be tolerated in my classroom," Mr. Hussein says tersely as Patrick's buddies giggle into their fists.

"But it's not homophobic to call something gay if it *is* gay, though, right?"

"That's enough. Ash, please continue."

Ash clears her throat. Her knees vibrate slightly. I'm not the only one who's nervous. "Vita's son would later call *Orlando* 'the longest and most charming love letter in literature.' We're going to debate that today. Jay will argue for, I against. My opening statement is that I do *not* think *Orlando* is a charming love letter because it is, essentially, the reduction of a real person into a stock character, who—while superficially attractive and charming—lacks any in-depth positive qualities. A person put on a pedestal. Objectified. Commodified. Their humanity reduced to tropes and niceties. Jay?" Her eyes flick toward me.

"Oh. I, uh . . ." The class stares at me expectantly. Mr. Hussein leans against his desk with his arms crossed, gifting us with his what I now recognize is an iconic eyebrow raise. I clear my throat a few times to buy myself some precious seconds. "I *do* think this novel is a love letter because . . . because just listen to how it's written." I open my book and read a passage I'd highlighted and underlined:

Thus, those who like symbols, and have a turn for the deciphering of them, might observe that though the shapely legs, the handsome body, and the well-set shoulders were all of them decorated with various tints of heraldic light, Orlando's face, as he threw the window open, was lit solely by the sun itself. A more candid, sullen face it would be impossible to find. Happy the mother who bears, happier still the biographer who records the life of such a one! Never need she vex herself, nor he invoke the help of novelist or poet. From deed to deed, from glory to glory, from office to office he must go, his scribe following after, till they reach whatever seat it may be that is the height of their desire. Orlando, to look at, was cut out precisely for some such career.

When I'm done, I look at the windows at the back of the classroom to avoid making eye contact with anyone. "Wasn't that an amazing description?" I say. "The book is *filled* with beautiful lines like that. Orlando is an awesome person, period, no matter his or her gender. Ash says that Woolf objectifies Orlando, but how is it objectifying when Orlando is so incredible that he, or she, or they, or whatever, is *beyond* gender? Just imagine meeting someone so great that it doesn't matter what gender they are; they're attractive in any way." When I'm done, my heart rate slows to a more reasonable pace. I'd started off by bullshitting, but I think I stuck the landing.

But Ash leans against the chalkboard shelf in that catlike way of hers, almost condescendingly relaxed. "But isn't that the problem? Orlando is described as the most beautiful and noblest of creatures, yet the novel specifically satirizes those aspects of them. Orlando seems perfect, yet even they get their heart broken and it really f—I mean, it messes them up. Real bad. They have an enormous house, beautiful dogs, throw lavish parties, and even meet their favorite poet at one point, but they never seem totally satisfied and struggle to complete their life's work, a poem they've been working on since they were a kid. And"—her eyes flash—"Orlando reeks of classism. When they run off and live with the Gyp—I mean, Roma, they initially think they're better off than the Roma because they have more bedrooms. Then one of the Roma makes Orlando realize they really haven't contributed much to society in the larger scheme of things. Sure, Orlando finishes their poem at the end, but it takes centuries. Honestly, if I was Vita, I would find parts of this story somewhat embarrassing, perhaps even offensive."

Ash's eyes shoot back to me. A ball of fire back in my court. I fumble out, "You make a good point, but at the end of the day, the novel is still a tribute, isn't it? In a time where anything other than heterosexuality was frowned upon, this was daring. I'm sure Woolf just used those devices to make the book look like an adventure story, so it wouldn't be censored to the max, so straight people picking it up could get a fun read without realizing how queer it is."

Ash smirks. "Woolf's intentions have nothing to do with my interpretation. That's like"—she tosses me a smirk—"Literary Analysis 101, dude."

Heat pricks my face.

"Not sassing your debate opponent is also Literary Analysis 101," Mr. Hussein says from his desk.

Ash shrugs, unbothered.

I sigh then draw myself up, standing straight. "If I loved someone, I would tell them how beautiful they are. I'm not a writer, but I'd create stuff for them, inspired by them, in my own little way. Art, poetry, film . . ." I clear my throat loudly and watch Ash's jawline get tighter the longer I speak. When I'm done, she throws her gaze toward the windows.

"But you can only see so much of the other person," she says, still looking out the window. "You're in love with the idea of this person, not the actual person. And that's dangerous. That's wrong. Instead of creating a fantastical, idealized version of someone, why not get to know their real self?"

Water wells up in my eyes. I use my newly developed skill of faking an itch and wipe it away. "But what if, try as you might, they don't *let* you get to know them?"

I feel the classroom's eyes swing back to Ash, eager to hear her rebuttal. Her foot bounces up and down for a few beats, and then she mutters, "Maybe they have a good reason for that."

Silence hangs between us. I sense our classmates twitching uncomfortably, but frankly, I don't give a crap about the debate anymore. Ash is still fixated on the window, lips pursed.

When Mr. Hussein speaks, I startle. "Jay, do you have anything to counter that?"

"No, Mr. Hussein." I shake my head. "I think Ash won the debate."

"Congratulations to Ash then." The class claps, but Ash doesn't look celebratory at all. She fans the dog-eared pages of her novel as she walks back to her desk. She sits, then lays down her head.

When the bell rings, Ash leaves immediately. I run after her. "What the hell was that?" I follow her long strides, struggling to keep up. "You embarrassed me in front of the entire class." She turns swiftly around a corner, but I stay glued to her elbow. "All that stuff you said. It was personal, wasn't it? You're still mad at me." I stretch my neck to read her expression, but she tilts her face away from me. Exasperated, I jump in front of her. She tries to go around me but I block her. Finally, she stops.

Ash stares at me. Or, rather, she stares at some spot below my eyes. "What do you want." No question mark.

"I don't *want* anything," I say, slightly breathless. "I mean, I'd like you to not embarrass me in public. And to stop shutting me out. And to talk to me. And let me apologize to you."

"That's a big list of wants for someone who doesn't want anything." She crosses her arms. "You embarrassed me too, you know."

I look away. The bell rings, but neither of us move from where we're standing in the middle of the hallway. People grumble as they step around us to get to their classes. "I could've done better, yeah," I mutter. "I was a jerk, but you've kinda been a jerk, too."

"Kinda?" She laughs. "But yeah. Okay. I guess we're due for a talk. How 'bout you come over after school. Three o'clock." She turns to walk away, but I give her a look. "Oh. Right. You've never been to my place. It's 3509." She strides past me and slaps me on the shoulder. I'm not sure what to make of it, and my palms start sweating all over again, but I guess this is as good a place to start as any.

. . .

It's 3:30. I know because I'm glancing at the time on my new iPod every thirty seconds. Ash's house is small and boxy. It hasn't been painted in years and it looks like it was built in the 1930s. All the dusty maroon curtains are drawn shut, and the yard is overgrown with weeds. It's starting to make sense why she's never asked me over.

The gate clicks open. I take a deep breath, but instead of Ash, a startled middle-aged Asian lady walks out holding garbage bags. She has long, messy, gray-streaked hair and wears an old sweater over pajama pants. She peers at me curiously before sorting garbage and recycling into bins. "Hello," she says in English. "You Ashley's friend, yes?"

"Yeah," I say.

"I am Ashley's mother."

I give her a polite nod. "How do you do, Auntie," I say in Cantonese.

"Oh!" She smiles, and it ages her down ten years. I would recognize that smile anywhere: slightly lopsided, proud, smart. It's identical to Ash's. "What a polite girl!" she says. "And so pretty! Your Chinese is very good too."

I don't think it is, but I just smile and nod. "Thank you, Auntie. I try."

She stands in front of me with her hands clasped in front of her. A small, slight woman, she's shorter than both Ash and me. Ash must get her height from her dad, but everything else I see in her mother. "Ashley says you are a very good friend," says Mrs. Chan. "You help her make videos for some contest, yes?"

"Yeah. I make her skateboarding videos."

Mrs. Chan shakes her head. "Aiii, I don't understand her skateboarding, but she's very good, isn't she? She's always skateboarding. Every single day. I tell her to do homework, but 'No, I want to go skateboarding!'"

"Yes." I smile. "She's very talented. Actually!" I fish my iPod out of my pocket. I've already downloaded most of my edits to it. "I can show you," I tell Mrs. Chan.

She shuffles over and peers over my shoulder. She's close enough that I can feel her breath and smell her. Unfortunately, she doesn't smell very good, like she hasn't showered in several days, and when I turn my head to speak, I can see and smell the oil in her hair. I tap play on the edit we sent to the Skaters Guild. Mrs. Chan falls silent and pays close attention. Her nose whistles with slight intakes of air whenever Ash does a cool trick, which is pretty often. She doesn't breathe at all during the three perfect tre flips in a row, the sick kickflip to manual, or the epic powerslides. She puts her hand over her mouth at one point, gasping as Ash falls hard from a failed back lip. The shot repeats and she sticks the landing this time.

When the video finishes, Mrs. Chan is silent for the few seconds it takes me to stuff my iPod back in my pocket. "She is very good," she says. Her eyes shine and she quickly looks away.

"Mom?" Ash struts up to us, skateboard tucked beneath her arm. "What are you doing out here?"

"Your friend showed me a video of you," says Mrs. Chan. "I did not know you skateboarded like . . . like that."

Ash shrugs. Her mother stares at her for a few seconds, and I stand there awkwardly, wondering if I should leave them alone. Then Mrs. Chan clears her throat and goes back through the gate.

"Your mom's nice," I say when she's gone.

Ash shakes her head. "My mom's a piece of work. I'm sorry you had to deal with her."

"No, I'm serious. She's nice."

We follow her mother into the house, and it turns out they live in the basement suite. The stairs that lead up to the main floor are jammed with boxes. The ceiling is low, the kitchen table covered with a cheap plastic tablecloth and piled high with empty containers. There's a faint smell of cigarettes.

The halls are constricted because they're crammed with unplugged appliances, empty cardboard boxes, and laundry. Ash slips through the clutter with ease, like a cat on a window ledge, and I struggle to follow her. Then she wrestles open a creaky door.

Ash's bedroom is small and narrow, but there's a very generous window looking outside at ground level. A faint breeze rustles a poster of Sleater-Kinney on the wall. Next to it, a bookshelf stuffed with hardcovers and paperbacks. Next to that, a table with no space to write on because it's carrying a plethora of trucks, bearings, and wheels. *Orlando*, dog-eared and scribbled all over in a way that would make any librarian gasp, lies open on the bedside table.

Ash sits down on the unmade bed with an expectant look. I sit at the foot of the bed. She goes first.

"So."

"So."

"What did Donna tell you?"

Straight to the point. I feel like I'm being pushed off a diving board, but I guess this was bound to happen. And it's long overdue. "That, uh, you brought drugs to a party and she got fucked up on them and had to go to the hospital. I'm guessing that's why you had to leave Mackenzie?"

Ash nods.

"So, it's true, then?" I wince inwardly, trying hard to keep a neutral expression.

"Sort of."

I wait for her to continue, but she seems on the fence about talking more. I try another angle. "What's she like, Donna?" Because I can't imagine someone with mostly dog and landscape photos on their Facebook doing drugs at a party.

Ash tilts her head slightly at me. "She's kinda like you, in a way."

This takes me by surprise. "Huh?"

Ash laughs. "No, she has a side of her that is *nothing* like you. But on the surface, yeah. She got top grades. Like, she's one of those people who don't need to study and can still ace a test." I nod. I hate people like that. "But she was also—I guess, she was really bored. You know, with all that extra time when you don't need to study. The fact that she did so well in school made it easy for her to get away with stuff. And I've never met anyone who could get away with *so much*. Like, she'd steal cosmetics and never get caught. She was also *really* good at talking. Which, you know, helped with the stealing. And somehow . . ." Here Ash lets out a regretful sigh. "She convinced me to do stuff with her, like shoplifting. I did it once." She winces. "Hated it. Almost burst into tears when I left the store. And when I hyperventilated from the anxiety, Donna *laughed* at me."

"So why were you friends with her?" I ask as nonjudgmentally as I can.

Ash looks away. "Well, we weren't exactly *friends*, for one. She was charismatic. She could convince anyone to do anything, including adults."

"If you guys weren't friends . . ."

Ash stares at the plaid pattern of her comforter, tracing the lines with a finger. "We weren't dating, if that's what you think. I found it weird that she didn't have a boyfriend because all the popular girls at Mac had boyfriends. So, when I asked and she confided in me that she liked girls, well, I felt special. And I thought . . ." Ash clears her throat and sniffs. "Well, I thought *I* was special."

I shift into a cross-legged position on the bed. "So, what happened at the party?"

Ash crosses her legs too, and one of her knees starts bouncing up and down. There's a hole in her jeans there, and she plays with the frayed thread. "It was Donna's idea to go to the Grade 12's after-prom. I didn't really care, honestly. Simon was having a party that same night with people I actually knew from skating, and I never cared much for the Grade 12s. Anyway, they told us we needed to bring drugs to get in. Pills, acid, something fancy. Enough for everyone. And"—she looks at me—"you know me, Jay. I don't touch anything that doesn't grow from the ground. But Donna gave me an ultimatum: we're getting drugs and we're going to this party or she'll never hang out with me again. And, well, I wasn't thinking."

She avoids my eyes as she continues. "We go to the skate park—together, that's the part she always leaves out—and we talk to this sketchy guy that everyone knows can get you anything. That was the first time I ever talked to him, I swear. Donna wants to get ecstasy first, but I'm scared of pills, so we compromise. Acid. He gives us a sheet and Donna pays 'cause, you know, I'm broke. All the way to the party, Donna's pissed 'cause she thinks we got ripped off. I tell her all you need for acid is a tab or two, but she says how do you even know each tab has acid on it?

"When we get to the party, everyone's impressed because they didn't think we could pull it off. Honestly, I think they just wanted an excuse to get rid of us because no one's even interested in the acid. I tell Donna to take just one tab, not drink, and see how she feels in an hour. I figure 'cause that's what you do with edibles, it makes sense.

"We get separated 'cause Donna wants to hang with these older guys. Then an hour into the party I find her slumped over the toilet throwing up. At first, I thought she was just wasted. But then she starts panicking . . ." She speaks faster now. "Jay, she was absolutely hysterical. Freaking the fuck out. I couldn't make sense of what she was saying other than 'help me, help me' and 'get me out of here.' I try to, but she won't budge. I ask the people around us for help, but they just laugh it off and say drink water. I was really worried though." She swallows and looks at me, eyes watery. "You have to understand, Jay. She was my best friend at the time, and I thought my best friend was gonna die.

"Keep in mind we were, like, fifteen. I didn't know how tripping works. I was scared for Donna—like, what if she died and I didn't do anything? So I call the ambulance and flush what's left of the acid— which wasn't much—down the toilet. I expected some paramedics to drive us home or something, but instead, a fleet of fuckin' cop cars show up. They must've heard the party on the phone and gotten suspicious. Some people get busted for weed and underage drinking and when it turns out the Grade 10 kid was the one who called the cops . . . well."

Her voice catches a little. Tentatively, I slide myself over so that I'm right next to her. She doesn't seem to mind, so I put a hand between her shoulder blades. Still no response, so I gently rub circles on her back. Then Ash sniffles and lays her head against my chest, right under my chin. My heart skips a beat.

"Donna says someone must have spiked her drink, but there's no evidence of that. Her family thinks I'm responsible, somehow, because duh, I'm the skate punk and she's the honor-roll kid. But I was stone-cold sober during that party and there wasn't anything on me, not even weed, not even cigs. And *I* was the one who called for help. So yeah."

"So you were in the clear?" I say.

Ash scoffs. "Legally, there wasn't much they could do. Socially? Totally different story. A rumor starts spreading that the Grade 10 kid who told on everybody was seen flushing drugs down the toilet. Even before the party, I'd been called a lesbian once or twice. So now the story that gets told at Mackenzie is that I'm some jealous dyke who drugged my crush at a party to hook up with her. Then was dumb enough to call the cops over a bad acid trip.

"Grade 11 is hell. Hands down the worst year of my life. Donna treats me like I don't exist. People knock books and food out of my hands and call me all sorts of homophobic slurs. The only people on my side are Dezzy and Matt and Logan. And Simon tried to give me advice and shit. But there was only so much they could do; none of us have ever been at the top of the school hierarchy.

"So, eventually I just stopped going to school. I'd just leave home and go skate. The school tried to get me to make amends or something with Donna, but fuck that. So they gave up on trying and suggested I start fresh in a new school.

"It just so happens my dad's boss lives here and needed a tenant so he makes a deal with him. Reduced rent for shitty hours and I get to go to school on the west side. Dad's either at work or asleep when I'm home, so we don't cross paths too often. Which is good because whenever we do, he makes sure to remind me of all the sacrifices he's made to keep me in school. And here's the worst part." Ash sniffs. "He's right."

I wait for her to continue, but she doesn't, so I guess she's done. "I'm so sorry you went through all that," I say, though I can practically hear the hollow knock of those words. I'm suddenly super tired, like I just went on a week-long hike and need a long, long nap. "You could've told me, you know," I add.

"I thought if you knew, you'd stop being friends with me."

On the contrary, I almost feel a sense of relief. Ash isn't a bad person. She was *never* a bad person. I feel terrible for ever considering that. I also wished Ash would've told me everything sooner, right when we met. But at the same time, a story like this is something you gotta earn. "You're absolutely still my friend," I tell her. She's still leaning against me so I squeeze her. Oddly enough, she laughs, the sound all bubbly because she's crying a little. We both are.

She squeezes me back then lets me go and wipes my face with her sleeve. She pinches a strand of hair that's hanging over my face and tucks it back. "I like you," she says, a statement that fills me with so much warmth I feel like a fireplace, "but you and I are not exactly cut from the same cloth, you know? Your parents give a shit about you. You're a straight-A student and so are your friends and your sister. You're not Donna—not by a long shot—but you're still in a totally different league."

I shake my head. "I don't fucking care."

She grins. "I don't fucking care either. It's just what it is."

We hug again then something crashes outside. Ash stiffens in my arms and a series of thundering footsteps rage toward her room. "Chan Hoi Lei! I told you not to put this behind the door!"

"It's my dad. He means my skateboard," Ash murmurs.

A man throws open the door, noisily eating a banana. He's dressed in an old T-shirt and work jeans, and his full head of black hair suggests he's probably younger than my dad. When he sees me, he pauses mid-chew, frowns, and then keeps chewing with his mouth open. "Who are you," he barks at me, no question mark. I freeze too, terrified, not sure if I should introduce myself (giving away my name feels . . . vulnerable) and debating whether I should call him "sir."

"She's my friend," Ash says, her voice dull and flat, and I'm relieved she's answering for me. "She came by to drop something off."

He gestures at Ash with his chin. "Where's your mother."

"Sleeping, I think." I've never heard Ash's voice so *small* before, not even during that last fight with Blake.

"I told you not to bring friends home," Ash's dad says in Cantonese.

"Dad," Ash says back in Cantonese, "she's Chinese."

"Hello, Uncle," I say hoarsely, also in Cantonese.

Her dad looks at me. "Make some instant noodles," he says to Ash then steps away.

Ash leans over and closes the door behind him. "Maybe you should lock it," I say.

Ash shakes her head. "He took off all the locks when we moved in."

I wince. "I should probably go."

Ash nods, but then she perks up, remembering something. "I forgot to tell you, we hit a thousand subscribers yesterday."

"Really?" Then I catch on. "'We'?"

She taps my knee with her knee. "Yeah," she says. "We make a pretty good team."

I want to kiss her, but it doesn't feel like the right time. Plus, I'm terrified her dad will see us. So I just smile at her in silence. Not awkward silence, victory silence.

"It's awesome that the channel's doing so well," Ash continues, "but the competition's pretty much over for me. Blake's not gonna drive me and I still need to pay him back for the guitar. He's threatening to call the cops if I don't."

I squeeze her elbow. "We'll find a way."

"How?"

"Well, I think I'm pretty resourceful, having netted a thousand subscribers," I say. "And you're not alone. *We're* not alone."

"What do you mean?"

"We have friends."

Ash walks me out. When we get to the kitchen, Ash's dad has his head in the refrigerator. He snaps up when we walk in. "I told you to buy milk. You didn't buy milk." He looks at us—well, Ash, mostly—and his eyes are black.

Ash stares at the ground. "Sorry," she mutters.

He slams the fridge door closed. "Do you know how hard I work all day? I come home and all I want is something to eat, yet my daughter won't even bother to boil water for instant noodles. It's just boiling water! So I pour a bowl of cereal, go in the fridge, and guess what? I can't even have *cereal* because my mentally challenged daughter can't even remember to buy the milk."

I shoot Ash a look, but her mouth is a line drawn taut. "I'm sorry," she says again.

"Be grateful you have me. Without me, you wouldn't survive a day in the world. You have no sense of responsibility. All you do is play with your skateboarding toys and dress like a gang member, steal my cigarettes and skip school . . ."

I must be invisible to him. Ash flicks her head toward the door and mouths "goodbye." She closes the door behind me quickly, but I can still hear muffled yelling from the other side.

I go home and spend the rest of that day thinking. Of all the sneakiness I've gotten up to this year, going to Kelowna will be my—to use a phrase I learned in AP English—magnum opus.

I'm sitting at my desk, staring out the window in a trance, when Wendy knocks on my door. She holds up a big envelope. "Ga Jie." Her eyes are wide, her mouth slack. "This is for you." The envelope's already open. "Sorry," Wendy mutters. "I opened it because I was curious. My bad."

I'm too distracted by my thoughts to be mad at her, so I take the paper out. I have to read the first sentence a few times and each word drops on me like a stone:

Dear Ms. Jessica Wong,

Congratulations! We are honored to inform you that you have been awarded the Grand Entrance Scholarship to the Amsterdam Institute of Art Bachelor of Fine Arts Program in September 2011. Your award amount is €10,000, renewable each year contingent upon your grade point average. We were highly impressed with your application and will be looking forward to you joining our 2011–2012 cohort.

Sincerely,
Anika Visser
Head of Enrolment, Amsterdam Institute of Art

The world goes quiet and my hands drop to my lap. Wendy is smiling at me. "Aren't you excited?!" she says. I stare at her. I don't remember the last time, any time, she was genuinely proud of my achieving something.

"Yeah." I carefully fold up the letter and place it back in the envelope. The Institute must have really liked that I edit I made, the video where nothing happens and everything happens. "Yeah," I say again. I feel weird, like my head is empty. All I can manage to come up with is "Yeah, this is pretty great."

CHAPTER 13

I start a group chat with Dezzy, Logan, Matt, and Ash so we can brainstorm ways to make money. Ash needs to get to Kelowna in a few weeks, but she also needs to pay off Blake's guitar. Unfortunately, Ash can't get more shifts at Simon's restaurant, so we need to get creative.

I look in my piggy bank at a lifetime's worth of birthday, Christmas, and Lunar New Year lai see. There's a lot here, but something holds me back from simply offering all this money to Ash. I don't think she'll take it well. Besides, €10,000 is a lot but it's still not enough to live on. I should save what I can. So I google "how to make money as a teen" and present my findings the next weekend everyone is at the skate park. Even Simon joins us.

"Sell stuff on Craigslist."

"Already done that," says Ash. "No more stuff to sell."

"Lemonade stand."

Logan snorts. "No one buys lemonade off anyone older than ten."

"Paper route."

"This isn't the eighties," Dezzy says. "Paper delivery people are adult dudes in vans."

"Babysitting." When there's a collective groan, I say, "Petsitting. Housesitting. *Some kinda sitting.*"

"I don't know anyone with pets," Matt says, "but I can draw up an ad and put it around my apartment complex?"

"No human babies, please," Ash says, wrinkling her nose.

I get to my last viable item. "Busking."

The guys look at each other. "I play guitar," says Dezzy.

"But you suck," Logan says. "I play bass in band, though."

"If we busk downtown, Jay and I can sell prints of our art," Matt says.

"You guys shouldn't do this."

We all whip around to Ash.

"*I* was the one who tossed Blake's guitar into the pool," she mutters, kicking the ground. "That's on me."

The rest of us exchange glances and I think of my lai see money again. Then Simon says, "Simple. We'll take a quarter of what we earn busking. I could use some beer money." He chuckles. "Oh, and I have an idea on how you can contribute, Ash."

I tell Ma Mi and De Di that the school is having a fundraiser for the next few weekends and that I'll attend all of them to complete my volunteering hours for graduation. "I thought you completed all your hours last summer," Ma Mi says, scowling. "I drove you to all those beach cleanups."

I shrug. "They updated the requirements."

"They updated the requirements and *didn't tell you*? The Canadian school system is so disorganized."

I manage to convince Ma Mi not to give the school an angry phone call by saying it was me who missed the fine print. She's annoyed, but it's not that many hours and I'll be home for dinner every time.

That weekend, we set up our clandestine busking station at Waterfront. It's warm and breezy. The tourists are already there, pointing at the mountains and wearing their "Canada, Eh?" T-shirts. Dezzy and Logan open their instrument cases to collect cash.

Matt and I hang prints of our artwork on a clothesline between two lamp posts. I had assumed Matt would sell copies of his comics, but he opens a duffel bag of vibrant prints instead. They're only postcard-size and printed with a shitty school printer, but the rich, saturated color palettes encased by bold, flowing black lines are mesmerizing. It's all two-dimensional, but it looks so alive, breathing, dynamic.

"I didn't know you paint," I say.

"Hey, us artists, we gotta diversify, right? Comics are great for the Internet, but paintings sell on the street." He's got a point there. "This is called Woodland style," he says, pointing to the images. "I learned it from my uncle who learned it from my grandpa. My uncle's, like, the best Ojibwe artist alive. I used to follow him around in his studio when my family visited him. My siblings and cousins preferred BMX bikes and chasing girls, so I think he saw me as his apprentice."

We call ourselves "local independent artists" (Simon says they're good buzzwords) and it works because tourists gobble up our stuff.

Simon gets Ash to stand between him and Logan with a cardboard sign: CHALLENGE ME TO A SKATE TRICK. $1 IF I CAN DO IT.

"What if someone, like, challenges me to do a friggin' backflip?" Ash mumbles, bouncing from foot to foot.

Simon shrugs. "Most people don't know trick names. Just . . . don't do that."

"Do what?"

"Stand there all derpy with your mouth open. Yeah, like that. Stop it. Do some freestyle tricks or something to catch people's eye."

Ash does what Simon says, and sure enough, it turns some heads.

A girl comes up and asks Ash if she can do a "flip-the-board thing," to which Ash does a kickflip and earns a loonie. A little kid asks if she can do an ollie. A toonie this time. Some office workers challenge her to a tre flip. Ash doesn't get it on the first try, but they give her a full five-dollar bill anyway.

Meanwhile, Logan and Dezzy take turns with their instruments. Logan is decent. Dezzy, on the other hand, while he can play chords fine, sings like a crow that smokes a pack a day. It's so bad that Simon quietly convinces him to pack it up after two crooning numbers.

When the sun starts to dip, we pour all our change into one of the guitar cases and count up a little less than fifty dollars. "What do y'all say?" Matt says. "Worth doing again?" There are mostly shrugs around the circle.

The following Wednesday, I'm packing up my stuff when David walks up to my locker and just stands there. After I stare at him with raised eyebrows, he finally asks, "What are you doing this weekend?" I tell him and it's his eyebrows' turn to fly up. "That sounds interesting. Way more interesting than tennis. Can I come?"

"You wanna bunk off tennis?"

He chuckles. "I 'injured' my knee last week," he says with air quotes. "I hate that place. I want to burn it to the ground."

"Don't let Ms. Watanabe hear you," I say. "You don't mind hanging out with Ash's friends?"

He shrugs. "Can't be worse than tennis."

Ash can't go that weekend because, cool enough, she's landed a dogsitting gig at Matt's apartment complex. So it's just me and Matt selling art, Logan playing bass, and Dezzy occasionally smoking with Logan. The day is slow, the sky is gray, and in an hour and a half, we've only made ten dollars and twenty cents. That's right, not even a full quarter, just two measly dimes.

David hangs awkwardly behind us, pacing and stretching. It suddenly hits me. I don't think David has any guy friends. It's not like he doesn't talk to guys. He does, but in the same way I did before I met Ash's friends: to coordinate group projects, to ask them what the homework is, that sorta thing.

"Jeez," Matt says, yawning and sliding down in the camping chair he was smart enough to bring. "Business absolutely sucks balls today."

I groan in agreement then feel David shuffle over to us. He clears his throat. Matt looks up curiously and David's eyes dash to the opposite side of his face. "Um, you guys got an iPod? Maybe you can play some music. Maybe that'll, like, attract some energy. Or something."

"Logan's playing music," I say.

"But he's just playing the bass part. I think you need, like, a full recording sort of thing."

"Dezzy's got a portable speaker in his backpack," Logan yells over. "Because he can't play shit."

Dezzy walks over to him and punches him in the shoulder. Logan punches him back, and soon they're scrabbling all over the place, cussing and laughing. David stares at them like he's contemplating whether to call the cops.

Matt sighs and goes digging in Dezzy's backpack. He takes out a portable iPod speaker and places it in Logan's guitar case then juts his chin at David. "Since this is your idea and those two are being useless, you got an iPod?"

David looks like he's been summoned to answer a question he wasn't expecting in front of the class. He looks at me, but I point at my artwork to indicate that I'm busy. Though, to be honest, I just don't want to put my new birthday iPod out in the open. So David reluctantly fishes out his Nano and hands it to Matt, who nods his thanks and docks it. The K-pop that comes out is louder than I thought the size of the speaker would be capable of, and David dashes forward to change the song.

"Wait, no! I love that song!" Matt says, pushing his hands away from the click wheel.

David blinks at him. "You like Big Bang?"

"Yeah!" Matt grins. "I *love* K-pop."

David just stares. Matt—with his lip piercings and chain belts—doesn't look like the kind of person who likes K-pop. Then again, who says people have to look a certain way to like K-pop? Who says they even have to be Asian? Besides, Matt has already outed himself as someone who likes Demi Lovato and Britney Spears. That's quirkier, I think.

"G-Dragon? I have a *massive* crush on him," says Matt, eyes sparkling.

David starts to relax a little. "Yeah?"

"Oh yeah. If I had the money, I'd dress up like him for Halloween." He thumps a fist against his chest, closes his eyes, and smiles. "'Heartbreaker' broke my heart."

"Yo." Logan flicks his hand against the back of David's shoulder. "I can't play this, man. Can you put on, like, Green Day or something?"

"Green Day?" I can practically see the sweat beads cascading down David's neck. He definitely does not have Green Day.

But the music has caught a few people's attention. Some Asian tourists point at us. A few people stop to look at our art. My art hasn't been selling well, which is disheartening. But maybe that's a sign that I shouldn't focus on it. Maybe I should focus on the thousand subscribers I earned through my filmmaking instead.

Logan shrugs and walks off for a cigarette break. An elderly couple buys a handful of Matt's prints, making him beam. He gives David a thumbs-up.

To my surprise, David beams back. He seems more relaxed now, his shoulders no longer scrunched up. His foot even starts tapping, and when the next song begins, I catch small, familiar movements in his hands and knees. Now, I'm no hardcore K-pop fan, but I've seen my share of music videos. You just do when so many of your classmates are Asian. "Dude, are you doing the 'Lucifer' dance?" I say.

David freezes and turns tomato red, but it's too late because Matt has noticed it too. "Dude!" he says, standing up. "You're doing that SHINee dance!"

David stares at us, chin ever so slightly bobbing to the beat. Then, it's like our watching him gives him a burst of encouragement because he counts a few beats and explodes into dance. Like, *full-on dance*. And it's *good*. Snappy when he needs to be, his joints popping and locking. Then liquid like oil, feet sweeping across the pavement, every movement precisely calibrated. David is dancing and he is fucking brilliant at it. David, the kid who cried under the bleachers when he got a C+ in gym. David, the kid who'd rather burn down his tennis club than play in it. My mouth falls open in amazement.

Logan and Dezzy return from their smoke break and stare. We all do. David's clearly practiced this as hard as Wendy practices Paganini. He's getting noticed, and a small crowd drums up around us. Logan kicks the open guitar case closer to him and people start throwing in coins. Even bills.

David performs the entire song, and when he's done we all yelp and clap and jump into the air. I hold my fist up to David, and he looks confused, so I take his hand and pound it. He smiles. There's nearly twenty extra dollars in Logan's guitar case. "Dude," I say. "I didn't know you danced. What, do you have a secret life or something?"

David leans forward on his knees, panting. "You would've seen this if you stayed on Halloween."

So he *was* dancing epically. "*That's* why everyone was calling you a legend?" He nods. "Gosh, Dave. I'm so sorry I missed that. Like, I'm genuinely, seriously—"

He shakes his head. "Forget about it. You've seen it now."

I nod and there's a weight off my shoulders that I didn't know was there. "How do you even find the time to practice? Aren't you studying, like, all the time?"

David shrugs. "Sometimes I can't sleep."

"Man, that was amazing!" Matt says, sidling up next to me. He holds up a hand, David holds his up in return, and Matt smacks it so hard David winces, but he keeps smiling. I don't remember the last time David was this happy, this proud of himself. Even after his offer from Columbia.

That Monday, David and I take our bag of coins and cash to Ash to crunch the numbers. I tell Ash that most of it is David's doing, and I expect her not to believe me. Instead, she smirks at David and says, "I knew you had a wild side to you." We dump out our earnings on the coffee table of the Grade 12 lounge, together with the fifty bucks Ash made dogsitting that weekend.

"This should more than cover gas and food for four people," I say. Ash is super nervous and wants as many people to come with her as possible.

"Wouldn't the bus be cheaper?" David says.

Ash shakes her head. "Then we'd have to stay at a hotel. They're expensive and they might not let minors in. Besides, I don't have a credit card."

"And mine's connected to my dad's account," I say. "So we're planning to drive and sleep in the car. No paper trail."

David tenses. "Isn't that illegal or something?"

Ash shrugs. "Not if we don't attract attention."

"By the way, Simon told me to tell you he can't drive us," I say. "He's got a shift that weekend and he really needs the money. He can lend us the car, but we still need a driver and I only have my learner's permit."

Ash groans and slumps onto the couch with her head between her knees. "How did I fuck this up?" she growls.

David shakes his head. "You didn't fuck up, you got the fuck away from a fucked-up situation." I nod in agreement, putting aside the fact that I've never heard David drop so many f-bombs in succession.

"Thanks," Ash mutters, "but leaving an asshole doesn't drive a car."

David clears his throat. "I can drive, you know."

"You only have your probationary license," I say. "You can't drive non-family members."

David says, "Well, we're already breaking who knows how many laws by sleeping in a car. Besides, Ash can be my, uh, sister. So long as I don't put the novice sign up, who's gonna check? And we're Asian—we can pass for thirteen or thirty, definitely thirty if I wear my tennis clothes." I'm shocked. David isn't one for breaking the rules. So I just stare at him.

Ash swivels around to me. "Okay. And you're definitely coming."

I had assumed so, but hearing it said out loud fills me with a new rumble of excitement.

"That leaves one more seat," says Ash.

"Matt," David says without missing a beat. When we whip our heads at him, he shrugs and says, "Well, he knows stuff, yeah? Like, how to read a map. And stuff."

Ash laughs. "Oh man. He told you about the time he and his cousins snuck into a music festival, didn't he?" She rolls her eyes when he laughs and nods. "I swear that incident is, like, his only personality." I try to remember when Matt told David this story on the weekend. I must have missed it.

When David and I walk to geography class later, I ask him how on earth he's suddenly so cool. "Well," he says, "I don't know if you've noticed, but this has been the hardest year of my life." I wince, feeling guilty again that I haven't exactly been present for him. But guilt-tripping me doesn't seem to be his goal. He just says, "So fuck it."

. . .

Of course, there's still the matter of dealing with our parents. Which isn't a big deal with Ash and Matt. Matt's parents are seasonal workers who are currently away, and Ash's parents are used to her pulling disappearing acts on the regular.

David and I, however, are on tighter leashes. But David has an idea. We take bubble tea and go to Sophie's the weekend before the competition. Her parents are out.

"Hey, Soph," David says, "we need a massive favor." Sophie nods, loudly slurping the pudding in her bubble tea while David fidgets. "I'm going away with Jay for a weekend and we need you to cover for us. Can we tell our parents that we're staying over at your place for a finals study marathon?"

Sophie looks at us, still slurping her tea. "Where are you two going?"

"Kelowna," I say, and her eyes go wide. "We're driving Ash to her skateboarding competition. It's very important," I add, somewhat unconvincingly.

Sophie looks at David. "And you're chill with this?"

"You know how I keep saying I want to do a big fuck-you to my dad at some point in my life?" So David's been really vocal about this. "This is that point."

"Huh." Sophie sits back thoughtfully then says, "You know what, I support that."

"Thanks," we say at the same time, and David tweaks a grin at me.

"But what do I tell my parents? What if your parents call my parents?"

"Your parents are super cool and liberal," David says, "so tell them Jay and I are going to an LGBTQ+ youth conference and we don't want our parents to know. Tell them it's all the way out in Abbotsford and we're staying with friends."

Sophie nods, slowly. When she sees my puzzled look, she sighs. "My mom has a bit of a savior complex." Then she smacks her lips and says, "Tell you what, let's do a photoshoot. Right now. Take out your books, sit around the dining table. Pretend we're deep at work. This way, if your parents call you, you can send them a convincing picture."

David gets to work right away. I just stand there and say, "Wow, Sophie, I'm impressed. I didn't know you . . . schemed."

Sophie scoffs. "I'm not *just* a nerd, you know."

After that, there's one more ally I need to meet with.

I call her into my room a few days before we leave. I get the urge to turn off the lights, get under the bedcovers, and talk around a flashlight, like we used to do when we were kids. But that feels like a lifetime ago. Instead, Wendy walks in quietly, closes the door, and sits down like she's attending an admissions interview. She nods seriously when I tell her my plan, never breaking eye contact. She doesn't say anything judgy or smart; she doesn't say a word at all.

I hand her a piece of paper. "Okay, I wrote down a list of possible situations and what to say in each of them."

She gravely takes the paper, as if receiving a contract.

"Wendy," I say, "can you handle this?"

She's deep into reading my list. "Uh-huh."

I push the paper away. "Seriously. And not just *can* you but *will* you. *Will* you handle this?"

She sighs. "Yes." When I continue staring at her, waiting for her to change her mind, she says, "This is important. My getting drunk wasn't, and you still bailed me out of that one. So, yeah, I'll handle this. Just promise me you'll be safe, okay?"

"I'll try my best. David's a good driver."

Over the next few days, I oscillate between unusual calm and sheer terror. Sometimes, I snap out of whatever I'm doing and think, *Huh, I'm running away from home.* Other times, I go into a spiraling rabbit hole of *Shit, what if my parents find out?* They will if we so much as get pulled over for going five kilometers over the speed limit. They will because I'll cave. I imagine Ma Mi having a heart attack and the whole family spending the night at the ER. Ma Mi will ban me from ever leaving the house and De Di will live in his office forever and never speak to me again.

I can't sleep at all the night before the great escape. I keep cycling between a feeling of impending doom and the realization that my bed is the warmest, safest, most comfortable place in the universe. When I hear the first birds at dawn, I realize that the me one year ago would never in a million years do something like this.

I laugh out loud.

CHAPTER 14

David and I wait by my gate while Ash uses the sidewalk cracks to practice. David looks at least twenty-five in a button-down shirt, gelled hair, and glasses. I wear my all-black band concert outfit and tie back my hair, which has grown into a messy shag that I need to lop off again the next time I'm in East Van. I feel ridiculous and uncool, but we look like two random adults on a mundane errand, and that's what matters. Ash, on the other hand, is rocking fresh red streaks.

A green station wagon screeches around the corner. Matt hangs out the passenger window as Simon drives. "Hey, David! Check out your horse!"

David makes a fluttery, nervous giggling sound.

Simon jumps out of the car, walks up to David, and says sternly, "You better take care of Carlene. Or else." When David turns pale, he laughs and claps him on the back.

As Ash and I load our stuff into the trunk, I catch Ash's I-need-to-talk-to-you eyes. "Are you sure you can do this?" she says quietly. Her face is the most serious I've ever seen.

"Of course," I say. I've never been so certain of something in my whole life.

"You know . . ." Ash lowers her voice. "I had to forge my mom's signature on the waiver for this. Because I'm under nineteen."

She says it like it's some kind of confession, and for a moment, I feel a stir of discomfort. But it's an old feeling, almost nostalgic. I take a breath and say, "You gotta do what you gotta do." Ash stares at me, as if still waiting for me to change my mind. "This is happening," I tell her again. "I promise."

She smiles weakly, and we slip in behind Matt and David. Simon tells Ash to make him proud. We wave goodbye to him while David pulls out from the curb. He drives at exactly the city speed limit, religiously uses his turn signals, and shoulder checks three times when he changes lanes. We drive in silence until we get to the highway, as if breathing too loudly will break the spell of getting away with our plan. Then, David merges into the eastbound traffic of the Trans-Canada Highway and it's like the rumbling of the road beneath us triggers a collective exhale of relief. We're not sneaking out. We're going on an adventure.

Matt digs around the glove department until he comes up with a CD. "Hey, it's the new Arcade Fire album!" He pops it into the stereo. I look sideways at Ash. She's got her hood up, eyes glued to the window. Staring hard, but I don't think she's admiring the mountain view. I send her a text:

u ok?

But her phone must be off because there's no buzz. So I look out the window myself, listening to Arcade Fire sing about growing up in the boring suburbs with no way out.

Hydro towers whip past us. Civilization grows sparse. We pass the

Langley farmlands, the Abbotsford suburbs, and the quiet Chilliwack streets. Big-box stores turn into warehouses turn into sprawling fields and then it's just trees and hills. When we get to Hope, we stop at a gas station to pee and Matt loads up on snacks and pop. Past Hope, the highway narrows but the drive is scenic and quiet. Matt and David start a deep and serious *Final Fantasy* discussion as if Ash and I don't exist.

I haven't told Ash about Amsterdam yet. I've been working on Project Europe the entire year, and I know Ash will be happy for me. And/or secretly disappointed. As weird as this sounds, I'm disappointed, too. I don't know why. It's like my coordinates have changed in the past few weeks. I'm not where I used to be and my destination has shifted.

If I leave, what will become of Ash and me? Not like we're *anything* right now. I've done nothing but study my ass off in recent weeks, and she's done nothing but train. Our paths have only crossed briefly at school and during those weekends at Waterfront. We haven't had "the talk." Even though it's been hanging over us like a giant asterisk.

Being in a relationship. With Ash. Can we do that? Can *I* do that? I've never been in a relationship. When I used to imagine being in one, I assumed it'd be with someone I met at university, like how my parents met. Someone who gets good grades and whose parents could become friends with my parents.

But Ash isn't going to university, and even if I weren't going to Amsterdam, the thought of dating someone gives me heart palpitations. I realize I've never really thought about dating because I've always seen it as something far in my future. And I've definitely never thought about dating a *girl*. I don't know any same-sex couples and I rarely even glimpse them in public. What if Ash and I get harassed on the street or kicked out of restaurants?

It all feels so real, so fast, and so serious. I look sideways at Ash's hooded head slumped against the window. I can still feel how it felt to kiss her that night because I've been replaying it over and over in my head whenever I lose focus studying or get bored in class. I wonder how Ash feels about it. Does Ash even want to date me? Or did she just feel like kissing me that night?

. . .

By the time we get to Kelowna, it's past sunset and my ass hurts. Logan had loaned us some camping gear and told us to try a campground— they're cheaper and seem less picky about age—but the campground we find is full. So we park at the very edge of an empty parking lot of a big-box store.

We take some camp chairs and snacks to a nearby park and settle in a quiet spot. Ash pulls out a huge bottle of Baileys. "Stole it off Blake a while ago," she says. "Call it alimony."

"That's perfect. 'Cause I"—Matt grins and pulls a small package out from his jacket—"have these." Ash takes the package, frowns, and sniffs. "Cuban cigars," Matt says. "Found them at the bottom of a box of my parents' wedding photos."

We use Logan's camp stove to heat up water for instant coffee then sit around a lantern in our camp chairs, smoking cigars and drinking Irish coffee like Mafia men. Even David tries a sip of spiked coffee before spitting it out. He smokes his cigar like a pro though.

Matt points his cigar at him and says, "So. When are you starting your dance career, D-Dragon?"

David laughs. "Um. Never?"

Matt looks genuinely offended. "Why not?"

David scoffs. "Because my dad would kill me? Because dancing isn't a job? Because I have to go to Columbia?"

"You *have* to go to Columbia?" Matt frowns. "Why do you have to do exactly as your dad says?"

"Because he's my dad," David says, like he's stating the obvious.

"Shit, if I did everything my dad said . . ." Ash doesn't finish the sentence, just shakes her head. Then she squints through the cigar smoke at David and says, "Look, Dave, the thing you gotta understand is that your dad is just a person, a mere mortal like you and I, Matt or Jay. He might think he's right about everything, but *no one's* right about everything. Like, that's just a fact."

I expect David to call Ash plain wrong, but he doesn't. "I don't know what else to do, though," he says.

"So go to Columbia," Matt tells him, "and figure it out. Study weird things, meet lots of people, fuck around." He shrugs. "It's not like he's following you to New York."

David gestures at Matt with his chin. "What are you doing after high school?"

"Probably a general program at a community college," Matt says, leaning back in his chair.

"I thought you were an artist, like Jay."

"Yeah. But I like to keep my options open." Matt shrugs. "I like cartoons. But I also like painting. And music. And video games."

"You should go to Korea and audition for one of those boy bands," Ash says to David, taking a huge draw off her cigar. I don't know how she does it. Mine tastes like old-people furniture. I wonder if they're from Matt's *grandparents'* wedding. "I think K-pop's gonna be the next big thing. 2NE1 is on YouTube's frontpage." She sits up, suddenly excited. "Mark my words, dudes. The next decade, we're gonna see Asians on screens everywhere. In music, movies, sports, skateboarding. And not just in kung fu movies or as the class nerd. White people are gonna take us seriously. Asian invasion!"

Matt raises his mug in solidarity and Ash high-fives all of us. I love it when she gets like this, and I make a mental note to get her and Wendy to hang out. I have a feeling they have more in common than they think.

Dezzy had loaned us his portable speaker, so Matt puts on some music for us to vibe to. It's a good night, full of laughter, minor tipsiness, and conversations. I don't remember the content, only the feelings. I'm stoked, Ash is stoked, we're all stoked. It's hard to put into words what exactly "stoke" is, but once you feel it, you know it. And I don't think I've ever felt this stoked.

Since it's getting dark and it's been a long day, we start heading to bed at around ten. Matt curls up in a sleeping bag in the popped trunk. David leans the driver's seat back and covers everything but his nose with a blanket. I fold myself under David's head across the back seat and Ash copies him, leaning back in the passenger seat. A gentle rain thrums against the roof of the car. That, and my friends breathing softly around me, lulls me to sleep.

· · ·

After a greasy breakfast at McDonald's, we head to the skate park. We get there early so Ash can warm up, and it's already bustling with bodies. Grown dudes carving bowls splattered with graffiti and throwing huge tricks off the staircases. Women with arms smothered in tattoos setting up tents. Gangs of teenagers hanging out and being loud on the sidelines. There's even a DJ spinning music. The weather is gorgeous and bright, not at all like the cloudy, DJless, and almost lazy skate park days I'm used to.

An energy drink company is giving out free samples, so Matt, David, and I slurp down a bunch and get all hyper. Ash skips out on it, thinking all the caffeine on top of her morning coffee will make her nervous. I notice that she's barely talking, just watching people while her leg jostles up and down.

We find a place on the grass to sit, and Ash says, "Guys, what if I don't win this? I need the money. I gotta move out."

We look around at each other. "There's more than one way to get money," David says.

"Exactly. David got money from dancing on the street," Matt says, and David promptly blushes.

Ash jumps from foot to foot. "This is my one chance to do something, get somewhere. I've got no skills other than this, and my grades are shit."

"You're good at English," I offer, but this doesn't seem to comfort her.

"I'm sure something will open up at Simon's restaurant," Matt says.

Ash looks at me then nods away from the group. "Jay?"

I follow her into a corner under a tree. She's jittering so much she looks like she's shivering, even though it's sunny and hot. "You'll do fine," I say.

She laughs nervously. "You sure? Because the last time I skated under pressure, I incurred a grand's worth of guitar damage."

"You'll do fine," I say again. "Those guys were posers. But here . . ." I look around. "The vibes are great," I say, and I mean it. I don't feel out of place here. Everyone's hanging out with their friends to watch some damn good skateboarding, and we're all stoked.

"But what if the Guild people just wanted a good laugh? What if they tricked me into coming? Fuck, I'm gonna fuck up and die, aren't I? I'll be the Skate Derp of East Van—"

I scoop her into a hug and squeeze hard enough that she has no more breath to finish her thought. She hugs me back even harder. I stroke her back. "You're not gonna die. And if you become the Skate Derp of East Van, I'll make T-shirts."

Ash shakes with a phlegmy laugh. "Jay, I fucking love you."

I stiffen, and when she lets go I feel like jelly.

Ash says, "I'm gonna miss you when you go to Europe."

"It's not set in stone yet," I say quickly, but she doesn't seem to hear me.

Ash runs off to warm up and I join the guys on the grass to watch. The park has standard street features like rails, ledges, hips, and stair sets. It's stuff that Ash is familiar with, but no two features are the same. Kinks, textures, and small variations in height and length can throw a skater off. Still, Ash always adapts well. A few kids are hanging out on the sidelines, arguing with their parents. When Ash flies past them with a huge 180, they shut up and stare.

Matt claps and cheers every time Ash lands something then yells unsolicited advice when she doesn't—mostly 'go faster' and 'commit!'"

David touches my folded knee with his drink. "Hey."

"Hey."

"You know, I was looking at Ash's channel the other night, and those videos are impressive."

"Well, obviously." I gesture at Ash, but David shakes his head.

"No, I meant the way you shot the clips and stitched them together. Even the music you picked. I would have thought a professional had done it."

I shrug. "I have a good camera."

David groans. "Don't you get what I'm trying to say, Jay? You're good at this. Film editing, cinematography, whatchamacallit. You should do something about that."

"What, go to film school?"

"Maybe."

A megaphone squeals. "Five more minutes before we start the women's invitational!"

Ash kicks up her board and walks up to us one last time so we can wish her good luck. When I hug her, I feel her breathe against me. Hear her swallow. I whisper, "You can do this." I hold out my hand and she slaps it in a swinging high five.

Ash is second to last in the lineup, with four contestants ahead of her. The oldest is a tattoo-covered thirtysomething. The youngest is fourteen, with quiet, focused eyes. Under-nineteens are required to wear helmets, so Ash is wearing mine. She's been complaining about practicing with it all week, how different and hot it feels. But it looks natural on her, almost like a toque, the red streaks streaming out of it like a fiery waterfall.

Several of the women know each other. They casually shoot the shit as they wait their turn. The announcer explains to us that each contestant will get three 45-second runs. Scores are based on difficulty and style, and the final score will be averaged out over the three runs. If a skater pulls off a hard trick, they can score big, but big tricks also have a higher chance of failure. I know Ash won't have issues with style, but she can sometimes psyche herself out with harder tricks. I'm not sure if she'll risk something bigger today or if she'll keep things simple and consistent.

The first few women give stellar performances, but the real shining star is Esther from Victoria. She's twenty years old and the only other non-white person, as far as I can tell. She must be nearly six feet tall and she wears neon ribbons in her braids. Her pumps are powerful and just one propels her at a dizzying speed, setting her up for good air. She lands everything, but her tricks—ollies, 180s, kickflips—are on the safer side.

"Next up, we have Ash Chan from East Vancouver."

Matt, David, and I go wild. I have never heard David yell so loud before. He screams so much his voice goes off pitch.

The announcer continues, "She's seventeen years old and a Grade 12 student at George Vancouver Secondary. Ash wants to thank her friends Jay, Matt, and David for getting her here today!"

A rainfall of claps as Ash walks into the park. I'm almost dizzy with excitement because the crowd has no idea the kind of awesomeness they're about to witness. Ash leans forward on her knees, her calf muscles tensing. Her shoulders rise and fall with big breaths in and out. Then, she runs forward.

She 50-50s the ledge. Solid. A few whoops. Then Ash pumps to the handrail and *bam!* slaps a huge backside boardslide. The crowd roars. She rolls towards the ledge and I hold my breath for a sick grind, but Ash can't quite lock in and falls off. Oh well, she keeps it moving and kickflips the hip. Then, back to top, she gains speed, crouches, and *wham!* A massive ollie over the seven stair. The buzzer sounds. Run one of three is done.

Ash skates past us for high fives, wiping sweat from her face with her shirt. I high-five her, but her eyes are focused elsewhere. We won't get to talk until later.

David slaps my arm. "Was that good? It looked good. Was that good?"

To be honest, I don't know how skateboarding contests work well enough to say, but the announcer calls out, "After round one, Esther Toussaint in first place, Terra Smith in second, and Ash Chan in third!"

"Holy shit, she's on the podium!" David exclaims. But Ash doesn't react. She's got one foot on the tail of her board, rolling it back and forth on its back wheels, her hands on her hips. Waiting expectantly for the next round to start.

In the second round, Terra gets the top score with an insane smith grind, but the crowd goes absolutely wild for Ash's varial flip. She doesn't fall the second round and gets to second place, just one point behind Terra.

When Ash rolls around again for high fives and water, David is jumping up and down. I think this is the first time David's ever been excited about sports. "Dude, you are so *in!*" he says while Ash chugs water and splashes it over her face. "If not first place, then second. If not second, then third."

Esther kills it in the third round. Terra falls twice—she's off the podium. When it's Ash's turn, my heart pounds like a hammer. Even from a distance, my eyes feel like they have zoom: I can see every detail of her face, every sweat drop, every crease in her forehead. She waits for the buzzer. It sounds off, and then it's just the *kunnng kunnng* of Ash's wheels echoing over a hushed crowd on the edge of their seats.

50-50 on the ledge with a 180 out. Half cab.

Front lip on the handrail attempt: Ash slips out and bails. But she loses no momentum, picks up her board, throws down, and keeps it going.

Backside noseslide on the ledge.

Heelflip on the hip.

Back to the top, and I see her go for it—the seven stair. Few of the women have attempted it, and the ones who have, like Esther and Ash, have only ollied. I watch Ash. I see every wrinkle of concentration, the laser sharpness of her focus. It's clear that, in this moment, nothing else matters to her. Not her dad, not memories of Donna, not school, not even me, probably.

Ash throws down. Zooms toward the stairs. Sets up her feet. Crouches low.

Kickflips.

And she lands it.

Clean.

The crowd must have been holding its breath with me the whole time because everyone absolutely explodes. People stand up and stamp their boards against the ground, howling and whistling. Ash fist-pumps the air, cruises around the park, and dishes out high fives.

The smile on her face is the biggest I've seen since the day we first ran into each other behind my house. She's laughing, actually laughing out loud. When she gets to where we're sitting, we lock eyes and, the moment her board hits the grass, she runs off it and crashes into me in a bundle of sweaty arms and sticky legs. I bury my face in her hair and squeal with her like we're kids. I say in her ear, "You've got it, you've *so* got it. You did so good!"

She pulls away, presses her forehead against mine, and closes her eyes. "Thank you." Something catches in the back of her throat—is she crying? She ahems then holds my head with both hands and kisses me on the mouth.

It's over and she's back in the ring before I can even comprehend that I've just made out with Ash in public. David stares at me like his eyes are about to pop out of his head, and Matt covers his mouth like an anime character.

When I gather myself enough to sit back down, David jostles me and giggles. "So the rumors are true. You two are a thing."

"We're not." Then I frown. "What rumors?" When David keeps giggling like a middle schooler I just sigh.

Thankfully, the announcer chooses that moment to shout into the loudspeaker, "You guys ready to hear our winners?" The crowd cheers. The announcer brings out a DIY yet colorful scoreboard and takes a piece of plastic off each name and score as he announces them. "In third place . . . Brianne James! Brianne wins $250 in cash." Applause and board slaps. "In second place . . . Ash Chan! Ash gets $500 in cash." We whoop and holler and stomp our feet. "And the championship goes to Esther Toussaint! One thousand dollars in cash!" The crowd roars, but we roar for Ash. "Congratulations, Esther! All our competitors today will also receive grab bags of gear from our sponsors."

Ash hugs and high-fives all her fellow contestants. The vibes feel fantastic—everyone's smiling, laughing, fist-bumping. I think they're all here to have fun first, win prizes second. I see Esther pull Ash aside. She talks at length about something and Ash nods along. Ash looks comically short next to her, but Esther doesn't do that tall-people thing where they bend down and talk to you. Rather, she leans back on her board, and her left leg is as hyperactive as Ash's.

When she's done, Ash comes and sits with us for the men's division. The men's tricks are way more complex and impressive, and maybe it's just me, but I like watching the women's more. The vibes are lighter and less competitive. At one point, Ash slips her pinky over mine, and thankfully, Matt and David are too engrossed in the competition (Matt explaining tricks to David) to notice.

Then it's time to hand out prizes. Someone shakes and uncorks a bottle of sparkling juice and splashes it all over the contestants. Ash swipes bubbly out of her eyes, laughing harder than I've ever seen her. She looks so relaxed, almost bouncy. I'm so stoked.

We wait patiently for photos to be taken, checks to be handed out. More handshakes. More hugs. Ash and Esther talk again with their phones out. There's a product giveaway where they toss stuff into the crowd—Matt gets a hat, I catch a T-shirt.

When it's all done, Ash runs to us and we all group-hug.

"Good show, good show," Matt says.

"You should have won, I think," David says almost angrily. "What an arbitrary scoring system."

"Nah, Esther's sick." Ash turns to me, eyes glimmering. "We exchanged numbers. She's moving to Vancouver next year after she finishes school here. She wants to organize something like a female skaters guild."

"Cool," I say, and then quieter: "You okay?"

Ash nods. "It won't pay off Blake, but it's a start. And now I have my foot in the door to the industry as a runner-up."

Matt sneakily produces three joints from his jeans pocket. "Let's celebrate."

I text Wendy the good news and she passes on her congratulations to Ash. Then, before she has a chance to call me, I text my mother the picture of David and me studying at Sophie's. *Working so hard!* she texts back. *Make sure you have a good dinner la.* I feel a slight twinge of guilt but quickly forget it when we get back to Carlene.

We order a big box of chicken nuggets for dinner and hotbox the car. When Ash lights the joint, passes left to me, and I inhale it like a pro, David's eyebrows jump to his hairline. When I hold it out to him underneath his nose, he looks awkwardly at his knees. "I've never smoked weed before."

"Up to you, bro," Ash says. "It's chill if you wanna pass."

I expect David to pass, but he pinches the joint from me and holds it carefully between his fingertips. He puffs, coughs, splutters, and scowls. "Huh. It's all right."

"I've got a good hookup." Matt winks.

David takes a few more tokes then stares at a spot between Matt and Ash, who are giggling about something I've already forgotten about.

"What're you staring at, Dave?" I say, my voice all scratchy from screaming and smoking.

He takes a deep breath. "If I can be sappy for a moment—"

"Yes! Do it!" Matt yells. "Boys can be sappy!"

David smiles. "Um. Yeah. So. So, this was fun."

Ash sucks at the last remnants of the joint. "That's not sappy."

He takes another deep breath. "There were moments over the past year when I wished I wasn't alive." We all go quiet. David's voice is thick. "I'd go to bed hoping I'd never wake up because of some undiagnosed disease. Or I'd be walking down the street and hope some psycho would randomly run me over. I thought, maybe if I was dead, my parents— namely my dad—would finally actually care about how I feel. But this" —he looks around, nodding at each of us—"this made me remember that there's a point to, well, everything."

Suddenly, I'm hugging David like he's a lifesaving piece of driftwood floating in the ocean. He hugs me back, and Matt joins the hug, then

Ash, and now it's the smelliest, sappiest cuddle pile ever.

"Ash, I'm sorry if we didn't get off on the best foot, but you're good people," David says. He looks at Matt, who's watery-eyed, too. "You're all good people."

"You're pretty fucking rad yourself, David," Ash says. "Don't ever change."

While Ash and Matt roll another joint, I say quietly to David, "Hey."

"Hey."

"I care about how you feel," I say. "You can come to me anytime. Anytime. I promise, I'll drop everything and come right over."

He smiles at me. "Thanks. You too."

My shoulders suddenly feel a lot lighter. I sit back and look around at my friends as they wipe tears and smoke out of their eyes. It's chilly in the poorly insulated car, but I've never felt this warm. Then Ash catches my eye and beckons with a jerk of her head: outside. I try to ignore David's insinuating look as we excuse ourselves.

Ash pulls our skateboards out of the trunk. I haven't ridden mine in forever and I'm all wobbly at first, but Ash gives me a "hurry up or I'm leaving you" look so I jump on my board and follow her out of the parking lot.

We skate for a block or two, me almost falling on every bump and sidewalk crack because I'm buzzed and it's been a while since I've skated. We get to another parking lot, a small one just behind a bar that's closed down. It smells like garbage, but there are brighter lights here.

Ash sits down on her board and folds her hands. "Do a kickflip."

I say, "I can't do a kickflip."

But Ash is dead serious. Non-smiling dead serious. "We're not leaving here until you land one."

I place my feet on my board, pop, and flick. The board rolls over lazily, like it doesn't want to get out of bed.

"What did I tell you before? Do it rolling."

Right. I do and get a better pop this time.

"You're kicking too early. Be patient."

Pop and flick. Pop and flick.

"Too late. It's like a quarter-second delay."

"I don't have a quarter-second watch, Ash."

"Shut up and do it."

"Someone's a bossy winner." Ash ignores me. I pop and flick, pop and flick. The board rolls better now. Lands back on its wheels. Then I land with one foot on.

"Chickenfoot!" Ash hollers. "Commit to it. Believe in yourself. Come on. Come *on*."

"Shut up and let me focus." I pop and flick, pop, flick . . . And then it's like I black out for a moment and my body forgets how to be afraid. I pop and drag and flick, the board spins, and it's like I've been transported to a dimension where time slows down because I see my board flip in slo-mo underneath me . . . and I force both feet back on.

Ash jumps up and slams the tail of her board so hard against a parking block, I'm afraid it'll split in half. "Dude! *Dude!* You got it, *you got it*!"

I step off my board, my heart thundering in my ears. "I did," I manage to choke out.

Ash grabs me by the wrist and hugs me, almost lifting me straight off my feet as she squeezes me hard. I squirm and she lets me go. "Hey," she says, slightly out of breath.

"Hey." I'm also kinda out of breath.

"You know." She can't seem to speak in complete sentences. "The times we kissed, they don't count." Hesitantly, she reaches out a hand, pauses in front of my face, and pushes back my hair. Then she kisses me and the night explodes. The world is silent and deafening at the same time. Like I'm blacked out but more awake than I've ever been. Like the kickflip, time slows and I feel everything and see everything like it's all happening in the third person—I see our hands curling around each other's waists, each tiny movement of our lips, her tongue, my tongue. It lasts a million years and a nanosecond because the next moment, she's pulling back and saying, "I think we should talk."

I nod, unconsciously brushing my lips with my fingers where she was just a moment ago. My chest is pounding, but she's right. "We should."

Ash scratches the back of her neck and looks at the ground. "I need to focus on moving out, graduating, and getting a job. I'm still recovering from my last relationship, and this . . . Don't get me wrong, Jay, you're a million times awesomer than that dickface Blake will ever be, but it's . . ."

"It's a lot." I have to admit, it's a lot for me, too. This time last year, all I worried about was getting into a good university. Something that had seemed tremendously difficult but in hindsight was super simple. But this, this is something else. This is real-life shit, not high school student shit.

"You get it," Ash says.

I nod. I feel an ache for that image in my head where we're walking down the hall with our boards. But I also feel my shoulders loosen, just a tad, as if I've let go of something I didn't know I was carrying. I take a deep breath, in and out. "Let's be friends. At least for now."

Ash says, "Right."

"And if something happens later—"

"It happens." Ash nods. I watch her, her deep-brown eyes framed by red strands under the yellow halo of the parking lot street lamp. "Besides, you're going to Amsterdam."

I look up at the night sky. You can see more stars in Kelowna than in Vancouver because there's less light pollution here. When it's nighttime, it's really nighttime. "I'm not going to Amsterdam."

Ash stares at me. "What? Did you not get in?"

"No, I got in." I'm suddenly overwhelmed by sleepiness. Twenty-four hours of road-tripping, sleeping in cars, eating junk food, and being intoxicated has finally caught up. "Actually, I got a ten-grand scholarship."

"Holy crap! Congrats, dude!" Her eyes narrow. "Wait—how long have you known? Why didn't you tell me? And why aren't you going?"

I stick my hands in my pockets and kick a stray rock. "I don't know. Back in September, I wanted nothing more than to leave. But I guess I never thought about why. I don't think Vancouver is the problem. In fact, I kinda want to stay now."

Ash chuckles nervously. "Don't tell me you're staying for little old me."

I laugh. "No, not you. I'm staying for me. And Wendy, Wendy needs me. And there's a super cool scene here that I've only just discovered. I think I'll defer my admission and take a gap year, make sure going to Europe is what I really want."

"Your parents won't get mad?"

I shrug. "They'll get over it."

Ash nods. "I, uh,"— she looks away—"I do love you, you know."

I allow myself to savor the moment for a whole second, let the smile run across my face, the feelings bubble up in my chest. And then I kiss her, just a peck. "I love you too."

She says, "Confession time. I do think Orlando is a love letter. The way Woolf sees Vita, flaws and all, and *still* writes an entire epic novel about her. I was—I was kinda fucking with you." She averts her eyes.

"So I'm right," I say.

She shrugs. "Sometimes." I laugh.

After a few moments of silence, I say, "Ash. Are you gay?"

Ash scratches her nose. "I don't know. Are you?"

"Maybe? I mean . . ." I scratch the back of my head. I haven't showered since Thursday, and my hair is starting to mat and stick. "I dunno." My voice drifts off, but Ash nods for me to continue. I just say, "Women are beautiful."

Ash scoffs. "Women are hot."

We hold hands and walk back to the station wagon. When we get there, David and Matt don't notice us but we spy them through the window, cuddling under David's blanket in the back seat and watching something on a phone. They giggle at something we can't hear. When Ash knocks on the window, they bounce away from each other like two positive ends of a magnet.

"Um, what the hell is going on?" Ash says.

"Nothing!" David splutters. Matt coughs and pretends to be busy on the phone. Ash smirks.

"You guys wanna share the tent?" she says.

"So you two can have car sex?" Matt says. "Please."

I give him a light cuff on the head.

We end up doing the opposite. Ash and I set up the tent behind the car under a few trees, and Matt and David sleep in the station wagon. I have no idea what they get up to all night, but the light is still on when I fall asleep.

CHAPTER 15

The next day, Ash treats us to a late-morning lunch of greasy pancakes, eggs, and bacon at a diner before we drive back to Vancouver. The weather is gorgeous and it's warm enough to not have to wear a hoodie. Compared to the trip here, everyone's more chill. I notice more details in the scenery and I feel like I'm on vacation.

We're about an hour and a half away from Vancouver when the car starts making weird noises. Panicking, David steers us onto the shoulder while the car does the equivalent of a hacking cough. "Oh my god, oh my god, oh my god," David stammers.

"Hey, at least there's no smoke coming out of the hood," Matt says, one hand on David's jiggling leg. He peers at the dashboard. "Oh. I know the problem." He chuckles. "Thing's out of gas."

"Goddamn it!" David seethes. "How the hell did I not notice?"

"Maybe you were distracted," I say. "You and Matt were *really* deep in that *Final Fantasy* talk."

David turns around in his seat, his face red. "You should've said something."

I throw up my hands. "Dude, I'm not the one looking at the dashboard all day."

"Well, maybe you should have noticed how weird it is we haven't stopped for gas at all!" David groans. "Now we're going to have to call our parents, right? They're gonna *kill* me. And if we leave the car behind, *Simon* is gonna kill me."

"We can just not tell him," Ash offers with a shrug.

"Or we tell him the beloved car he inherited from his dead dad is rusting away on the side of the Trans-Canada Highway," Matt says, chuckling.

David glares at him. "You're not helping." He jumps out of the car and slams the door. Matt wears a look of guilt and hurt.

"Well, we're not calling anyone's parents," Ash says and exits the car too. In the side mirror, I see her walk to the side of the road and stick her thumb out.

"Shit," Matt says, pursing his lips.

"David's just not the best at handling stress," I say, shrugging.

He sighs. "I'll go talk to him." He gets out and I'm alone now, so I text Wendy. I ask her to google what to do in a situation like this, but she freaks out on me before I've even finished explaining. So I just tell her we'll try to find help from other drivers and that unless I call her for help, we'll be home by dinner.

It's twenty minutes before a truck pulls up and offers to drive us to the nearest gas station. Ash and I go with the driver while Matt and David stay with the car. The driver smells like stale cigarettes, but I doubt we smell any better. He's very talkative and keeps asking Ash how old she is, where she's from, where she's *really* from, and whether she has a boyfriend. Fortunately, the guy has a strict schedule and can't drive us back to our car. So, after we buy a jerry can of gas, we get a lift from an elderly couple in an RV going the other direction.

In the end, it all works out. Sorta. Matt and David continue their video game conversation and it morphs into a deep discussion about politics and identity, which I've never heard David discuss with anyone. I start recognizing landmarks by sunset and go to text Wendy, but my phone is dead. Warehouses turn into big-box stores. Farms turn into suburban developments turn into condos. But the moment David rolls onto my block, my skin crawls with dread: my entire family is standing on the sidewalk in front of our house.

David wordlessly pulls up to the curb even though I want him to floor it back to the highway. But it's over—the weekend, the contest, everything. I look at Ash, who pats my hand. I'm so nervous I'm scared I'll pass out.

When I get out of the car, Wendy runs up to me. "I'm sorry, I'm sorry, I had to tell them. I was so worried about you, and then your phone was off, and they wanted to call the police, but I convinced them not to, and then you said you'd be home at this time, and—"

"It's fine." And just like that, I'm calm. There's nothing I can do at this point anyway. "It's my fault, I didn't notice my phone was dying."

Ash hands me my board and my backpack. "You'll be fine." And I guess she's right. The worst my parents will do is yell at me. I'm certain they won't kick me out of the house or threaten to not pay for my tuition, both of which are very possible consequences for Ash and David.

I drag my feet to where my parents are standing, and Ash trails behind me. Ma Mi's hands are on her hips. De Di looks haggard. I open my mouth to say I'm sorry, but before anything comes out, Ma Mi scoops me up in her arms. Carries me clean off my feet. I didn't know she was even strong enough to do that; she never exercises.

"You're okay, you're okay, God has protected us!" She's practically sobbing. I don't remember the last time my mother even touched me.

I glance at my dad, confused, but all he looks is relieved. "Are you hungry? Thirsty? Are you hurt?"

"Well, she definitely hasn't showered," says Wendy, wrinkling her nose.

"Go. Get in the shower. Just leave your clothes outside and I'll wash them with ours," Ma Mi says. "Justin's coming over for dinner and we're having sushi."

I raise my eyebrows at Wendy, and she says shyly, "Yeah, I finally told them about him."

"Jesus," Ash says from behind me, "your parents are the coolest."

"Ashley!" Ma Mi blinks, as if seeing her for the first time. "Do you, uh, need anything?"

She smiles. "I'm good. Your daughter has made me richer."

Ma Mi looks confused but nods politely at her.

I tell my friends to text me once they're home, and I book it to the shower. The scalding water is comforting, but my mind runs a mile a minute. No one has yelled at me, but that's because we were outside, in public. My parents are probably waiting until after I get out of the shower.

There's a lot my parents don't know, like my gap-year plan. Should I tell them now? And should I come out to them, or is this the wrong time? Then I start thinking about all the final exams I have to study for and the essay on Victorian poetry I owe Mr. Hussein. Ugh, real life sucks. I miss the road already.

I dry off and dress myself as slowly as I can. When I get downstairs, Ma Mi, De Di, and Wendy are sitting at the dining table, talking in hushed voices. They shut up when they see me. Wendy stares at the table, wiggling her leg in the way De Di hates. Any other time, he'd be barking at her to stop, but tonight, he doesn't seem to notice.

I sit down. De Di clears his throat, eyes glued to his folded arms. Then he says mechanically, "Why didn't you tell us?"

I can't help but scoff. Ma Mi opens her mouth, but De Di shoots her a look and she restrains herself.

"Obviously I couldn't tell you what I was doing," I say. "You would have said no and told me not to butt into other people's business."

"Of course!" Ma Mi practically bursts out. "You could have been killed in a car accident. Someone may have tried to kidnap you. You are very lucky to be safe, Wong See Kar. Very lucky la." She grips the edge of the table as if she's about to fly off into the air. "And why did you get David involved? Why, we ought to call his parents—"

"No!" I instantly let go of any pride I'm wearing and plead to her with my eyes. "David's parents will hurt him. Or kick him out of the house. Or—"

De Di says, "We won't call them." Ma Mi looks confused for a moment. But seeing something in De Di's face, she sighs and looks away. "Jessica," De Di continues, voice steady, "of course we would not have let you go to Kelowna by yourself. But if you had told us what was going on, perhaps we could have helped in some way. We could have bought bus tickets for your friend. Something. You just had to ask."

Just ask? *With all due respect, De Di, I think you have epic hindsight bias.* Of course, I don't dare say that. I just shrug and say, "But you guys don't even like Ash."

Ma Mi and De Di exchange tortured looks. De Di sighs. "Well, she's not our favorite person—"

"She's my best friend," I say. "I care about her a lot. I'd do anything for her. She's been dealt some bad cards in her life, and I just wanted to help. And I did," I add quickly. "I helped her win second place. She's in a better position to move out of an abusive home now. Isn't that a good thing?" *I did a good thing,* I tell myself. *I did a good thing.*

"But none of that was your concern," Ma Mi says. "How could you have slept in a car for two nights without telling us?"

"I'm eighteen." I try not to growl. "I can do whatever the fuck I want."

Ma Mi bristles at the f-word. "But we are your parents and you live in our house!"

I stand up. "Then it should be no surprise to you that I want to move out as soon as I can."

Ma Mi glares at me without speaking and then pushes back her chair with a screech and stomps out of the room.

"Jessica. Don't talk to your mother like that." De Di's voice is soft but crumbly.

"I don't care," I say, my chest feeling tight. "Ma Mi doesn't understand."

De Di closes his eyes, takes a deep breath, and lets it out very slowly. "Your mother was very worried. All we want is for you girls to be safe, so don't ever, *ever* do something like this again. You're lucky everything worked out. Next time you need help, ask us. And if you don't like what we have to say . . ." He shrugs. "Well. I guess you *are* eighteen."

I'm still angry, but I say, "Okay."

"Obviously, we have to punish you," De Di says. "No TV, no computer, and no skateboarding until you're done with your exams. Well, unless you need the computer for school. But I'm taking my camera and the MacBook back."

The doorbell rings. I hear Ma Mi open the door and say in her fake discount-requesting voice, "Oh, you must be Justin! Hello!"

Justin walks in with a goofy grin, an ironed shirt, and two platters of sushi. And for the next hour, we pretend there's nothing wrong. Justin delights my parents with his chopstick ability and a few phrases of Cantonese he's painstakingly perfected. To my surprise, he nails the tones. Most English speakers can't speak passable Cantonese because they can't do the tones, and without the tones, you might as well be speaking gibberish.

My parents' energy levels replenish as dinner progresses. Ma Mi loses her fake voice bit by bit, and by the end of dinner, I think she's genuinely impressed with Justin. She asks about his family, his plans for university, what he wants to be.

"An environmental lobbyist," he says, before looking at Wendy with a proud smile. "And I believe this one wants to become a journalist."

Wendy looks away and blushes. I expect Ma Mi to correct Justin and say Wendy wants to be a doctor, but she's got her mouth full with California roll.

After dinner, Wendy and Justin watch a movie in Wendy's room. Ma Mi tells Wendy to keep her door wide open. De Di assigns me the dishes and locks himself in his study, clearly exhausted from all the parenting he's had to do today. Ma Mi busies herself with tidying the table and dries every dish and bowl the moment I set it on the drying rack. Whenever there's silence between us, she rapidly fills it with critiques of my dish-washing technique or complaints about how the sushi was mostly rice and not enough fish. "That boy is smart, but he obviously doesn't know anything about sushi. There were twelve cucumber rolls on that platter. Twelve! What a waste of money. Next time, we're taking him to that discount place on Main where they give you sashimi an inch thick."

"Justin seems nice," I say, hoping to steer the conversation somewhere positive.

"He is. A smart boy. But any children he and Wendy have will be quite dark—"

"Mom!" I try to pick my words carefully. "You might not know this, but many people these days would find what you just said racist."

Ma Mi shrugs, but she doesn't disagree with me.

After the dishes are done, I go to my room, shut the door, and embrace the peace and quiet. David had texted me when he got home earlier, but I'm still worried about him, so I call him.

"I just beelined to the shower," he says, "but everything's okay. Parents were in the living room watching K-drama and one of my sisters is sick so that commanded most of their attention. I think I'm safe."

I breathe a sigh of relief. "Good."

"Sophie told Min about what we did, and I think she's a little pissed we left her out of it. But at the same time, Sophie said she was impressed."

"Thank Sophie for me if you see her," I say. "I'll talk to Min in band. I hope she gets to leave home soon too, to be honest."

I feel David nod from the other side of the phone. "She's going to McGill, did you know?"

"That's awesome." A small part of me wishes I were going somewhere too, but then again, who's to say I'm not? There's a lot in Vancouver I *haven't* gone to. "Well, thank you. Again," I say to David. "Like, for everything. I know this was a big risk for you."

"No, thank *you*. This weekend was, like, the highlight of high school," he says, and I catch a leftover trace of adrenaline in his voice. "And you're right, your friends are cool. Matt is awesome."

Ash had texted me earlier, too. I call and she tells me her dad yelled at her a bit, but he assumed she was at a friend's house. Then she finally told him she's moving out after graduation. When I ask her how he reacted, she said he just walked outside to smoke without saying anything.

Without a computer, I decide to reread the stack of pamphlets on my desk. Then, there's a knock on the door and it's Ma Mi, carrying a bowl.

"Tong sui," she mutters.

"I'm full," I tell her.

She sets it on my desk anyway.

"I'm full," I say again.

"I brought it all the way up here."

I relent and taste a spoonful of the dessert. It's not her best batch, but whatever. "Thanks," I say.

Ma Mi grunts and leaves.

"Um, Ma Mi?"

"Ha?" she yells down the hall.

"I'm sorry I made you worry."

Another grunt. The subject doesn't come up again.

CHAPTER 16

When I tell my parents I want to defer my Amsterdam admission, they look like they don't know what to do with their faces. I brace myself for the moment Ma Mi will call me out on threatening to leave during our argument about Kelowna. But she must have forgotten about it because all she says is "Oh" and "What will you do for a year? Stay home and skateboard?"

I roll my eyes. "Of course not. I'll get a job."

"But you have a scholarship." De Di is scowling, seemingly trying to comprehend why anyone would want to take a gap year.

"It doesn't pay for everything. I still need to pay for airfare, food, and other stuff. I want to make some money first. Besides"—I look away—"I'm not sure if I want to go to Amsterdam at all anymore." Ma Mi sits up, but before she can say anything, I cut in. "But if I decide to live at home for university—and that's a big if—I insist that I come and go as I please. Stay out as late as I want without calling. I'll pay rent if that's what it takes. I need boundaries, and if you cross them, I'll move out."

I fold my arms over my chest. De Di and Ma Mi look at each other. Then, De Di chuckles. "Our daughter is negotiating with us like we're a rival business!" Ma Mi doesn't look amused, but her body loosens up when it's clear De Di isn't taking this too seriously. "Well, she is no longer a child," he says. To me, he adds, "All right, so long as you let me know what days you'll be home for dinner. I do need some notice, okay?"

I nod. "Okay."

Ma Mi says, "But what will you study? Do you really need a whole year to figure it out?"

"You wouldn't want me to do half a program, hate it, and quit, right?" I keep my voice even. Mature. Which is harder than it looks when you're speaking to your parents like this for the first time.

Ma Mi and De Di exchange a glance and then slowly, reluctantly, they nod their heads.

. . .

The last two weeks between our road trip and the end of the school year whip by. After our Kelowna shenanigans, I try to keep my head down and my grades up. Meanwhile, Ash is in Ms. Watanabe's office a lot, and she's not always happy when she comes out. One time, I catch her sitting on her skateboard outside in the rain, smoking cigarette after cigarette. "What's up?" I ask her.

"Everything's fucked is what's up."

"What do you mean?"

She's vibrating with rage while she blows out a smoke plume. "No one will rent to me, and since I'm not nineteen, I can't sign a contract anyway."

"But if your dad's such a piece of shit, surely there's a way for the government to make an exception?" I offer.

Ash shakes her head. "I don't want to get the government involved. Dezzy and Simon were in foster care for a year, and they said it was hell. See, the government just messes everything up."

Going home that afternoon, I feel heavy, soaked through with all sorts of complicated feelings. Sadness because Ash has so much going against her. Relief because I don't. But it's weird. Ash did nothing to deserve her bad circumstances, and I did nothing to deserve my good ones. That night, when I see Ma Mi hunched over the sink doing dishes, I walk up behind her and without a word give her a big hug.

She tsks. "What is this now?"

"Nothing," I say. Ma Mi pats my arm with a wet hand.

Matt visits our school a few times. I don't know if it's because he has a free block or if he skips, but he shows up randomly at lunch and after school. Which is cool because when it comes to skating, the more the merrier. He sessions with Ash and me and then goes for bubble tea with David. The two of them drink *a lot* of bubble tea.

And just like that, we finish high school. I get eight As and two Bs. I even get one of the highest averages in AP English, second only to— you guessed it—Ash. She wins an award at the graduation ceremony for earning the top grade. Not even aware of the award's existence, she stiffly shakes the principal's hand and they both look shocked in the photo.

Matt shows up at our graduation, which I find odd at first. But when he walks off with David and I see them joking and laughing about something out of earshot, I develop a theory.

Min catches me staring, sidles up to me, and muses, "Aren't they adorable?" She tilts her head. She really does think they're adorable. When I'd explained to Min that we only told Sophie about Kelowna because her parents were progressive, she'd said, "That makes sense, I guess. My mom would *not* have helped. But I would've. If I could." I hadn't quite believed her then, but now I do. Min probably figured out Matt and David before I did.

After the ceremony, De Di takes our family out for sushi. While we sit drinking tea and waiting for our food, two middle-aged women walk in with twin girls. One of the women is Asian with long hair and the other has short, spiky blonde hair. The kids are mixed-race. Ma Mi watches them take a seat on the other side of the restaurant and says, absentmindedly, "I wonder what their relationship is?"

De Di chuckles. "Can't you see? They're fai lok yun."

I scowl. "'Happy people'?"

"Gay," Wendy mutters next to me.

De Di muses, "I think that's the first time I've seen a Chinese or Asian fai lok woman who doesn't look like a man."

"Why are you so surprised? It's not like gay people exist in some countries and not others," I say. Wendy tosses me a cautious look.

De Di shrugs. "I rarely see Chinese gay people."

"You probably have. Gay people are more common than you think."

"Well, I really haven't."

"Maybe you have and you just didn't know," I say, trying hard to keep my voice flat. "It's not like all gay women have short hair." Ma Mi laughs nervously at that. I brace for her to say something like "or else our daughter would be gay!" but luckily, she doesn't. She stops laughing when she realizes she's the only one doing so.

De Di sips his tea. "We don't go to the same places gay people go to."

"Like where?"

"I don't know. Parties. Parades. Fashion shows?"

"Sushi restaurants?" I say, tilting my head.

De Di looks confused. I think he thinks I'm laying a trap out for him. Ma Mi—also looking genuinely confused—says, "Ah Nui, what's going on with you?"

I squirm in my seat and my ears feel hot. I feel Wendy's eyes watching me tensely, and I'm so glad she's here right now. "I just think, De Di, that you should be open to the fact that gay people are everywhere, in all races, all areas of life. For example, I happen to be gay."

De Di and Ma Mi both freeze. De Di has a mouthful of tea and Ma Mi's got an edamame bean in her chopsticks partway to her mouth. Their eyes are as wide as the bowls holding their soy sauce. Dread gushes through me. Did I time this poorly? Am I ready for the inevitable barrage of questions? Then again, how could I have done this any less awkwardly? Besides, it's my graduation day. They can't get mad at me on my graduation day.

Our waitress comes by and slides California rolls, sashimi, miso soup, salad, and udon in front of us. She cheerfully names each dish as they grace the table, but she might as well have been talking to herself because it's like my entire family has forgotten how to speak. "Enjoy!" she chirps before slipping away with a strained smile. As fast as she can, probably.

Ma Mi clears her throat and starts busily putting food on Wendy's plate and mine. De Di stays frozen for two more seconds before his body relaxes into nervous laughter. "Ah Nui, don't scare us! You're not gay."

"But I am," I say, ignoring the stack of food Ma Mi is piling onto my plate.

De Di stops laughing and clears his throat. His face tightens into seriousness. "You think you're gay?"

"I know I'm gay."

"Are you sure?" Ma Mi puts salad on my plate and reminds us all to eat our vegetables.

"Yes, I'm sure."

"But you're still young! You're only eighteen. I didn't start dating until I was in university. I didn't meet your mother until I was twenty-one. You have plenty of time to figure out these things."

"I've spent a lot of time figuring it out, De Di, and I'm pretty sure I'm gay. I like women."

Ma Mi winces ever so slightly. De Di scowls. "I'll talk to Dr. Kwan. See if we can get you a therapist. You can figure things out with a professional."

"I don't need a professional, De Di. I know myself."

De Di sighs. "Why not? I've never heard you talk about this before—"

"De Di, I'm not seeing a counselor."

Wendy coughs softly next to me. "Just let her be, De Di."

De Di sighs again and shakes his head. "But—these things—"

"De Di. I'm sure." I want to sound strong, but my voice, weighed down by emotion, sounds hoarse and unsteady. When I look at my mother, she's chewing loudly, as if hoping to drown out the conversation.

De Di sighs one last time and says, "Let's eat and talk about this later."

Of course, we don't talk about it later. When we get home, it's like the conversation never happened. Which I'm honestly grateful for. I'm exhausted. I text Ash about what happened.

dude, that's sickkk, she texts back. *you got balls.*

there was less drama than i expected, I text. *in fact, i might have to do it AGAIN at some point because my dad doesn't seem to believe me.*

honestly, that's probably the best reaction you coulda gotten from ur parents. i wouldn't tell my dad in a million years.

yeah. i guess you're right. it's not about the guts, tho. it's about feeling safe.

· · ·

Now that he's done stressing about universities, David has a ton of free time, and I think it makes him anxious. He's constantly calling me up to hang out only to get flustered when we do. I offer to teach him skateboarding, but he freaks out the moment the board rolls an inch underneath him, so I let him teach me K-pop dance routines instead. They're pretty fun, and since it's so hot outside, it's nice to spend the days in David's family's cool basement practicing dance moves.

One day, I notice David's quieter, dancing harder than usual. When we take a break, he paces the room drinking bubble tea while I fan myself. Then he blurts out, "Matt and I are dating."

I'm too exhausted from the workout to act surprised. "Cool."

He stares at me. "You know?"

I roll my eyes. "Dude. It's so obvious."

He frowns. "Not as obvious as you and Ash."

"Ash and I aren't dating."

"Wait, really?" He sits down next to me, eyes wide.

"Don't change the subject, asshole," I say to him. "How did it happen?"

He smiles slightly. "We became official last night." He sighs. "He's so awesome. He's like no one I've ever met before."

I smile too. "I know that feeling."

"We're so different in many ways, but also . . . kinda similar? He gets shit done," David says. "You know, he just got one of his comics published in a magazine. He told me last night."

"Whoa." I'm impressed.

"I feel as if we've been taught there's only one way to work hard. Study, go to university, get a job that earns six figures," says David. "But Matt's got a killer work ethic too, you know?"

I nod. Just like Ash.

"It sucks because I'm going to Columbia and he's staying here. We've been talking about an open relationship, and honestly, I'm scared. But also, like, I'm willing, you know? To take the risk?"

I want to hug David, but I'm drenched in sweat and so is he and I can smell the hug before it happens, so I just squeeze his shoulder. "Dude.

I'm so happy for you, man. I love you."

He pats my hand. "I love you too. But"—he scowls, almost worried-looking—"what do you mean you and Ash aren't together? Are you guys all right?"

"Oh, we're totally cool. It's just . . ." I shrug. "It's complicated, you know? I've been enjoying the space, honestly."

"You can talk about it with me," David says.

"I know."

"Even when I'm at Columbia. I'm gonna make it a point to call you at least once a week."

"I know. We'll talk about it. Just not now. I kinda need to figure it out first."

. . .

I brace myself for a sequel to the sushi restaurant, but it never comes. We see other obviously gay couples in more restaurants over the summer, but no one comments on them. I'm convinced that my parents have lost their memory when I overhear this one night:

". . . all those movies and TV shows that are popular these days that say being that way is totally normal," Dad is saying.

"Like what?"

"The one she loves watching, with the vampires and vampire-hunting girl."

"Well, if she's wrong, she'll figure it out eventually."

"She better soon, or you won't have grandchildren."

"We have two children."

"Wendy being as ambitious as she is, don't you think she'll sacrifice family for a career?"

"Ga Jie can be ambitious. You don't know."

Huh. My mother calling *me* ambitious.

Eventually, I decide to stop worrying about an argument that may never happen. It's summer, after all—a rare few months out of the entire year when it doesn't rain every single day. I skate as much as I can. Ash picks up as many Burger Truck shifts as possible, so I only see her on weekends when she shows up at the park with the guys or when we attend one of the local contests she signs up for—and she signs up for a ton of them. She's met a lot of people, including professional filmmakers, and our schedules never align anyway, so I take a break from filming and skate for skating's sake. I get my kickflips more consistent. I learn manuals. I practice ollieing on and off stuff. Next stop: boardslides.

But I can't spend the whole summer skating, of course. I need to keep my mother happy, and it's not like I'm going to become a pro skater like Ash, so I enroll in a film editing class at the community college. Then I get a part-time gig at the Burger Truck too, just cashier stuff, and it's not nearly as easy as I thought. All my life I've been raised to see service jobs as being just for people whose grades weren't good enough for university. But I get my fair share of embarrassment. The first day of work, I have to fill out a tax form and I keep bugging Ash for help. She looks at me like I have two heads because she's been filling out forms for her parents ever since she could read. It also takes me several tries and many exasperated sighs from a very patient Simon to cash out properly. The first time I do it without needing him to recount or fix my mistakes, I feel like I've run a marathon. The first paycheck I get, I buy a mini-rail so that I can practice boardslides in my laneway.

Ash and I don't work together for long, though, because the week after I start, she scores a position at the Clamshell, this skate shop in New Westminster that's run by Esther Toussaint's brother. I'm happy for her, though it means we see each other even less. But maybe that's a good thing—to get some space.

. . .

On Sundays, I pick Ma Mi up from church and we have lunch at her favorite Hong Kong–style diner in a sleepy corner of Richmond. De Di uses his Sundays to prep for work in the upcoming week, and Wendy spends her weekends either studying or hanging out with Justin, so it's just Ma Mi and me.

At first, I dread spending one-on-one time with my mom, but it turns out to be more peaceful than I expect. Since I'm done high school and I'm working, my mom doesn't have much to grill me about. Lunch is therefore spent in peaceful silence. Ma Mi drinks milk tea and I drink iced coffee. She reads the church bulletin and I often bring a paperback. (I've gotten more into reading—I blame Mr. Hussein and Ash.) The church bulletin can only occupy Ma Mi for so long, though, and she can't stand the pause between ordering and receiving food at restaurants.

"How is work going?" she asks one time, spinning her mug in her hands.

I keep my eyes on my book. "Fine."

"Only a month left until you're done your summer job."

"I told you before, Ma Mi, I'm working at least until the new year."

"Did you look at the catalog I sent you? It's a very nice art program on the Island. Painting. Sculpture—"

I flip a page. "I'm more into film these days, but thank you."

"I'll look for film programs then." She drums her fingers on the ceramic. "How's Ashley?"

"She's fine."

"Where is she going to school in September?"

"She's not."

"Oh. So she's doing a gap year like you?"

I put down my copy of *The Bell Jar* and sigh. "I don't know."

"Oh." The waiter comes by and deposits a bowl of roast duck noodle soup in front of Ma Mi. That's the efficient thing about Hong Kong diners: they bring your food out as soon as it's ready, no waiting-for-everyone-else's-dish nonsense.

I consider returning to Sylvia Plath, but something pricks the back of my mind. Spinning my iced coffee straw, I clear my throat and ask Ma Mi, "Hey, how's De Di?"

"He got a contract position overseas and they're not asking him to move, so I think he's doing well."

The waiter returns with a casserole of baked Macau-style Portuguese chicken on rice. It's still bubbling, so I don't dig in yet. "I mean . . ." I clear my throat. "I mean, how is De Di with . . ." My voice dribbles off.

Ma Mi digs into her noodles with her chopsticks, focusing her eyes on the food. "I don't know. I think he's thinking about it."

"I heard him say he thinks I'm just confused by *Buffy the Vampire Slayer*. It's a TV show," I add when she gives me a puzzled look. "But I'm not. I've known something was different about me for a long time."

"I think . . . I think we're just surprised because you've never talked about this."

It's my turn to sigh. "Well, I'm talking to you now." I force myself to take a deep breath to calm down then say "It's not like we're a family that talks."

Ma Mi scowls. "What do you mean? We talk all the time!"

"About universities and careers and grades. The news and classical music, on a good day. But not stuff like this. Stuff like . . . feelings."

Ma Mi weighs that for a moment then says, "I suppose you're right."

"Like, Wendy was afraid you'd get mad at her for seeing Justin."

"Mad at her? Why would we be mad at her?"

"Because you and De Di are always saying how young people shouldn't date in high school."

"But Wendy will be okay. She's so responsible."

"Then you should tell her that, Ma Mi."

"Oh, she knows."

I shrug. "It's still nice to hear that sometimes."

We eat quietly for a few minutes. Then Ma Mi says, "Your father just needs time."

I look up at her through the steam coming from my food. "How about you?"

Ma Mi scoffs. "You're my daughter and I haven't stopped worrying about you, have I?"

I smile. "Thank you for accepting me, Ma Mi."

Ma Mi makes an awkward snorting sound through her soup noodles.

Later in the car, after she scolds me for not making a tight enough right turn, Ma Mi says, "I didn't learn to drive until I got to this country. We just didn't need to, or couldn't afford to, back in Hong Kong. But for you kids here, learning to drive is a rite of passage whether you need to drive or not. Oh, much better," she says when I make another right turn and execute it perfectly this time. Ma Mi continues, "How we grew up and how you did. So different."

· · ·

People start leaving in August. Sophie goes to Mount Allison and Min leaves for McGill a few days after. Dezzy starts his culinary course and can't go skating much anymore. Then Ash, Matt, and I see David off at the airport when it's his turn to go.

David and Matt have an emotional, if subtle, goodbye because David's family is there as well. I see them secretly squeeze each other's hands before David walks through security.

Matt is quiet on the train ride back to the city, arms crossed, one leg over the other. Ash and I don't feel like talking either, so we just stare out the window. Then Matt clears his throat and says, "I've been thinking."

We both turn to him. "Yeah?" I say.

Matt looks out the window and says, thoughtfully, "I think I might be Two-Spirit."

Ash fist-bumps him. "That's sick, man."

"Congratulations!" I say. "So you're basically coming out to us?"

Matt says, "I'm not sure 'coming out' is the right term for it. And to be honest, I want to learn more about it first, maybe talk to an Elder."

We hug him.

Sometimes, on my days off, I go downtown. Sometimes, I skate. Other times, I kinda just wander around, ride the bus, and people-watch. I watch an old man get on the bus with an enormous bag of recyclables, sit behind the driver, and leaf through a bus flier. Next stop, a man decked out in neck-to-toe in tattoos wheels his wheelchair into the disabled spot with two deft pumps of his arms. His wife or girlfriend sits on the ground in front of him and holds his hand. Two men get on at the next stop, one pushing a baby stroller, and everyone has to shift around to make space. I'm standing up now, but I don't mind. There's so much to see. It's funny. You can ride through the city for years and only notice concrete. But if you slow down and actually look around, you'll see that everyone has a story. And it's almost sad how there will never be enough time to hear each one.

The bus crosses the Burrard Bridge. To the west, the sun hovers over the calm waters of False Creek, getting ready to set. Downtown is a shimmering sea of glass. I listen to music and watch the city dance by me. Skateboarding has made me see the world differently. I look at ledges, curbs, rails, stairs, ramps, and concrete features I don't even know the names of, and all I can imagine is grinding, sliding, wallriding, or kick-flipping and ollieing over them. Even if I can't do those tricks (yet), the streets look like an empty canvas begging to be painted over.

The bus passes the nightclubs on Davie, the designer stores on Robson, and god knows how many pot shops on each block. At Waterfront, I get off and look across the harbor to the North Shore. The mountains—pale-blue giants—stare back at me. I pick out the shapes Ash taught me to recognize: the double humps are the Lions, the one with the big ski-run scars is Cypress, and the one with the faintly visible wind turbine at its peak is Grouse. In a few months, the whole range will be sprinkled with a layer of frosty snow. It'll be magical. It hits me that I live in one of the prettiest cities in the world.

· · ·

It's a sunny Labor Day weekend and I'm practicing boardslides. I cut my hair again last week, and that lack of extra weight is making all the difference.

"Look at you. Going pro already." Ash rides up, carrying two bubble teas.

"Thanks," I say, taking my drink. I mean it. It must have taken Ash a long time to get here. She lives in Burnaby now with Simon and Dezzy, sleeping behind a folding screen on their couch and paying a few hundred dollars in rent.

Ash sips her bubble tea while squinting at my mini-rail. She looks the same but also different. Black shorts and a dark-red plaid shirt. Sunglasses perched on her head, hair tied back with the red almost completely gone. A bandanna hangs out of her pocket and a Clamshell pin sits on her collar. She holds her drink out to me. "Happy friendiversary."

I smile. "Happy friendiversary." We clink plastic cups. "So," I say, "how's your mother?" The day Ash moved out was a shitshow. Her mother kept accusing her of abandoning the family, of driving her father to hypertension, of ruining their lives with what happened at Mackenzie. Ash kept going back and forth on the move, and if it wasn't for me, Dezzy, and Logan being there, I think she would've caved. In the end, Ash's mom shut herself in the bedroom and Ash said through the door that if she ever wanted to leave, Ash would support them both in their own apartment. She didn't get a response.

"Funny thing," Ash says. "I saw her at the park. I think she thought I didn't see her because she walked away without saying anything." She shrugs. "I'm not sure if she was there looking for me, or if she finally decided to get out of the house. But I'm trying not to overanalyze it. I'm making money and I think I can get my own place by next year; I'm good."

I want to tell her she's incredible, but I just smile. Then I get my laptop bag from the shade. "Hey, let me show you something."

We sit down against my garage, side by side, and I open my laptop to show her my wireframes. Ash had introduced me to Esther, who told me all about the women-led skate organization she's starting. I volunteered to build the website.

"Whoa. Sick. You have a real knack for this, J.W." She loudly slurps her tea and clicks around the website, looking through the different sections: About, Programs, Merch, Videos, Blog. "Dude, the Pacific Girl Skaters Guild is gonna be huge."

"Those are all just placeholders," I say, "but I figure we could host women-only clinics or something. You should teach."

"Oh, fuck yeah. We should do something for kids. I love teaching kids. Man, that'd be a dream job." Ash isn't wrong. She's been mentioned in a couple of Google reviews from parents who take their kids to the Clamshell. I was surprised that Ash is the kind of person who's good with kids (she hated my babysitting fundraising idea after all). But she says it makes her feel like her grandmother. She said even though her por por didn't know how to skate, her being there and cheering her on made Ash unafraid to fall. And when it comes to skateboarding, not being afraid of falling is, like, 80 percent of the battle.

"Wendy says we can apply for government funding if we incorporate ourselves as a nonprofit," I say. "I think my parents would be willing to lend us some startup money for equipment, hiring, insurance. At least a little bit."

Ash clicks her tongue, a grin growing across her face as her eyes dart around the screen. The laptop is frying up in the sun, though, so I tuck it back into my bag as soon as she's done.

Ash says, "So, how are you? Are you okay?"

I squint at her through the sun. "Of course I am. Are you?"

"Yeah. I mean, all things considered, yeah." She crosses and uncrosses her legs. "I've been going to therapy. At the youth center, where it's free. It's actually really awesome."

"Dude, that's *sick.*" I mean it.

"Yeah." She plays with a hole in her denim. "But, like, you're good, right? You don't need therapy?"

"Dude, everyone needs therapy." We both laugh because most of the people we know absolutely do need therapy, members of my family included. "But I'm fine. Honest."

"You're still not going to Amsterdam?" Her eyes seem tense, and maybe I'm imagining it, but I see a tinge of guilt.

I shrug. "I'm thinking of doing film here. Film and journalism, maybe. Wendy's got me thinking more about social issues lately. Maybe I'll produce for the CBC. How about you? You think you'll ever do more school?" I hate admitting it, but it's still weird to me that Ash isn't going to university. Way in the back of my head, I can hear my parents disapproving of anyone who chooses not to. But those voices have gotten quieter, and I'm starting to wonder if they were my own voice all this time.

Ash says, "I don't know. I just want to survive the next year. Make my rent on time."

I nod. "That's legit."

"I think you'd be awesome at filmmaking," Ash says.

I nod. "I could do it for the Guild. Remember the guy at the park who recognized me from YouTube?" I started my own channel shortly after graduation. And maybe it's because I upload a lot of videos—of Ash, of our friends, of myself commenting on them skating—but they've been *really* taking off in the past few weeks.

Ash rolls her eyes. "Oh god, not this again."

"Hey, I'm not saying I'm famous. But it's still nice to be recognized!"

We sip our drinks. Ash sucks hers down noisily, the liquid almost gone. I prefer to keep my liquid-to-topping ratio balanced so I don't get stuck with hard-to-reach leftover toppings at the end.

"Do you think you'll ever come out to your parents?"

Ash breaks the seal of her cup and tilts it, using her straw to shovel pearls into her mouth. "Probably not. I don't plan on speaking to my dad if I can help it. And my mom—well, we'll see. She's a bit of a wild card."

I nod. I can't imagine having to make a decision like whether to speak with your parents or not. I think about mine. De Di's likely in the kitchen making his afternoon coffee. Ma Mi and Wendy are probably in the living room, watching a Korean drama. I can hear Ma Mi yelling at the TV every time she thinks something doesn't make sense. And I can see Wendy counterarguing her with a textbook in her lap. She always has a textbook nearby, even if she's not reading it—as if its mere presence will let her absorb knowledge through osmosis. In other words, it's a typical long weekend. Well, for my family. Some people might think it weird that my parents ignored my coming out, but I'm happy with the way things are. Maybe that's the thing about Chinese parents. They don't say "I'm proud of you" or "I accept you." Instead, they stay up to make sure you get home in one piece, make you coffee, and bring you dessert even when you're not hungry.

"Jay?"

"Yeah?"

Ash shakes her cup, finds it empty, and plops it down next to her board. "I think the next few years are gonna be pretty wild. I have contests lined up. In Alberta. Ontario. Even the States. Maybe sponsorships." Makes sense. Ash's channel has been blowing up, and almost every time our group gets together at a skate park, someone I've never seen before comes up to her because they know her from the Clamshell, around town, or YouTube.

"That's sick," I say. "Are you nervous?"

She squints up at the sky and of course, she doesn't answer me directly. "Hey, can you promise me something?"

"Depends," I say.

She smirks. "Let's make this a thing. Get together and skate on Labor Day."

I nod. "I think I can do that."

Without answering, Ash jumps up and starts sessioning my mini-rail. I watch her while I finish my bubble tea. When I'm done, I try a few boardslides myself and she gives me pointers.

Ash gets ready to go when it's almost dinnertime, but I sense her hesitating. "You know, I was thinking . . ." She's turned away from me, facing the laneway, frozen mid-stride. "Do you wanna, like, maybe get dinner sometime?"

It occurs to me that Ash and I have never eaten dinner together, just the two of us. I shrug. "Sure. Yeah."

She looks over her shoulder at me and I smile. She smiles back.

"Cool. I'll look up some places." She puts one foot on her board, pauses, and then glances at me again. "I'll see you around."

"Yeah. See you."

She blinks. "Love you."

I grin. "Love you too."

She pushes forward on her board and I watch her fluttering hair disappear around the corner.

I can smell the winter melon soup De Di is making. I pick up the mini-rail and store it in the garage. I walk up to the back porch and look out at the mountains, listening to the Naked and Famous in my earphones. Take a deep breath. I look at the neighbor's garage, at the ramp where Ash did a shove-it exactly one year ago. I imagine myself in her place, what I can try there tomorrow. Pop shove. Half cab. Kickflip. And maybe someday, a tre flip.

Author's Note

When I was a teenager, my hobbies were everything. I was a skater, a guitar player, and when I got a MacBook, a cinematographer. When I was sixteen, I started writing what would later become *Crash Landing*. At the time, it was told from Ash's perspective and represented who I wanted to be if I was cooler and edgier. In reality, I was an honor roll nerd working on my piano diploma, and I just wanted to make my parents proud.

As I got older, I realized that life is about more than just good grades. I met people whose priorities were different from mine. I started connecting with the "types" of people my elders once warned me away from. And the kids I once thought were too cool for me? They didn't have it all figured out either.

Crash Landing is about finding your people. Not in the sense of a clique, though; it's about finding people who accept all the different parts of you. Despite sharing a similar cultural background, Jay and Ash are polar opposites in many respects. Yet they're drawn to each other by the same source of stoke: four wheels and a plank of wood.

Writing *Crash Landing* has been my playground. It's the book that I needed when I was younger, one that (hopefully!) says it's okay to be who you are and love the things—and people—you do.

Char
Vancouver, 2023

A Note on Language and Culture

On Language

Jay speaks English to her parents, who speak Cantonese to her. Jay's parents' speech should not be taken as a direct translation from Cantonese, but I decided to pepper some Cantonese words throughout. The romanization used in this book is not an official system; I simply wrote the most intuitive pronunciation I could with the help of my dad (thanks, Dad!) and our consultant Ambrose Li (thanks, Ambrose!).

In Cantonese, two words can have the same pronunciation but different tones. I decided against writing out the Cantonese tones because they can be quite confusing to read in English. I also decided against including Chinese characters because as a Canadian-raised child, Jay would probably not be able to read them.

I encourage readers to explore this language if they're interested—Cantonese has a lot of personality, and there are at least six tones!

On Culture

Crash Landing is written from the point of view of Jay Wong, who (much like me!) is of Chinese (Hong Kong) descent but born and raised in Canada. This story reflects how Jay sees the world and the people she meets. Representation is very dear to me as a queer writer of color, but my story should not be taken as a complete representation of the queer Asian diaspora or even queer Asians in Vancouver.

As a kid, I couldn't find many books about girls who looked like me and who loved doing the things I did. The few books I found that featured Asian characters tended to be historical, serious, and often sad. What would have been awesome was a book simply about growing up—starring characters who just so happen to be Asian and queer.

Queer Asian voices are still underrepresented, and I am honored I get to share mine. But I am just one voice. If this story resonates with you and your identity, that's awesome. But if it doesn't, I hope you'll write your own story, one that represents you.

Acknowledgments

Publishing a book has been my life's dream, and it wouldn't have been possible without the dozens of wonderful people in my life.

First and foremost, a big heartfelt thank you to Kaela Cadieux, Jieun Lee, and Annick Press for taking a chance on my story. Thank you for making space for queer authors and authors of color. And a thank you to my copyeditor, Dana Hopkins; my proofreader, Mary Ann Blair; and Ambrose Li, who provided valuable feedback on Cantonese romanization. Finally, big thanks to JB Gallego for illustrating an incredible cover!

Next, I'd like to thank my mentors: my professors Alison Acheson and Nancy Lee for teaching me the art of children's literature and novel writing; Amber Dawn, for being inspiring as always; and Tish Silvers, for witnessing me all these years. A big thank you to Danny Ramadan, for suggesting I submit this book to Annick in the first place. And shout-outs to friends I look up to—Amy, Wren, Yilin—for your continued mentorship and support.

Shout-outs all around to everyone I hung with in Buchanan E at the UBC Creative Writing program. A big thank you to the Foxy Army writing group for workshopping an early draft and getting stoked, and thank you to Rachel Rose for being one of my first beta readers. You guys have made me the writer I am today.

The biggest of thank-yous to my expert readers Diamond Yao, Anna Zeitner, and Elijah Forbes for lending me your knowledge and experience. And thank you, Kristin Ebeling, for your expert feedback on the ARC. You folks influenced major decisions in this book, thereby making it more authentic to the communities I wrote about than if I'd gone it alone.

Writing requires knowing a lot of things, from how difficult it is to

278

kickflip a seven-stair to realistic school policies. Thank you B, Michaela, Jeemin, and everyone I phoned, texted, and chatted with who shared their practical and emotional insights so that I could make this story believable and strong. Oh, and another thank you to Kaela's group of friends for your important last-minute input!

This book would not exist without my friend Cherrie. She let me try her board in Grade 7 and, well, the rest is history. A special shout-out to Rose Archie for sharing your stories, the Latebloomers Skate Club for getting me stoked on skating again, and all the friends I've made through skating. You know who you are ;)

Thank you to my family, chosen and blood, for your undying support. Thank you, De Di, for answering my random texts about Cantonese language and culture. Thank you, Juliet, my brother from another mother, for always being there for me. Thank you to my friends, the parents of those friends, friends of my parents—I am so privileged to have such a loving community.

Finally, I thank the two most important people who have since passed on: Ma Mi and Por Por.

Por Por: you raised me, taught me my ancestral language, and were my primary caregiver and friend for the first eight years of my life.

My mother was an English teacher and an avid reader who read to me every night as a child. She would translate literary classics into Cantonese to tell them to me and later, when I could read on my own, just sat and read beside me every night. Every. Single. Night. Ma Mi: I am who I am because of you, and every accomplishment I have is also yours. I miss you every day.

Li Charmaine Anne (she/they) completed a BFA in Creative Writing and English Literature at the University of British Columbia, and shorter works of hers can be found in Canadian journals. **Crash Landing** is her first novel.

Charmaine's inspirations include skateboarding, snowboarding, music, birds, the Pacific Northwest where she grew up, and the people and ideas she has encountered. She believes that stories create a more just world: by sharing our narratives and listening to those of others, we become more empathetic citizens attuned to the strengths and needs of our neighbors.

Charmaine gratefully acknowledges that her work takes place in the traditional, unceded, and ancestral territories of the Coast Salish Peoples, mainly the xʷməθkʷəy̓əm (Musqueam), Sḵwx̱wú7mesh (Squamish), and səlilwətaɬ (Tsleil-Waututh) Nations. Indigenous Peoples have been producing art and literature on this land for countless generations, and without their stewardship of the land, Charmaine's work would not be possible.

Website: licharmaineanne.ca
Instagram: @chartheshark